THE BLOOD WITCH

IVY ASHER

Edited by Polished Perfection

Cover by Book Covers by Seventhstar

Chapter Heading by Ricky Gunawan

For all the Untidy Joseph lovers.

1

Warm lips press against my cheek, and I lean into the tender touch. It feels warm and familiar, and I don't know why, but I need it so much right now.

"I'm here," a strong, deep voice assures me, and I search for the source like a sunflower seeks the sun. "I'm here," he tells me again, and then those warm lips are on mine, gentle pressure coaxing me lovingly from the darkness.

I drink him down, parting my lips for his and deepening the tentative connection that feels dangerously fragile between us. There's a wrongness to that feeling. What's between us should be strong, impenetrable, but instead, it's on the brink of shattering and I'm afraid.

Desperation roosts in my chest, and I reach up and thread my fingers into thick, silky hair. His tongue teases mine, and I lap up the desire and heat that's being fed to me, shivering as the chill in my bones is chased away. Large, strong hands cup my cheeks as the kiss turns frenzied, needy. I moan, the sound begging for more, and an answering chuckle has me sucking on his bottom lip and then giving it a teasing nip. Satisfaction moves through me at his answering appreciative groan, hunger dripping off of it as thick as fresh honey.

Yes. This is how it should be, I exclaim internally as the connection I feel in my chest starts to heal. *This* is right, I affirm as the tether brightens and grows thicker, more secure.

"Rogan," I pant, breaking the kiss so I can demand more, but as soon as his name leaves my lips, it's the key to unlocking the truth, to unlocking everything that happened.

Images assault me. Prek blowing a powder in my face. Rogan holding my limp body as he negotiated his place at the table. The feel of a needle in my neck, whatever was in the syringe stealing my fight and my consciousness. It all slams into me with brutal unforgiving force, and I'm thrown into reality like it's a freezing ice-coated pond. I breach the surface of my Rogan-fueled fantasy with a gasp, sitting up as alarm pumps in my veins. My heart is a speedy staccato of panic, and my eyes don't adjust fast enough to everything around me. Rogan sits back from the edge of the bed I'm in, surprised, his green eyes taking me in, uncertainty and worry alight in his examination. My surroundings are out of focus, but I see him.

All I see is *him*.

His coffee brown hair, the scar kissing one side of his face from eyebrow to cheekbone. The guilt in his moss-green stare. Rage surges in my blood, replacing the traces of alarm that were just there. I burn with fury, and the concern on Rogan's face shifts to wariness.

"Get the fuck away from me," I snarl as I try to blink into focus the world just past Rogan's unwelcome visage. I scramble back from him, sheets tangling around my limbs until I'm stopped by a wall, trapping me between it and this duplicitous witch.

"Lennox, please," he counters, his features beseeching,

entitled, as though he has any right to look at me that way, any right to be heard or to plead his case.

I'm not interested.

I wipe at my lips, as though I can wipe his searing presence away, disgust and confusion warring inside of me. "Where am I?" I demand, rubbing my eyes as though it will finally bring my surroundings into focus.

What did they give me?

"Lennox, you need to understand the *why*," Rogan insists, and I scoff, shaking my head in disbelief.

"Get away from me right now, or I'll make you," I growl at him in warning, trying and failing to move back even more as he reaches for my hand.

Is he serious? Does he really think, after everything he's done, I'll just sit quietly while he defends himself? What does he think he can say that will erase what he's done, erase the betrayal and selfishness?

"Please," he begs, the word quiet and filled with emotion.

I don't sift through everything I hear in his one-worded petition, because I can't get past the hint of hope I hear in his plea. It makes me want to pluck that hope from the air between us and crush it in my hands. I want him to watch just what I think about his supplication, about his need for understanding. How can he think for a second that there's any coming back from what happened? He destroyed anything that could have ever been between us with one little word.

Seno.

The simple incantation he's used far too many times to knock me out swirls in my mind, laced with Rogan's commanding voice and topped off with treachery. Hurt hurtles through me, but I drown it in anger. This witch gets nothing more from me. Not my pain. Not my loss. And certainly not my sympathy.

I glare at him, sitting feet away from me, unmoving and unwilling to heed my warning. He still isn't taking me seriously. The thought I had—just before I was knocked out by whatever he and the Order gave me—was that I would make him wish he'd never laid eyes on me. I focus on that promise as magic fills my limbs and retribution fills my heart.

An incantation trickles into my mind, and without any thought, I seize the magic in a death grip and let it pour out of my lips: *ikur woor essenna ih beshee vot dhono sava ru.* Terror overtakes Rogan's gaze, and he opens his mouth to say something, but all that comes out is a pained groan. He grabs at his torso with both hands, and every muscle in his body tightens as he heaves out an agonized bellow.

The raw sound of his pain lashes out, and I try to fling it away from me. I harden myself against his agony. He hurt me, and now it's time he hurts. Rogan looks up imploringly, his face mottled with purple like he's been holding his breath for too long. Blood starts to drip from his nose, and then there are crimson tracks trailing from his eyes too. I can see the questions and betrayal in his accusing stare before the green of his gaze is lost to the blood pouring out of them.

A flare of satisfaction sparks through me, but when Rogan falls to the ground and starts to vomit up blood, I'm knocked from my perch of vindication by a wave of uncertainty. Magic pours out of me, and I try to ignore the disquiet of my thoughts. I remind myself that he deserved this, wrapping myself up in a thick blanket of justification. He betrayed me. Violated my trust. He had this coming.

Blood pools below the bed I'm still sitting on. At least I think it's a bed; I still can't make out anything besides

Rogan. He convulses on the ground, and it's so hard and brutal that I prepare to hear the sound of cracking bones at any minute. He chokes, wet gasps breaking up the sound of retching. It's so violent and graphic that my stomach turns in rejection of what's happening before my eyes. Salt floods my mouth, and I clasp a hand over it to quiet the cry that tries to escape.

I try to pull the magic back, to stop what's happening, as death-twitches fill Rogan's limbs and blood pours out of him.

That's enough, I tell myself as I struggle to gain control. But it's as though the magic spilling out of me is slippery and I can't get a hold of it.

"That's enough!" I scream, cracks sounding off around me as Rogan's bones give up and shatter. "Stop!" I beg, but acid crawls up my esophagus, and the next thing I know, retribution comes pouring from my mouth. The coppery taste of blood fills my senses, and before my vision blinks red, I see my own blood start to pool around me. I've never felt anything like the pain that chases through me in this moment, and I'm lost to the heaves of blood pouring from me.

The ground rushes up mercilessly to meet me as I fall. All I can hear beyond my own dying is Rogan's voice when he told me, *what happens to my soul happens to yours. What happens to my bones, happens to yours. We are bound now, and unless I remove it, there isn't a thing you can do to change that.*

My body starts to convulse, and I know it will be over soon. My thoughts race, and the taste of blood in my mouth is replaced by the bitter taste of regret. What will my Grammy think? What will become of the line? Will Tad and Hillen forgive me? Will they ever know what happened?

Agony tightens like a fist around my heart, and all my

questions, all my twisted thoughts of retribution and justice are replaced with paralyzing fear.

What have I done?

The magic is lost to me, I couldn't rein it in if I tried. The damage is too great to ever take back. I try to blink blood from my vision, and my terrified, dimming stare settles on empty green eyes. Eyes that have looked at me in so many different ways. With betrayal. With attraction. With hope. And now with death. I stare into Rogan's now lifeless eyes, and I want to ask why, but in my head, I hear the answer loud and clear...*we did this to each other*.

The sensation of falling takes over, and oddly, I land on something hard. With a gasp, I'm yanked from my own death, and I find myself on a dark wood floor, blinking and gasping as I sit up. Panic claws at my throat, and I cough hard to clear my airway of...nothing. There's nothing in my throat. No blood. No death. Nothing. And yet the sour taste of regret still sits on the back of my desert-dry tongue.

I look around frantically, taking in what appears to be a small, swanky apartment, but Rogan's not here. He's not lying next to me, dead on the floor in a puddle of blood. His lifeless eyes may haunt my future dreams, but they're not staring back at me from the ground. I clutch my chest, my heart racing from the nightmare I just woke up from. The poor battered organ beats furiously, clearly disbelieving that what just happened wasn't real.

Was it a prophecy? A foreshadowing of sorts? Or just my fractured mind trying to fix everything that happened?

A glass of water sits on the black side table next to the king-sized bed I just fell out of. Bubbles line the inner walls of the glass, leading me to believe it's been sitting there awhile. I grab for it and gulp it down greedily. I need to wash the taste of loss from my mouth, rid myself of the guilt I'm swimming in even though what just happened wasn't real. I didn't kill Rogan.

"Just a dream," I mumble to myself as I wipe my mouth with my forearm and stand up.

I'm wearing the same gray T-shirt and jeans I had on before. They don't look worse for wear, which—despite what the flat tepid water might indicate—makes me think I haven't been down for long. My legs feel unsteady and weak as I put my weight on them, and I feel all fluttery and fragile like I'm recovering from the stomach flu or something. That thought conjures images of Rogan puking up blood, and I cringe away from the imagined flash of his pain.

"Just a dream," I repeat, but I feel as though it might be more of a warning.

I survey the dark wood of the apartment around me. Deep browns and blacks offset light gray fabrics on the bed, sofa, and chairs. It's a studio style setup. I can see a living room, a kitchen, and a door that leads to a bathroom, I hope, with another door that looks like it's the entrance and exit to this space. I'm not sure what to make of my surroundings.

When Prek and Rogan dosed me, I expected to wake up in some kind of cell. Bars and polished concrete wouldn't have surprised me, but this...I don't know what this means. Did Rogan change his mind and steal me away to wherever this place is? Has someone else rescued me?

I eye the door, unsure about what to do. Do I make a run for it? I mean, even if I can escape, how far can I get? With the Order looking for me, a yet-to-be-confirmed possible kidnapper hunting down Osteomancers, and the unresolved issue of Rogan and me still being tethered, the odds aren't good. Do I wait for Rogan to appear and then force him back to his aunt's place to remove our tether? Is that even possible if one half of the connection wants to use the other half? What if Rogan isn't the one who brought me here, then what?

My head aches from the weight of the issues that are bearing down on me. Doubt, confusion, and questions apply more and more pressure to my already exhausted mind as the seconds tick on. So I push all of it aside and focus on the most pressing issue I'm dealing with right now.

I have to pee like a racehorse.

I stumble on unsteady legs over to the bathroom, some semblance of a plan forming as I plop down on the porcelain throne, sighing in relief as the floodgates are opened. First phase of the plan: empty the tank. Second: refill it by tracking down some food. And lastly: tear this place apart looking for clues as to who owns it, and then go from there. I flush and wash up, surprised by what I find in the mirror staring back at me. Once again, my expectations of my reflection are far from reality.

I feel weak and shaky and expect to find a reflection that looks as haggard as I feel, but that's not what's staring back at me in the mirror. I look good. Like, *really* good. There's a healthy glow to my tawny-beige skin. I appear pumped full of vitality, and oddly, I'm practically photoshop smooth. I got a dose of *refreshed* and *beautiful* when I first bound the bones to me, but *this*...this is next level. I don't just look *Osteomancer* good, I look *Queen of all the Bones* good.

I rotate my face in the mirror and poke my plump lips and smooth skin. I fight the urge to raise my hands above my head and shout *I have the power* He-man style. I lean in closer to the mirror and fluff my tresses. Damn, even my typically unruly hair looks tamed by professionals. I angle my head this way and that, the cinnamon-toned streaks that break up my dark brown mass of curls, adding dimension. And shockingly, every strand on my head looks luminous and frizz-free. I stare at myself dumbfounded, my golden brown irises staring back at me curious and looking a little too haunted. I look away before that gaze can suck me in and remind me of just how painful my reality is.

Time to get serious. No more marveling over *Extreme Makeover: Magic Edition*, it's time to focus on what the hell to do now. With a roll of my neck, I try to shake the exhaustion from my limbs. I find a loaf of French bread, a Coke, and some butter and call my hunt for food over. I shovel bites into my mouth like I've taken up speed-eating as a profession, dropping crumbs all over as I search the small but lavish studio.

I get even more bewildered when I don't find any clothes in the drawers and nothing hanging in the armoire in the room. There aren't any pictures or personal effects in the entire place. It's empty of anything other than furniture, home decor, some toiletries, and food. On closer inspection, what I thought was a blank white wall turns out to be a massive blackout shutter. I try to open it, but it seems I need some kind of remote or elemental magic or something.

I take a huge bite of bread as I start to search the living room for some device that opens things when I hear two faint beeps, and then the door to this place opens. I whirl around, my heart sprinting like it's racing Shelly-Ann Fraser-Pryce for a new world record, with worry and alarm on its back. It isn't Rogan's annoyingly handsome face that spots me from the doorway, it's Prek's surprised russet-brown stare that meets mine.

The Order member who attacked Rogan and me hesitates at the door as though he wasn't expecting to see me. I log the reaction, intent on examining it later, but there's no hesitation in my bones as I lunge for him. Too late, he blasts wind my way, but I'm close enough to swing and slap him across the face with half a loaf of French bread before a cyclone tries to pull me away. Instinctually, I infuse my bones with magic, making them heavy, unmovable, and locking myself in place.

He shoves more magic at me, but I grit against the onslaught and step forward, closing the distance between us one forced step at a time. Magic is calling on me to crush him, tempting me with the thought that a simple incantation could make him dust underneath my sneakers. I reject the idea immediately, echoes of the nightmare I had just before I woke up here still looming over me menacingly and undeciphered. That and, like it or not, Prek is an Order member. They may not be playing by the same set of rules of honor and morality that I am, but I can't start a war with the Order. Not if I want to live. Or try to get out of whatever fucked up situation Rogan has forced me into.

I kick his feet out from under him and aim another kick at his ribs just as soon as his back hits the floor. He doesn't anticipate that I would try to *physically* fight him, which seems stupid given the bread slap that I landed seconds ago. It makes me question the kind of unprepared idiots the Order hires, but then he rolls away from my kick and pops back up, a pissed-off look in his eyes. I return his angry look with one that screams *fuck you and the broom you rode in on*, and we both ready our stance.

"Useless dimmers, I'm going to kill whoever made this one too strong," Prek growls, but whatever he's talking about isn't for me, it's more like he's making a to-do list for after he beats my ass.

I ball my fists and bring my hands up, ready to go toe-to-toe. Prek's jaw tightens, accentuating his square jawline. He's clean shaven now, no black beard to cover up the smooth dark skin of his cheeks or to hide his buxom lips. "I don't want to fight you, Osteomancer, but I will if you force me to," he warns, tense and waiting for me to strike.

I give an indignant snort in response. "Could have fooled

me with the way you've now attacked me...*twice*," I point out, adding an extra sprinkle of irritation on the last word. "Where am I?" I demand, looking past him into what looks like a simple apartment hallway.

Why the hell would Prek bring me to his house?

It's on the tip of my tongue to ask where Rogan is, but I swallow the question down, determined to choke on it if it will keep the words from escaping my lips.

"You're in Chicago, at Order headquarters. You're safe, I'm not here to hurt you," he declares, his body relaxing ever so slightly.

Sucker.

I feign a kick, and he rotates his body away from mine to keep me from landing anything. I take advantage of his twist away and land a fist to his back, right in the kidney. Prek grunts, pained, but recovers quicker than I expect. His fist connects with my cheek, and my head snaps to the right. The vertebrae in my neck pop in objection, and I feel my lip split from the force of the hit. I growl, menacingly, suddenly rethinking this whole *bones to dust* thing my magic was pitching earlier, but my anger is drowned out by an outraged bellow, and suddenly Rogan is there grabbing Prek by the neck.

Rogan lifts him off his feet as though the Order member weighs nothing. "Don't you *ever* touch her again," he snarls in his face, and Prek claws at the hand around his throat, his legs kicking and searching for purchase to no avail. "I have let you have your temper tantrum long enough," Rogan yells at him. "You want a shot at me, here I am. But you will *never* come for her again, or so help me by the goddess, I'll kill you. Your ignorance or innocence will no longer be a factor, do you understand me?" Rogan warns, shaking Prek once for good measure.

"What is going on here?" an authoritative woman

demands, marching into the room and assessing the scene. She looks like she's in her mid-fifties, with gray streaks peppering her otherwise light brown hair. She's dressed head to toe in a black military-style uniform with yellow symbols embroidered on the collar and cuffs of the pristine shirt that's neatly tucked into her pants, which are neatly tucked into shit-kicker boots.

"An overdue lesson," Rogan growls, his eyes never leaving Prek's. They stare at each other for a second longer, and then Rogan lets the Order member go.

Prek drops to his feet, but he doesn't crumble to the ground like I expect. He coughs and sputters as he rubs at his throat and pulls deep breaths into his starved lungs. He shoots a glare at Rogan, but there's something else in his gaze, suspicion, confusion, I'm not quite sure what it is, but I don't get to examine it any closer as the woman barks a command at Prek to *speak*.

"Apologies, Major. I entered Osteomancer Osseous's quarters to deposit clothing. She was awake ahead of the healer's schedule and attacked me. I attempted to de-escalate the situation, which is when Kendrick attacked me from behind," Prek recites, straightening up to attention at the woman's commanding presence.

I look down at the ground and find a black bag with clothing spilling out of it. I look up, my eyes landing on Rogan's, and I quickly snap my gaze away as though I've just accidentally touched a hot surface and am trying to keep from getting burned.

"I was told you'd keep your pets on a leash," Rogan lobs at the woman venomously.

"And I was told that you'd keep your feral ways to yourself," she snaps back. Her brown eyes find mine, and we study each other. "I am Major Griego," she offers and pauses, waiting for me to complete the introduction ritual.

I say nothing.

Amusement flickers through her stare. "You are in the Chicago head of the Order, and you've been brought here for your own protection."

"Funny," I retort with a hollow laugh. "*Brought here for my protection* feels a lot like assault and kidnapping," I tell her, pointedly looking from her to Prek and back again. I refuse to look at Rogan. I want to scream and rant at him and then banish him from my presence forever, but right now, I'm trying to figure out if it's better or worse for me to put on a united front.

"Nobody thought to just ask me, give me a heads-up that I was in need of bodyguards? No? Instead, I get a needle to the neck? I mean, you guys make one hell of a fucked up first impression for an organization that's so worried about my safety and protection," I point out.

She nods once as though she understands my vitriol and isn't offended by it in the slightest. "I am sorry for the circumstances surrounding your arrival here. We did not know what to expect from someone who had aligned themselves with a renounced witch. We took extra precautions to protect us and you, but I can see how it would be received as, how did you put it...right, a fucked up first impression," she tells me, her gaze filled with understanding and a cheeky smile pulling at one side of her lips.

"I assure you that you are not a prisoner here, and we will not treat you like one. We're here to keep you out of the hands of whoever has taken all the other Osteomancers, nothing more and nothing less. You are not confined to your quarters. You are allowed to leave the building, but be aware that a security detail has been assigned to you, and they will accompany you wherever you may wish to go for—"

"My protection," I interrupt, shaking my head in irritation. "Yeah, I got it," I huff indignantly, wanting to rub my temples and the headache blossoming behind them. I stop myself, refusing to show any weakness in front of this witch. "So, I take it your team is my security detail?" I ask, my annoyed glare settling on Prek.

He nods once.

"Right, because that makes sense. Stick me with the crew of witches that tried to kill me, but hey, it's for my protection, right?" I snark at Major Griego, shooting her a look that says *come the fuck on, you really think I'm buying this?*

"We weren't trying to kill you," Prek defends, but one look from the Major and he goes ramrod straight and silent. I raise an impressed brow despite my irritation.

Sign me up for that super power.

"Captain Prek and his team have been assigned for your protection. Each of them will forfeit their life if that means keeping *you* safe. I understand things between you started off aggressively, but make no mistake, no harm will befall you at their hands," she assures me.

"Does that look like no harm," Rogan interjects, motioning to my split lip and the warm line I can feel slowly dripping from it.

"She was attacking me; am I not supposed to defend my —" Prek immediately shuts up again as a small impatient noise escapes the Major.

"Are you equipped to handle this, Prek?" she questions, her brow raised in judgment, and he stiffens even more.

"Yes, ma'am," he barks in response, and weighted silence creeps in all around me as some kind of unspoken exchange goes on between them.

Major Griego flicks her hand in my direction, and I feel the slow trickle of blood running down my chin stop and my lip knit together. My cheek ceases its throbbing, and my head clears of pain. Shock moves through me as the Soul Witch does what Soul Witches do best, she heals me.

A *thank you* almost pops unbidden out of my mouth, but I crush it between gritted teeth, refusing to be polite and well-mannered after everything that's happened. I figure my Aunt Hillen would understand if she were here.

"That doesn't change what happened," Rogan declares, the healing clearly less impressive to him.

"Why do you even care?" I snap at him with daggers in my eyes as they finally fix on his.

Well, so much for a united front. "You're the reason I'm even here. If I weren't, things like this"—I gesture to the blood stain on my shirt—"wouldn't be happening." I turn from him dismissively and focus back on Major Griego. "If I'm free to go wherever I please, then can I go home?"

She hesitates for a beat and then nods. "We have some questions we need you to help us with, but once that's done, yes, you may go anywhere you like, so long as you keep your protective detail with you."

I appraise her, studying her features and looking for any sign of deception, anything that might give her away. I doubt it's all so easy, answer a few questions and I'm on my way, but a small spark of hope flickers to life in me anyway.

I look over at Rogan, debating my options. He's furious. Anger radiates off of him in waves, and it puts my hackles up. If anyone in this room has a right to feel enraged, it sure as fuck isn't him. My nightmare flashes to the forefront of my mind. I can see Rogan's pleading gaze, his need to try and make things right. Well, that sure as hell isn't the look he's wearing in real life. There's no apology etched in his features, no pleading tone begging me to hear him out. He looks as though I've wronged him, and it makes my blood boil.

"Fine," I agree, tearing my gaze from Rogan's searing

unapologetic stare. "I'll help in any way I can, on one condition."

"And that is?" Major Griego asks. I can see in her eyes that she already knows, but the formality of voicing it is important.

I return my seething gaze to Rogan. "Keep him away from me," I declare flatly.

Rogan's eyes flash with something I don't want to interpret before a gale of wind shoves him mercilessly out of the apartment, and the door slams shut behind him.

"My pleasure," Prek declares, a punctuation to what just happened.

But instead of it making me feel better, that same sense of foreboding I felt after I woke up from the nightmare settles in my stomach. I stare at the now closed door, and all I can hear is an echo reverberating in my mind of my last thought as I lay dying in my dream.

What have I done?

2

"Would you like a tour, Osteomancer Osseous?" the Major asks me, pulling me from my conflicting thoughts.

My head and heart are at war, and just like with all battles, I know there isn't going to be a true winner. I don't know why I feel this way. I have every right to be angry, to be livid for the rest of my life, but even though that's true, something is screaming at me that choosing to be pissed forever is deadly. That Rogan won't be the only one suffering. Maybe it's the tether. Maybe it's warping my emotions and trying to drive us together, but even as I think that, it has a hollow ring of wrongness to it.

"Leni," I correct the Major. "Call me Leni."

She nods once and steps further into the studio-esque apartment. She clasps her hands behind her back, taking in the mess I created when I was searching for clues of who lived here. The cushions on the couch are upturned, the rug pulled out and folded in half. The baubles and books decorating the shelves on one wall are on the ground and scattered. There's an explosion of bread clumps and crumbs by the front door, and I rewind my memories and take a mental snapshot of the look that was on Prek's face when I slapped him with the loaf of French bread earlier—you know, to laugh at later.

"These are to be your quarters while you stay here," the Major declares, and inwardly I groan. Maybe they have someone who can bibbity bobbity boo all this shit back the way it was before I tore it apart.

The Major plucks a small white remote from a drawer in the TV hutch I didn't notice before, and with one click, the wall of white shutters begins to rise. Night greets me on the other side of the windows, so do the city lights all around us. I realize the Order's hub is one of the many high-rises dotting Chicago's skyline. I knew the High Priestess resided here, but I didn't know the Order did too. I suppose it makes sense though. We're more or less hiding in plain sight in a big city like this, and it's clear to see why the ruler of witches would want backup nearby and accessible.

I hate that my mind wanders to Rogan with that thought. I don't want to care about how he feels being so close to his mother, or why he would have chosen to come back here after everything that's happened to him in this place. I brush all my questions and unearned concern aside, tuning back in to what Major Griego is saying.

"The Order resides in the entirety of the building. You have access to anything other than the top twenty levels and anything below the basement."

That peaks my curiosity, but I don't bother asking what's on those floors or why I'm not allowed near them. It's not like she's going to actually tell me.

"We have housing, training, food, and entertainment all on the premises. There are maps in the elevators that will aid you in finding your way around, but your guards will ensure you're where you want to be," she points out, and I have a hard time not reading into what that might mean.

Her brown eyes study me for a moment. “I’m sure by now you’ve felt the drain on your magic. It can be alarming at first, but you will get used to it. The building has protections in place for its inhabitants, it’s nothing personal. We all have to endure the dimming of our abilities here, and it should become an afterthought soon.”

I work hard to school my features. I don’t want to show the slightest bit of shock or bewilderment. One, because I don’t feel any kind of drain on my magic at all. In fact, I feel quite the opposite, like I’m a juiced-up magical battery. The other reason I don’t want to give anything away is that I suspect Order members are given something that makes them immune to whatever drain or dimming she’s referring to. Prek cursed *the dimmers* when we were going at it, as though they affected him more than they should have and *that’s* why I got the better of him. But I don’t think that’s what happened.

Point for me, that he’s more focused on his inability to magic me into submission instead of realizing that these *dimmers* didn’t affect me and my ability to magically fight him at all. The only reason he’s not bone dust on the hardwood is because I wanted to know what I was up against, what was happening here. But that picture is getting clearer and clearer, and I’m becoming really grateful that I still have access to my magic the way I always have.

I look over at Prek. He’s still standing at attention, his eyes focused on nothing as the Major continues to talk up my new prison. I don’t care what she says about this place and all the amenities it harbors within its walls, we both know it’s just a swanky oversized holding cell. She can sweet talk me all she wants about how I’m free after I answer some questions, but based on what I’ve been told, the Order has contingencies for their contingencies, and somewhere in that mess is the plan that they could trade me for the other missing witches, just like the ransom note stated.

"There are eight suites on this floor. You occupy one. The renounced occupies another, and your protective detail is housed in the remaining suites," she tells me, moving toward the door. "We can tour the facilities, and then, if you're ready, sit down and discuss why you've been brought here," the Major tells me, turning to see if I'm following her.

I pause, not overly interested in finding out if the Order has a juice bar. I'm also not eager for the interrogation to start, although I am hoping I can glean some information from whatever it is they're going to ask me. But first, I need to call home.

"My phone was lost in the accident that Prek and his team caused," I start, hoping to capitalize on the Major's previous annoyance with Prek and his dis-Order-ly behavior. "I need to get a new one, and I need to check in with my family. They'll be worried, I haven't spoken to them in..." I pause, trying to calculate how many days have gone by. "How long was I out?" I ask, hating that I don't know the answer already.

Seriously, what is my life that this has become a normal question?

"It's eight p.m. on Wednesday night," Prek offers, finally breaking his silence, and relief filters through me that I haven't lost another day, just a handful of hours.

"I need to call my family," I repeat simply, unsure if this is going to be allowed or not.

I feel as though I'm calling the Major's bluff. This could go a couple of ways. She could deflect and try to distract me from what I'm asking. Flat out refuse to let me. Or she could hand me a phone. I'm not sure which direction she'll take. We both know there is more to this than my protection, but I don't know if she'll show her hand this soon. Not when they want something from me, or at least I'm assuming that's why I'm really here.

We watch each other for a moment, and then she nods once. "I'll arrange for one to be sent up immediately. Prek, with me." And with that, both Major Griego and Prek leave, the door shutting quietly behind them.

I almost expected Rogan to be out there, waiting to barge back in to threaten Prek some more and hurry along whatever is going on, but the hallway is empty. Annoyingly, there's a part of me that's relieved by that and a part of me that's not. I release a weary breath and look around my new quarters. I start to pick up everything I haphazardly tossed around when I assumed this was someone else's home. The lights from the bustling city all around me bleed into the apartment, and it's a far cry from the trees and fresh air of Tennessee.

Traffic moves like choreographed ants far below me, and I stand and watch it as the knot of feelings in my chest tries to untangle itself. The nightmare, or warning or whatever it was, still sits in the forefront of my mind, but so does the hurt and betrayal I feel. It's like I'm stranded in the middle of an ocean without a life raft or trustworthy person in sight.

I can still smell Rogan, feel his shirt pressed against my cheek, my tears staining it one by one as he carried me against my will away from his aunt's house. I can feel his arms around me as his actions shattered what we had, what we were. How can I be tethered to someone who would do that to me? His aunt said that everything happens for a reason, that maybe the connection was written in the stars, but how could *this* be what fate has in store?

I look around me, at the foreign home in a foreign city. I'm more lost than I ever have been in my life. If my dream is a warning, I can't kill Rogan, and what's worse is that I don't even know if I want to. I want him to hurt, and I want him away from me...forever. Unfortunately, I don't think I can run from him or from the Order. I doubt I'd be allowed to get away, but I also don't know how I'm supposed to be in the same room with him. I don't think I can interact with him or get past what he did.

A knock at the door startles me. I jump, jolted from my melancholic imaginings and move to open it. Conveniently, there's no peephole. I hope it's just a messenger with a phone in their hand for me, and no one else. But as I crack the door hesitantly, I'm forced to huff out an irritated sigh. The *messenger* with a phone in his taunting hold is Prek.

I open the door wider and try to reach out and pluck the device from his grasp, but he uses that opportunity to push his way into my quarters.

"Hey! I didn't invite you in," I snap as he moves past me and parks his unwelcome ass on a low-back stool he pulls out from the eat-in nook in the kitchen.

"I'm your protective detail, I don't need permission," he announces evenly, sliding the phone across the counter toward me. I move to catch it, his entitled, blasé attitude grating on my last nerve. I glare at him, taking in his cocky countenance. He's not much older than I am, decked out in an all-black military-style uniform with yellow embroidery that I think indicates his rank in the Order, but I'm not sure. The onyx of the uniform against his dark skin, bald head, and short neat beard makes him appear shadow-like and lethal. He clearly thinks entirely too much of himself, and I suddenly feel as though it's *my* duty to correct that.

"Well, go stand outside and shine your head or something. You're sure as hell not welcome in here."

Yeah, I'll have to work on better material than that.

"No can do, *Leni*," he quips. "The Major gave me strict orders to get that back when you're done with it and to not leave you alone while you have it," he informs me, his chin tilting to indicate the phone in my hand. He looks like some brownnoser who's been put in charge, and you know he's just *loving* the power that's been bestowed on him.

Heat burns in my cheeks, and anger boils in my stomach. "Who the fuck does she think I'm going to call? Why on earth would *my* conversation need to be monitored?" I demand, power welling in my chest, ready and waiting to be called on. I work to internally calm down, no use showing that I'm not as affected as I'm supposed to be by their security measures. I need to save that surprise for when I can take firm advantage of it.

Prek shrugs arrogantly in response, and we stare at each other for a beat. I get the distinct impression that he wants me to argue, to try and fight this or maybe him in some way. I'm not sure what he has up his sleeve to level the playing field this go-round, but I'm not interested in finding out. *Fucking weasel.*

I pull in a deep breath in an effort to keep from doing something I might regret. My eyes never leave Prek's cocky stare, and I silently replay in my head what he looked like the night I almost killed him on the side of the road. He can smirk at me all he wants, thinking he has the upper hand, but we both know who won when we went head-to-head. It should probably concern me that such a morbid thought offers me comfort and reassurance, but I don't question it. I've done enough questioning in my lifetime, and look where I ended up anyway. No. Now it's time to become what was always written in the stars. Now it's time to embrace everything that's happening to me.

"Fine," I concede, looking down at the phone and opening it. I punch in Tad's number, grateful for the night he forced me to memorize it *just in case*.

"Leni, is that you?" he greets me, and a calm washes over me at the sound of my cousin's voice.

"It's me," I confirm, my shoulders sagging as if my body wants to fold in on itself with sorrow.

"Lynyrd Skynyrd, where in goat balls have you been?" Tad demands frantically.

I bark out a weary laugh. "Goat balls?" I tease, melancholy and relief dancing together in my chest. "Is Hillen there?"

"No, she's at Uncle Glen's, helping with Jill. Don't be jealous of my creative swearing skills, and don't change the subject. Where have you been? I've only tried to get a hold of you a kabillion times in the past couple days," he informs me, and my relief is quickly replaced by worry.

"Why, what happened?" I ask as my mind starts whipping up worst case scenarios like Julia Child whips up egg whites.

"What? Nothing," Tad reassures me. "I mean, other than my gaydar is still intact and active, oh, and someone broke into Grammy Ruby's shop, well, your shop now—"

"What? Do they know who? Did they take anything?"

"Not that we can tell. You have the grimoire and the bones, right?" I look around me as though I expect them to be right there, but then I remember that I left everything at Rogan's house. An itch to summon my bones just to make sure I can starts just beneath my skin, but I'm not sure if that's something I should be able to do with the wards they've set around this place. I debate if I should go into the bathroom and try, but I figure that will just make Prek even more suspicious.

Shit.

"Yeah, I have them. Did they get into the apartment?" I ask, pacing. I need the movement to help ground me, to keep me from losing my shit and leaving this place whether they want me to or not.

"No, just the shop. It was pretty trashed, broken bottles

and tipped shelves, but it doesn't look like they robbed the place."

Flashes of Rogan and me wrestling around the shop when he first made me his familiar play in my mind, and I cringe. We left the shop trashed. I thought I'd have time to go back and clean it up, but I wasn't able to before Rogan and I hopped a ley line to Tennessee.

"Oh shit, Hoot!"

How did I forget about the stink pot until now? Who is looking after him and Rogan's skunk while we're here? I add it to the pile of questions I need to ask Rogan the next time I see him. Dammit, that sure is going to put a crimp in my *he's dead to me* plan. How am I supposed to never speak to him again when he's the only one who can answer these questions?

"Hold up, Tad, what makes you think the shop was broken into?" I query, holding my breath for his answer.

"Because it was trashed."

"But were the front doors locked or open? Any windows broken?" I press as I recall myself pulling potions from shelves and chucking them at Rogan's head.

"No, the doors were locked and the windows fine, just the damage inside. Ma called Grammy's necro buddy, and he came and smudged. He said there were two distinct magical signatures there last, and then one he wasn't sure about. He said it was off, like milk just past the expiration date," Tad explains, and confusion trickles down my spine.

The two magical signatures could easily have been Rogan and me, but the third, I'm not sure what that could have been. The tether maybe? Our magic is supposed to be separate, so maybe tethering it makes it resonate as off? I rack my brain for other explanations. Could it have been Grammy Ruby, like her magical signature was starting to change as her body failed? I dismiss that option almost as soon as I think it. The necro knows what death and its trail feels like. No. This must be something he's not experienced before. I huff out a frustrated breath and add this question to the Rogan pile too. Maybe he's heard of tethered magic feeling different to necros. At the least, he can ask his aunt about it if he hasn't.

"Okay, thank you, Tad. I don't know about that rotten magic part, but the mess in there is from Rogan and me. Remember how I told you about the fa—" I cut myself off and shoot a look toward Prek. He's cleaning dirt from under his fingernails and pretending to not pay attention to every word I'm speaking. "Remember how Rogan and I met?" I correct instead. "Well, we left that mess behind," I explain, mentally crossing my fingers and hoping that Tad won't say anything about familiars or tethering or anything that Prek might overhear that would create even more problems for me.

"You ride that dick yet?" Tad asks instead, and Prek chokes out a cough, making it clear that he can hear both sides of this conversation loud and clear. "Is that why you were ghosting? Too busy screaming his name to pick up the phone?" he teases.

"No!" I shout a little too emphatically, and I can practically hear the raised eyebrow that I know Tad is giving me on the other end of the line. "There will be none of that...ever," I add, feeling my face heat with embarrassment and anger.

"Leni, the dick gods have blessed you, how can you be so ungrateful?" he starts, pausing to pull in a breath that will fuel a lecture that I'm sure will scar me in some way.

"He fucked me over," I blurt before Tad can get going. "And no, I don't mean he fucked me; he lied to me and screwed me over," I clarify, humiliation, betrayal, and hurt painting my tone.

"What do you mean? What happened?" Tad demands, his voice now dead serious, not a hint of teasing or levity in sight.

"He's not who I thought. He was renounced, outcast. He tricked me and then sold me out to save his own ass," I explain, leveling a look on Prek, who's no longer pretending not to listen. I can see him filing this information away, looking at me now as though I'm more victim than perpetrator.

"Sold you out? Wait. Where are you?"

"I'm in Chicago with the Order. They forced me here against my will for my own protection."

The phone is snatched from my hands, and I'm whirled around by the shoulder until I'm chest-to-chest with Prek, staring into his annoyed brown eyes.

"What are you doing?" he questions, holding the phone away from both of us. I can barely hear Tad's worry-filled, shouting voice on the other end. "You're making trouble for your Lesser family. There are no Lesser authorities that you, or they, can turn to. You're setting them up either to spill secrets that will get them killed or to spend a lifetime searching for a place they'll never be able to see with their own eyes," he practically growls at me.

"A lifetime?" I challenge, pouncing on that statement. "I thought I was free to go after I answered some questions? Why would they go a lifetime without seeing me if that's true?"

His eyes bounce back and forth between mine, like he's quickly trying to calibrate what I'm about and how to answer me. He lets out a breath that tickles my face, his arrogant mien disappearing out of nowhere.

"Tell him you're fine and you're going to call him tomorrow," he commands, and I raise a brow and offer him a look that says *fat fucking chance.* "I'll explain what's going on, and you *will* call him tomorrow. Protect your family, and tell them to stay where they are."

Now it's my turn to study Prek's face, to try and read what he's not saying and gauge what I should do. I reach for the phone, and Prek sets it back in my palm.

"Hey," I greet as Tad releases a barrage of worried *hello*s.

"What happened? What's going on, Lennox?" he demands, and his use of my name and not a nickname shows me just how freaked out he really is.

"My babysitter didn't like what I was telling you," I state evenly, and Prek reaches for the phone again. I skip back from him and hold up a hand for him to give me a minute. I watch him debate what to do, but he doesn't try for the phone again or close the distance I just put between us.

"Are you safe?" Tad demands.

"Yes," I answer, not hesitating even though I'm not entirely sure if it's true. Like it or not, getting my family involved in all of this isn't wise. What can they do when they're up against the witch police?

"Who was the first boy I kissed?" Tad questions suspiciously.

"Brennan Skeen," I answer, approving of his test.

"Okay, and what did we make for Halloween when you were eleven?"

I smile at the memory. "Poodle skirts."

"Who was the first guy to break your heart?" Tad challenges, and I close my eyes and swallow the emotion his question conjures.

"My father," I answer with a pained whisper.

I hear Tad's relieved sigh before he asks again, "Are you safe, Leni?" The concern and tenderness in his tone makes my eyes prick. I suddenly wish I were at home on my Aunt Hillen's couch with a pint of ice cream and a *Hunger Games* marathon queued up on the TV. I would tell Tad all about how Rogan hurt my heart, wrapped up in a soft blanket, with his advice and jokes to cushion my fall.

"I'm safe," I reassure him, filling the pummeled cracks in my heart with resolve and determination.

"Okay, now put me on speaker phone, please?" he asks, and I pause, not expecting his request.

"What?"

"Speaker phone, please?" he chirps, and after staring at the phone for a second, I do as requested.

"You're on speaker phone," I announce curiously.

"I don't know exactly what you're about there in the Order, but I want you to listen closely," Tad practically snarls, and I look over at Prek. "You may think I'm just some Lesser, some simple human who could never pose a threat to you, but I want to tell you that you'd be wrong. You fuck with Lennox, you fuck with the entire Osseous clan, and you should know we are skilled and we are relentless. *You* can be gotten to. Your family can be gotten to. Am I clear?" he asks, and a smile pulls at the corner of my mouth. Of course Tad would go full *our family will beat your ass*, I'd do the same for him.

I'm surprised when, instead of rolling his eyes and saying nothing, Prek answers. "Very clear."

"His name is Prek," I insert, just in case.

Prek shakes his head at that but goes to sit back down on the stool by the kitchen.

"I'll call you tomorrow," I assure Tad, ready to grill my new Order babysitter for some answers.

"Okay, Lens, but if I don't hear from you, shit's going to go down," he states louder than he needs to. "Oh, and tell Rogan if I ever see him again, I'm going to fuck him up."

I chuckle, picturing average-sized Tad trying to fight the muscled skyscraper that is Rogan.

"Don't you laugh at me, Lennard. It's always a fair fight

when the little guy has a taser," Tad chirps cheerily, and I crack up.

"I love you," I tell him, my heart aching with how much I wish I were there with him.

"Love you, Leni, keep your head up, and I'll talk to you tomorrow."

I hang up and blink back the tears of longing and helplessness that try to breach my lids. There's always something about talking to family that makes you feel vulnerable as fuck. I feel that so much in this moment, like I've been grated raw and now I'm exposed. Prek clears his throat as though there's any way I could have forgotten about his intrusive presence already. Without looking at him, I hold my hand out with the phone, and he takes it.

"Ready for questioning?" Prek asks casually as he pushes to his feet.

"As I'll ever be," I snark, rubbing both my hands tiredly over my face and sighing.

He moves to the door, and I prepare myself. Time to get some answers, one way or another.

3

"Okay, Prek, tell me what the hell I've landed myself in the middle of," I ask as I follow him down a corridor, away from my quarters to an elevator. The carpet and walls are almost the same color of gray, and it feels a tad too claustrophobic for my liking. We pass dark wood doors, and I wonder which one Rogan is staying in. I tell myself it's so I know which one to avoid and not because I'm looking for him, but I'm not sure if it's all the way true.

"I don't know what Rogan told you, but we're not the bad guys you think we are," Prek answers as he presses the button to call the elevator a little too hard.

I scoff and shake my head, annoyed. "Rogan is irrelevant. I don't think you're the bad guys because of *him*, I think you're the bad guys because you blew a car *I* was in off the road and could have killed me," I inform him.

"Rogan *isn't* irrelevant," he counters. "He's a pariah, and *you* were with him. By association, you can be held to the same standard as he is, and *he's* dangerous."

I throw my hands up in frustration. "I didn't even know

who he was until…" I try to recall what day it is again, and remember it's still Wednesday.

Was it really just this morning when Rogan and I stood in his kitchen, spelling and spilling secrets?

I look down at my hand and see that my ring is gone. Dammit, I just spelled that earlier. *Did I lose it somehow, or was it taken from me?*

"This morning, actually, I didn't know who he was until this morning," I repeat defensively. "I had no idea when he showed up in my shop that he was a renounced witch."

The elevator doors open to an empty car, and Prek doesn't say anything as we both step in. He pokes the button for floor eleven. I look up and see that we're currently on floor thirty-seven before the doors close and we begin to move down. I lean against a wall and rub at the back of my neck. I'm tired and run down both physically and emotionally. The side of my neck stings a bit, and I realize that's where they stuck me with whatever knocked me out. I want to ask if it was Rogan or Prek who did it, but in the end, it doesn't really matter.

"Just tell me what's going on," I finally ask, breaking up the silence as we descend. "Leave the Rogan shit out of this. I don't know what the issue is between the two of you, but it has nothing to do with me."

Prek turns his head to study me for a moment and then faces forward again without a word as the elevator stops.

"Rogan is as good as dead to me," I declare emphatically as the doors slide open, revealing none other than the asshole Rogan Kendrick himself. He towers over both of us, and I immediately stiffen at the sight of him. He fixes a severe stare on me, the likes of which tell me that he heard my last statement and doesn't like it.

Good. He can smolder all he wants. Burn himself up for

all I care. I'm done falling for the tall, dark and broody bullshit.

It doesn't go unobserved that, unlike me, he's sans an escort. Then again, what do I expect? It's clear the Major isn't a fan, but I know Rogan cut some kind of deal to be here, and it seems that deal included free rein of the place and a constipated, priggish manner while he's here.

Prek elbows past him without a word, and I do the same, throwing a few more elbows than are necessary. Rogan takes it, stoic and confusing as ever. Prek leads me further into floor eleven, which has a busy precinct feel to it. I see the yellow robes of Order members coming and going. Witches in offices working or talking with other groups of witches. We pass the beehive of activity, Rogan's imposing presence on my heels the whole way.

I feel like I'm holding my breath. Will he say anything? Do I want him to? I have so many questions, and yet I simultaneously wish I could never see him again. I want to dropkick the part of me that's quietly hoping he will fix this, as if there's something he can do or say that would make everything he did okay, but I know that's bullshit. Nothing can erase what happened. I'm also assuming that he even has something to say, that he realizes what he did was wrong, but I'm not getting that impression, and that ties me in knots too.

The hustle and bustle grows more sedate the further we walk, and I observe a small maze of closed doors that have an odd pattern to their arrangement. It isn't until Prek opens one and I'm herded in that I realize why. I'm brought into a well-sized conference style room with modern cushy chairs surrounding a stark white oval table. I take in the massive rectangular mirrors that make up two of the four walls, and I know exactly what this kind of room is used for.

Without a doubt, I'm here to be interrogated.

I stop in my tracks as apprehension floods my system. It's like being called into your boss's office without warning. I know I haven't done anything wrong, but tell that to my racing heart and the adrenaline that just shot into my system.

"Have a seat," Prek instructs, and that sets off even more panic. Which chair do I choose? Will they read into my selection?

Oh she sat on the end, she's guilty!

I do my best to swallow down my unease, telling myself it's irrational. They told me they had questions, and here I am to answer them. I had no idea it was going to be in this kind of setting, but it changes nothing. I haven't done anything wrong.

I select the chair farthest from the door—that's not on the end—and sit down, opening and closing my fists in my lap in an effort to release the tension thrumming through me. I keep picturing button-down-shirt-wearing detectives on the other side of the reflective glass, drinking stale coffee and jonesing for a cigarette. It's a stupid visual. I know this room and what's happening on the other side of the faux mirrors won't be like anything I've ever seen, or even heard of, on a TV show.

This is the Order. They have magic to observe and deal with *all* kinds of things. Witches that track vitals and feelings, that can hear lies. They could have a mind reader behind one of these walls of glass for all I know. And for what witches can't do, there are amulets and potions that can. There's no telling what's built into the walls of this place or what could be standing on the other side of the mirror. I'm sure they surprised me with this setting on purpose so some witch can get a baseline on my emotions or dig into my head or something.

"If you're reading my mind right now, here's a scarring slideshow of what STDs look like. You can thank my high school health teacher for the trauma. Also, go fuck yourself," I snap in my mind, looking over to the expanse of mirror across from me.

Movement pulls my attention from my mental sabotage efforts, and I see both Prek *and* Rogan turning to leave. Bewilderment stomps out my trepidation, and I shoot out of my chair.

"Wait. You're not being questioned too?" I demand as Rogan moves to exit the still open door.

He turns back to me, a bored look on his face. "I've already been questioned," he replies, his tone far too dismissive for me to ignore in my current state of freak out. When he turns to leave again, as though that's all the explanation I'm owed, I lose my ever-loving shit.

I drop every barrier I've been using to hide my magic from him, and reach for the tether that connects us. I may not be able to magically flex outside of myself in this place —not yet anyway—but I sure as hell am about to let Rogan know that I'm coming for him. I wrap my essence around our connection and pull with everything I have. I syphon his magic so brutally and proficiently his knees buckle and he goes down. I hear him gasp in pain as I call on our familiar link and take every ounce of ability stored in his gargantuan body.

If our connection was a true witch-and-familiar connection, I could kill him by doing this. I could pull his entire essence into me, extinguish the light in his very soul if I were cruel enough, but I can't. The tether between us allows him to pull right back. But if I drain him thoroughly enough, it will take him time to recover and build up the magical strength needed to either replenish or syphon back what was taken.

What I'm doing is painful and violating. I'm leaving him vulnerable, weak, and right now I couldn't care less. It all happens in a matter of seconds. Prek barely has time to turn around to see why Rogan is on the ground before the damage is done.

"Just like that, you'll leave me here to fend for myself?" I snap at Rogan as he shakily tries to push up from the floor. His eyes rise to meet mine, and the fury swimming in his gaze makes my heart constrict painfully in my chest. "Not even a glint of apology on your face for what you've done to me?" I demand, hating the frail wobble in my tone that breaks through my rage. "You dropped me dead center into all this shit, and I can't get so much as a heads-up from you?" I gesture all around me, furious that I'm here, livid that I didn't get a say in it. "Well, how do you like it, Rogan? How does *vulnerable and fucked* feel to you?" I snarl, dropping back down into my seat, wrath worming its way around my chest and begging for more.

My blood sings with ability, my magic calling for retribution, but it also triggers an echo of what I felt in my nightmare. I breathe through the anger and pain churning at my core, reminding myself of the warning in that dream. I play back what it looked like and felt like to kill him, and then I recall what it felt like to die right alongside him. I acted on raw emotion in my dream, retaliating without a second thought, but I ended up drowning in my own rage, suffocating on my own blood, wishing I didn't know what the taste of regret was like on my tongue. I tamp down my fury and struggle to get a hold of the hurt bleeding out of me.

"What the fuck is wrong with you?" Prek asks, looking from Rogan to me and back again, obviously perplexed and irked.

"I fell," Rogan grumbles, and with great effort, he pushes to his feet. He dusts off his dark wash jeans and the emerald-green shirt he's wearing, but when his eyes meet mine, I discover it's not revenge or fury that I see in his stare. No. His moss-green gaze is filled with agony, with loss. The torment he fixes on me when his gaze connects with mine is so visceral that I can feel the ache of it to my very marrow. It shocks me. Catches me completely off guard. Before I can respond in any way, Rogan blinks, shuttering his stare, and then he turns and steps out of the room, the heavy solid-wood door closing behind him.

I ache from what I just witnessed, and I hate that I'm just as confused as I always am when it comes to him. I can never find my footing with Rogan Kendrick, I'd be stupid to think I ever will. I touch the side of my neck where a needle was shoved into it and let the sting of pain ground me. It doesn't matter what Rogan shows me now, what he tries to convince me is true about him. I've seen enough to know where caring about him gets me. I look around the room and shake my head in disgust. It gets me here, in an interrogation room, alone.

I'm not sure how long I sit, waiting, stewing in anger. I feel too full of magic. It's as though I went too hard at a power buffet and am now stuck in public and can't unbutton my pants to make room for my ever-expanding stomach. I'm uncomfortable as hell, but the only way to relieve myself of this feeling is to give some of the intense amount of magic I'm holding back to Rogan, and I won't do that. So instead, I sit in this chair, shifting my weight every couple of minutes like a kid who has to pee, growing more and more irritated and worried by the moment, and wondering why no one has come in to talk to me.

Did my magic suck set off some kind of alarm? Did my

temper get the best of me and give me away? Are they fixing the wards on this room as we speak so they can leave me as powerless and weak as Rogan is right now? My mind shoots off in a dozen different directions, each imagined scenario worse than the one before.

I put my head on the table and sigh. It's a good thing I'm not actually guilty of something. I'm clearly the kind of person who would crack like an egg, confessing to shit I wasn't even in trouble for until I spilled every deep dark secret to the authorities in a fit of tears and panic. Ugh, I'm pathetic.

As though that were the magic word to make the door to the room open, it unlatches and swings open, allowing four witches to file into the room. I blink a couple of times as though I've been stranded in a desert and I'm trying to make sure they're not a mirage.

Note to self, too much magic in your system makes you a little batshit.

I clear my throat and sit up, trying to get a hold of myself.

One of the witches is rockin' a severely tight ponytail and harsh angular facial features. She sits in a chair away from the rest of us and pulls out a tablet, as though she's this meeting's minutes taker. Two witches sit across from me, a male with long wavy blond hair and gray eyes, and a Judi Dench-looking woman—if Judi Dench dyed her cute pixie cut black and wore too much eyeliner. The seat next to me is pulled out, and a beautiful woman with black eyes, bantu knots in her hair, and skin a shade darker than mine sits down. She's just a little too close, and all at once I feel like a cornered cat that's being threatened with a bath.

My magic pulses in my chest, restless and responding to my discomfort. I feel it start to crawl up my throat, begging me to tell it where to go and what to do, but I swallow it back down and keep my mouth shut.

"Hello, Miss Osseous. My name is Eleanor," the Judi Dench-looking witch introduces. "This is Orion," she continues, gesturing to the man across from me. "And this is Fiona."

I look next to me and nod at Fiona in greeting before looking back to Eleanor. I expect her to introduce the witch sitting against the wall, tapping away at a tablet, but she doesn't.

"We'll be asking you some questions today and taking notes for our case. It shouldn't take too much time, and as long as you're honest and forthcoming with answers, everything should be easy peasy," she declares, scrunching her nose and smiling wide in an overexaggerated expression of friendliness.

It immediately puts me on guard, and I watch the trio warily.

"What does the name Nikki Smelser mean to you?" Eleanor asks me casually, her stare cryptic and watchful.

Well, okay then, I guess the pleasantries are over.

I shrug, not sure where she's leading me. Marx told us that he was questioned about his involvement with the search and my grandmother's dream, but I don't know if the Order is aware that he told Rogan and me that. Maybe this is some kind of a test?

"I know that the bones gave me the name Nik Smelser when I was at Elon Kendrick's house," I tell her, working through how I can answer truthfully but not provide context and details that will give away that I might know more than they realize. "I assumed it was a man's name, but your use of Nikki is either some kind of weird aim at familiarity or Nik is a woman," I add, hoping my suspicion is right and I didn't just get caught in any kind of trap.

"Yes, Nikki Smelser is a woman. An Animamancer at that," she offers, the look on her face conspiratorial, like we're just two girls gossiping while we get manis.

"She's a Soul Witch?" I repeat, confused, and she nods enthusiastically in answer. I pause for a beat, trying to work out what this could mean. "But...not the Soul Witch that was reported missing with the other Osteomancers?" I query, placing this new nugget of information with the other kernels that I already possess.

Why would someone take three Osteomancers and two Animamancers? What's the connection between the Bone Witches and the Soul Witches?

The vision I had the day I was at Elon's house of him leaving with a pack on his back and his familiar, Tilda, in tow reminds me that the *taken* status for all of these people is still unconfirmed, but I don't say anything, instead wanting to see how much I can get out of the Order before they realize I'm fishing.

"Okay, and you think she's the one who took the others?" I ask, looking to the witches around me as though the missing pieces to this puzzle will be written all over their faces. I glean nothing.

"Well, it's too early to say that, but she's most definitely the person who wrote the note asking to trade them for you," Eleanor states, tilting her head to the side and scrunching her brow in a comical display of bad acting. "Now why would she do that?" she queries, staring past me as though the empty space behind me will whisper the answer to her.

"Do what, write the letter?" I ask, fighting the urge to look behind me and see exactly what the old witch is staring at.

Eleanor tsks. "No, not that, my dear. Why would she

trade them for you?" Her blue eyes focus back on me, and she waits patiently as though she expects me to answer.

"How would I know?" I defend, starting to get irritated. This is a waste of time. If Nik Smelser is the one who took the other witches, why are they talking and acting like I might have had something to do with it?

Orion conjures a picture out of thin air and slides it across the table to me. The woman staring back at me has brown curly hair, glasses, and a kind smile. She's pretty and has a small dimple in one cheek. Her eyes are almost the same mocha brown as her hair, and there's a clear and perceptible happiness in her gaze.

"This is Nik Smelser?" I ask, feeling even more confused. This does not look like the kind of person who kidnaps other people. I mean, what do I really know, looks *can* be deceiving, but this woman...yeah, I just don't see diabolical or unfeeling written anywhere in her features.

"The very one," Eleanor answers, and I start to wonder why the other two witches are here when Eleanor is the only one who talks.

"And you're sure *she* wrote the note?" I press, not convinced at all that there's not something we're missing here.

"There's no question," Eleanor confirms.

"May I see it, the note?" I ask as I slide Nikki's picture back to Orion.

"I'll have it brought up for you," Eleanor chirps happily, but when none of them get up as though they're going to get it, I assume either someone on the other side of the glass is getting it or my seeing the note will happen some other time.

"Your grandmother had an odd dream that she felt the need to report. She worried it could be a warning of some sort, a prophecy perhaps. Did she discuss what she saw with you?"

I try hard not to roll my eyes at her question. Why do I need to go through this with them, didn't they talk to Marx already? Didn't he tell them that he and Rogan told me about the dream. That I didn't even know I was the next in line, let alone have deep conversations about potentially prophetic visions with my grandmother.

"Can we just save ourselves some time here, and I'll just tell you that I don't have anything to do with these missing witches. I didn't know I was going to be chosen when my grandmother passed. We never talked about her work or her magic. I had no idea that my grandmother had a dream that bothered her. I don't know Nikki Smelser. I never met the missing Osteomancers. I have nothing to do with this other than I was asked for help, by a stranger, and I agreed," I state evenly, hoping we can skip past the part where they suspect me and dive right into trying to find who really is behind all of this.

"And why did you agree to help...*a stranger*?" Fiona asks, her voice smooth and intoxicating.

I almost jump in surprise when someone besides Eleanor finally speaks, but luckily I keep my butt firmly planted in the seat. *Vox Witch alert*, my senses scream, and I work to not get lost in the creaminess of her voice.

"Because that's how it works," I answer simply, looking at each of them with judgment-tinged bewilderment. They all know the give and take Osteos deal with when it comes to our magic. "I read for people the bones choose, I help those my magic encourages me to," I add as though these Order members need the reminder.

"And your magic chose Rogan Kendrick?" Fiona presses.

"Yes," I declare confidently.

Eleanor's gaze slides quickly over to the mirror on the

wall to my left before returning back to me, but I don't miss it. Who is she looking at? Rogan? Someone else?

"How old was your grandmother when she passed?" Eleanor asks, and I'm taken aback by the abrupt change in subject.

"She was eighty-three."

Eleanor's eyes grow more intense as the next question spills out of her mouth. "And who found her body?"

I open my mouth to answer, but I'm forced to pause. I almost said my Aunt Hillen, but that's not right. Tad told me that someone had called them with the news. Was it Magda? No, that can't be the case because Hillen called them to rub it in that they didn't have the bones. They also didn't have the Grimoire long enough to read through it and destroy it. If she and Gwen had found Grammy Ruby the day before, that Grimoire would have been toast by the time I showed up looking for it.

Unease settles in my soul as I respond the only way I can. "I don't know."

Eleanor's thin eyebrows jump with shock, but it's obvious it's feigned. There will be no Oscar awards in this witch's future, that's for damn sure.

"How do you not know? Were the necros not called in?" she asked, over-the-top shocked.

"Of course they were, it was natural causes, *that* was undisputed."

"And how do you know that? If you didn't see your grandmother's body, don't even know who did, how can you be sure?" she queries innocently, but there's a conniving glint in her blue eyes.

I want to say *because I was told so*, but the argument sounds weak even to my ears.

"Were you close with your grandmother?" Orion pipes up out of nowhere to ask.

"Yes."

"But not close enough to discuss magic with her, to know about her troubling dreams, or her standing in our community?" he goes on, the judgment clear in his voice.

Flustered, I want to tell him to fuck off, but all I can say is, "We didn't talk about magic, that was the way I wanted it, and my grandmother respected that."

"Not want to talk about magic?" Eleanor exclaims loudly as though she's never heard a more absurd statement. "Why ever not? Was your duty as a member of your line treated so cavalierly?"

I flinch slightly at the jab. "No, but contrary to popular belief, not everyone wants to be like you. Magic isn't the be-all and end-all for some people."

The three witches around me laugh as though I've just delivered the best stand-up routine they've ever heard. It bounces around the room offensively and lands like bird shit on the ground at my feet.

"What was the *real* reason, Lennox? And don't think the lies you've been telling yourself for far too long are going to hold any sway here," Eleanor snaps, all pretense of the jovial elderly woman she's been playing up until now, gone.

I glare at her unimpressed. "What? The kindly grandmother routine not working for you the way you thought, so you just drop it all together?" I accuse. "Did you really think I'd warm up to the inadequate job you just did of trying to emulate my grandmother? That I'd be too grief stricken to see right through that crap?"

Eleanor chuckles, but there's not an ounce of genuine humor in it. "Lennox, you can talk to whoever you want, the attractive friend," she declares, gesturing toward Fiona next to me. "The calming father figure," she goes on, tilting her head toward Orion before pointing at herself, "the representation of a lost loved one. You could even spill all your secrets to a girl you feel sorry for, the one you want to help," she adds, pointing behind her at the witch with the tablet, sitting separately from the rest of us.

"This is the collection that our analysis showed would be most effective, but if this isn't to your liking, I can call in the gay BFF option, the stern authority figure, or my personal favorite: handsome and broody. Truly, Lennox, you can pick your poison, but in the end you *will* answer our questions. You *will* tell us everything we need to know," she states matter-of-factly.

Heat rushes to my cheeks and anger simmers in my stomach. I'm an idiot. Here I was thinking I had one up on them. That I was staying one step ahead, milking them for information and navigating their stupidity, but they've been playing *me* the whole time. Probably before I ever even set foot in this room. Eleanor just bitch-slapped the overconfidence right out of me, and now I'm at a loss for what to do.

I clench my jaw and breathe through the embarrassment and frustration I feel. I thought I was smarter, that I was dealing with a bunch of amateurs, but it was the other way around. I'm the rookie here, and it's obvious that I have no idea what I'm up against. I sit back in my chair and fold my arms over my chest protectively. Eleanor's eyes light up with the movement, like she takes it as my waving a white flag of surrender.

"Good," she coos cruelly. "Now, where were we, yes, that's right...what was the real reason why you and your grandmother didn't talk shop? Why was she so willing to leave a descendant in her line, one who she knew could potentially inherit, so ignorant?"

Pain slams into me like a massive, unexpected wave at the beach. One minute, I'm appreciating the feel of warm sand and cool ocean water, then the next, I'm being pulled under and drowning in it. Flashes of my father's face, his note, and the devastation left in its wake hollow me out, and I wish I could climb inside of myself instead of having to answer these pointless painful questions.

I shake my head, pissed that I'm here, that they're forcing this hurt to resurface, and all for what? Is this really about them trying to understand me, my grandmother, the prophecy she thought she had? Is there more to this than I realize? I struggle to find my footing to see where this is going, but I can't. I tell myself to just get it out, answer their stupid questions regardless of how invasive or useless it might be. Witches are missing, and if this gets them to focus on finding them, then it'll be worth it in the end. I fix a resigned stare on the bitch of a witch sitting diagonally across from me, the *fuck you* clear in my fiery gaze, and with a deep fortifying breath, I answer her question.

"When I heard *chondrosarcoma* for the first time, it was the scariest word I'd ever heard. I was sixteen and didn't know what it meant. When my dad explained that it was cancer and that it was very advanced, I thought my world was over. And then I heard the words *bone cancer*, and it was like all my worry turned into sparrows and just flew away," I tell them, gently shaking my head at the memories, at how young and dumb I was then.

"Most people wouldn't feel excitement at the words *bone cancer,* but most people didn't know a Bone Witch. I just knew my Grammy Ruby would save the day. After all, what's cancer compared to *magic*?" The rhetorical question floats on the tension in the room all around me, and I look up at the ceiling, blinking back the emotion and fury welling in my eyes.

"I dove headfirst into the spells and potions and remedies that should have cured him. We attacked chondrosarcoma with everything we could, human treatments or witch, it didn't matter, we went for it. For two years, getting my dad better was all I could focus on. But it didn't matter what my Grammy Ruby made or magicked, he deteriorated right in front of our eyes. I couldn't make sense of it, and instead of accepting that not even magic can save everyone, I worked harder to find some spell, some tincture that would keep my dad with me. And then he died."

My throat grows tight as too many feelings all try to spill out of me at once. I'm quiet for a moment as I struggle to rein it all in. Fiona takes my silence as the end of my story.

"You turned your back on magic because it didn't do what you wanted it to?" she snarks, her tone painting me as a petulant child who's been having a temper tantrum for far too long.

I release an empty chuckle and shake my head. These people may think they know who I am, what I'm about, but they don't know shit.

"No," I answer simply, a sad smile taking over my face. "My dad never even gave the magic a shot."

Confusion sneaks across Fiona's features, and I fight the urge to slap it off her face.

"You see, I found this note in my dad's things when I was forced to pack them up after he died. I found boxes of untouched potions, neatly packed and protectively wrapped in his closet. It seems he wouldn't take them, but he also wouldn't waste them, so he saved them. Each and every remedy my Grammy and I had worked on for years was just sitting pristine and untouched. His note said that he loved me, and he hoped someday that I would understand, but that he's with my mother now, and he's happy."

The smell of stale carpet and magic wafts up around me, and it's like I'm sitting in that closet again. I can feel the notebook paper in my hands, smell the faint hint of cardboard. I remember looking down at my dad's slanted scrawl, his words simple and direct, just like they always were when he was alive.

He said he loved me, but he left. *He* was happy, but did he care that it shattered *my* happy?

A tear rolls down my cheek, and I blink, mentally pulling myself from the small space in the trailer I grew up in. I look over at Fiona, leveling her with my anguish. "I didn't turn my back on magic because I didn't get what I wanted, I walked away because I wanted *too* much from it. Putting all your faith in someone, in some*thing*, is dangerous. I made sure it never happened again. My grandmother understood how I felt. She knew there was no pushing me on this. Besides, we thought my cousin would be the chosen one."

I say the last part out of habit. I now know that wasn't the case, but in the end, it didn't change anything. My Grammy knew I needed time, that I needed space to find the beauty in magic again, the power in it. These people may not get that, but she did, and I'm eternally grateful that she loved *me* enough to let me find my way.

"What if I told you that your grandmother didn't push you to learn magic like she was supposed to, *not* because she empathized with your situation, but because she never intended to pass it on to you?" Eleanor spews, her face smug and her eyes predatory.

The statement is so random, so ludicrous, that I bark out an incredulous laugh. "I'd say you didn't know my grandmother," I answer simply, done with the questions for the day. I need to get out of this enclosed hell hole and breathe some fresh air. I need to sit with the emotions I just dug up and let them settle once again.

"No, Osteomancer, I'd say *you* didn't know your grandmother very well," the elderly witch snaps, and with her vitriol goes my last ounce of patience. I open my mouth to tell her to go sit on a wand, but she cuts me off. "You may not have known Nikki Smelser, but do you want to know who did?"

Orion conjures another picture and slides it my way. The photo bumps against my arm, ricocheting back a couple of inches before going still on the table. A familiar cherubic face looks up at me. One I've seen in a frame in my grandmother's house since I can remember. It takes me a second, but as I study it, I start to see.

Large brown eyes stare up from an adorable little oval face. Short brown curls stick out every which way, a happy smile stretched wide on the kid's face, exposing a single dimple. She didn't have glasses then, and her face hadn't yet started to morph from the squishy cheeks and button nose of a child into the beautiful woman that she becomes. But there's no doubt...I'm looking at Nikki Smelser.

Befuddlement clamors through me as I take in the little girl's picture I've seen and dismissed a thousand times.

"Your grandmother was close friends with her grandmother until she died, and Nikki became her successor. Ruby looked in on the Soul Witch from time to time. So imagine our surprise when this otherwise innocent seeming witchling appears to be smack dab in the middle of an attack on Osteomancers," Eleanor sneers, looking far too *cat that got the cream* than I have the patience for.

"Oh, she's good, your grandmother. She had us looking at the pawn, thinking it was the queen. We were all chasing our tails until we searched her apartment and found the *one* loose end she forgot to tie up." Eleanor taps the picture as though it's all the damning evidence she needs. "We couldn't figure out where you tied into all of it, why trade them for you, but now it's obvious..."

She pauses dramatically, and I can see in her eyes that she wants me to ask *what*. Well, she can keep on waiting, I'm not a marionette, and she sure as hell isn't my puppet master.

Eleanor's eyes sparkle with excitement, and the tension in the room rises. "Your grandmother is alive, Lennox. *She's* the one behind this. But don't worry, we're going to find her, and when we do, we'll make sure she's dead for real this time."

4

Rage blazes through me, and my magic flares in response.

"Are you trying to get your ass beat?" I seethe as I push up from my chair and lean toward the witch, who has no idea who she's fucking with. The other Order members in the room all shoot to their feet, eyes wary and looking off to the mirrors as though they expect help to come rushing in at any moment, all except Eleanor. *She* looks delighted, like it was her sole purpose in life to make me lose my shit. The eagerness I see in her demented gaze gives me pause, and I think through why she might be pushing me so hard.

Her revelation spins around in my mind.

The declaration.

The threat.

Does she really believe Grammy Ruby is alive? Is this some kind of trick? I want to completely reject the notion that somehow my grandmother faked her own death, but after everything I've seen and learned since the bones chose me, I don't know if I can.

Rogan was just telling me that magic in a line doesn't

have to only pass through death. It can be relinquished and then...*they leave, they live the rest of their lives as Lessers.*

But even if that's true, I recall when I first discovered the bones in my apartment. I know I felt my Grammy watching over me as I opened the pouch and sealed the bones to me. There have been other times where I've distinctly felt her presence, and there is no way any of that happened if she was still alive.

Right?

As though Eleanor can see me talking myself down, she lobs more of her twisted theories at me. "Think about it, Lennox, why would this kidnapper go through all of this trouble to get to you? It's because your grandmother wants her power back, because she doesn't realize we're on to her, but we are now!"

A boom thuds from the other side of the mirror across from me. The surface of it vibrates from the force of whatever hit it. I expect someone or something to come crashing through it, but nothing happens other than the loud sound drawing our attention.

Just then, the door to the room opens. A young man walks in, gloved hands holding what I presume to be the ransom note. He glances around the room like he's unsure what he's supposed to do with it. Eleanor looks from the paper to me.

"Don't believe me, Lennox? See for yourself. Call your bones. We know you can. Spill them on the table, see if they'll clue you in on what else your grandmother has planned."

She snatches the note out of the man's hands, but before she can so much as turn to fling it at me, she throws her head back and releases a blood-curdling scream. An alarm sounds off all around me, but all I can see and hear is Eleanor screaming as her body erupts in blisters as though she's burning somehow from the inside out. The paper in her hand starts to smoke, and I'm terrified that this witch is going to spontaneously combust right before my eyes. I'm frozen in place as her skin starts to char and split.

Another scream demands my attention, and I look over to find Fiona scrambling away from her fellow Order member. She's shrieking something about demon magic and to clear the room, but I'm so muddled with shock that I don't move. Lights flash all around me, but all I can see is Eleanor as parts of her hands start to flake off like burnt paper on a breeze.

Arms wrap around me in a tight band, and the next thing I know, I'm being pulled from the room, the echo of Eleanor's screams and the smell of sulfur and ash chasing after me as I'm pulled to safety. Everything around me slows, I'm hyper aware of what's happening, and yet it's as though someone activated drunk-sloth-mode in my settings. I can't seem to respond to anything in real time.

Shouts to *get her to safety* bounce around the hallway I'm being carried down. Someone kicks a door open, and suddenly we're pouring into a stairwell. Booted feet pound loudly on each step as we start to climb up. Everything feels disorienting with alarms blaring and lights blinking all around us. I want to tell whoever has me that they're going the wrong way. You're supposed to go down when there's a fire, not up, but I can't make my mouth work. I feel like we're rushing into an apartment that looks like the one I was in before, but I can tell it's not mine. Everything is in the same place, but the colors are different, the knick knacks on the shelves aren't the ones I remember throwing around when I was searching my quarters for clues.

I'm set on my feet, and a tall man leans down until his face is in line with mine. Wild green eyes stare back at me, the scar running through one side of his face making him look far more formidable than I know he is. I stop that line of thinking immediately. *I don't know anything about him*, I remind myself. Well, nothing beyond the fact that I can't trust him anyway.

As though Rogan can see that conclusion form in my shock-filled stare, I watch as his eyes harden. I can practically feel him putting on his armor in protection from what he sees in my gaze. It breaks me a little that this is where we are. It wasn't very long ago that I was looking into his eyes and seeing *possibility* there. Now all I can see is my weakness.

"Is she okay? Did she get hit by any residual curse?" a voice asks, but Rogan's eyes never leave mine.

"No, she's just in shock. Is the rest of the building secure? Do we know if there were any others?" Rogan demands.

Others?

"No, they're doing a sweep now," the other voice responds, and I realize it's Marx.

"I need you to clear the room," Rogan quietly tells his friend, and I blink, shutting Rogan's face out of my mind for a millisecond before I'm once again staring at him.

Internally I try to rally, to mentally slap myself and shout *snap out of it*. But my feet stay planted, and my eyes stay fixed as though I'm the moth and Rogan's the flame. Or maybe I'm the flame, and that's why I can't do anything other than stand here and feel like I'm burning up with confusion and fury.

"Team, let's sweep the floor, make sure there's no surprises planted about. Rish, Bridger, watch the door, if anyone but us tries to approach, put them down."

Yes, sir sounds off all around me, and even though I don't look away from Rogan's face, I hear witches scurry out of the room on Marx's command. The sound of the door closing and a lock being put in place registers to my ears, and yet I stand, brokenly staring at the man who's betrayed me every chance he's been given.

Silence wraps itself all around us until eventually Rogan breaks it. "Are you okay?" he asks me, his eyes searching mine for answers.

"No," I surprisingly respond, my voice flat and distant.

"Are you hurt?"

I take stock. *Am I hurt?* Eleanor's scream reverberates in my mind, and I flinch against the playback of the sound in my head.

"Not physically," I voice quietly.

Geez, is Rogan part Vox Witch and he forgot to tell me about it, or does my drunk-sloth-mode come with an auto-answer setting?

"What was that?" I ask shakily, relieved that I can form the question and not just stand here and spit out answers like I'm still in that interrogation room.

"They'll run tests to confirm, but I'm pretty sure it was a demon curse," Rogan tells me. There's awe and worry lacing his tone, and it makes me feel as though he's surprised by what he's saying.

I don't know much about demons other than they're powerful and parasitic. They feed off the essence of other living beings, but I have no idea why a demon would be involved in any of this. Questions fire off in my mind, zinging by too quickly for me to grab any and force them out of my mouth. I have no idea what this means, but judging by what I just saw, I'm no safer here in the heart of the Order than I was outside of this place.

"If I had touched that note before she did…" I start, but the adamant shake of Rogan's head makes me trail off.

"She knew better, she knew she shouldn't have handled any evidence without proper precautions in place. She put us all at risk with her blatant disregard of protocol. They wouldn't have let you handle that letter without protection," he reassures me, but I'm far too busy putting myself in Eleanor's shoes to really hear him.

I shake off those thoughts and rub at my eyes as though it will scrub the image of what happened to that witch out of my mind. "Why would a demon do that? I don't understand how that fits with everything else that's happened?"

Rogan puts his head back, stress and exhaustion radiating off of him. "I don't know. Demons are rare and don't usually involve themselves in witch business. They have no political aspirations, no desire to be part of the hierarchy, as far as I've ever known. They have their underworld and thrive in that atmosphere." He pauses, his eyes lost in thought as he works through possibilities, better equipped than I am to suss them out with his vast experience of the magical world.

Meanwhile, I can't help but look at all the shadows in the room suspiciously. *Am I being hunted by demons?* Worse yet is that I don't know if *that* possibility is better or worse than the idea of my Grammy faking her death and potentially kidnapping witches.

"The Order has experts in demon magic. They'll study what occurred, break down the purpose of the curse, and figure out why that happened. Until then, Lennox, we need to be careful. Whoever is behind this breached the Order once, they could do it again," he warns me, and I swear the room feels like it grows colder by degrees.

I'm back to side-eyeing the shadows when Rogan releases a deep sigh and presses his forehead to mine. "Lennox, I know you're mad at me," he starts, and I despise that breathing him in feels comforting to me. People who are assholes shouldn't be allowed to smell good or feel safe. My instincts should be warning me away from him right now, not dosing me with the warm and fuzzies.

Traitors.

"I need you to give me my magic back," he finishes, the breath of his question tickling my lips, and finally the warning bells I've been looking for inside my head go off.

Something snaps inside of me, and I shove him away.

Note to self: when drunk-sloth-mode is accidentally activated, hate *is the off switch.*

"Are you for real right now?" I demand incredulously, and Rogan steps back into my space, crowding me, confusing my senses. I back up to keep him away and hold up a hand in warning.

"This isn't about *us*, Lennox," he argues. "I'm vulnerable, and I can't be, not here, not with demon magic breaching the Order," he attempts to reason, but it falls on deaf ears.

I cross my arms over my chest and glare at him. "You'll make it work, Rogan. I know I did when you forced my hand the first day we met or when you drugged me and shoved me into this den of vipers," I snap, not an ounce of sympathy in me for his plight.

"I didn't have a choice," he defends. "Elon is in trouble. This was our best bet at finding him as quickly as possible. We needed more resources than what we had access to. Our best shot was to take advantage of what the Order was offering."

I stare at him, gobsmacked. "You didn't have a choice?" I repeat as though there's no way I heard him right. "Oh, you had a fucking choice, Rogan, you just didn't choose *me*. Don't get that twisted in your conniving little mind. The Order didn't offer *us* anything; you went to them for a fucking trade. Me for what you wanted. Don't paint your decision with bullshit martyrdom and forced-hand nonsense," I lob back venomously.

"No, Lennox, I didn't have a choice. I was never in a position where I could choose you. It was always about finding Elon. Always. I owe him that much."

"Then owe him," I shout, moving to get in Rogan's face. "Owe him whatever you want, but don't sacrifice me to pay *your* debt! Don't fuck me over because your guilt when it comes to your brother overrides whatever decency you had or trumps whatever the hell was happening with us!" I yell, furious.

"There is no *us*," he counters with a snarl, and I reel back as though he just slapped me. "There can't be when Elon's not safe. Don't you understand? I failed my brother before. You have no idea the torture he went through. I can't let myself get distracted, I can't put anything before him and *his* safety!"

I shake my head and look around frustrated. "I get that. I do. But why the hell are you kissing me then? Why are you trying to get to know me? *You* are the one who ignores and crosses the boundaries *you* say you have, not me!"

"I know," he shouts back, throwing his arms up in a gesture of complete frustration. "I didn't plan on *you*. I didn't see *you* coming. It was all about Elon, about finding him and fucking up whoever took him. Then suddenly *you* were there, and I was just pulled into your orbit. I couldn't have stopped it if I tried, and I did try," he confesses, running his fingers frustratedly through his rich coffee-hued hair.

"Is that supposed to make me feel better?" I growl, his words pissing me off even more.

Rogan starts to pace with a growl of exasperation. "No, I'm just trying to make you understand."

"I'm not the one who needs to understand, you prick, you are!" I bellow, stepping into his path. "It was never about choosing. I would never have asked you to. It was about trust. You could have come to me and told me the deal, told me this was the only way," I yell, gesturing all around me. "I promised I would help you, and I've done everything in my power to do exactly that."

I step closer to him, dropping my voice menacingly. "You forced a familiar bond on me and then stuck a needle in my neck to seal a deal *you* made," I seethe. "You know the longer our magic stays tethered, the worse it will be for us, and yet you didn't even *try* to fix it when you could have."

"There wasn't time," he bites back, his eyes pleading. "I was such a fucking idiot, Lennox. I didn't even get the clue when you first told me, I was too busy thinking about what happened in the kitchen between us and then what Marx dropped in our laps. I was distracted, and I almost fucking missed it," he shouts, panic and self-loathing dripping from every word, his face crumpled with anguish.

"Missed what?" I scream back, thoroughly incensed and tired of all the cryptic shit.

"Run," he clips back, pained. "I almost missed *run*." His voice breaks on the word, and I swear I can hear his heart shattering in his chest. "It was a code. It meant there was trouble and to come fast. We hadn't used it in a while, I don't know why I didn't get it right away. I was outside after Marx left, I went to text him a question, but Elon's text messages were right above his, and that's when it hit me." He paces closer, talking quickly and agitatedly using his hands as he explains. "It was a stupid inside joke. We had gotten shit-faced after we'd won a fight with the latest group of *extractors* our parents had sent our way."

My heart constricts at his words, at how casually he delivers them as though your parents sending bounty hunters after you is an everyday occurrence and not worth focusing on. I stomp out my empathy for him like someone stomps out an uninvited fire at their feet. Nope. I'm not falling for his *the world is against me* crap anymore.

"We joked about needing a Bat Signal. I said I'd message

him *we ride at dawn* and he'd know to get his ass over to me. The next thing you know, we were both putting on fake Texan accents and tipping imaginary hats."

Rogan is lost to the memory, his head tipped back as he recounts the details. I work to hang onto my anger, but it's hard when I keep picturing a drunk Rogan sauntering around his house and saying things like *howdy* and threatening to duel his living room furniture.

"Elon shot up out of nowhere, riding an invisible bucking bronco, but instead of shouting giddy up now, he shouted *ready up now* and his voice cracked like a teenage boy's in the process. I don't know if we've ever laughed as hard as we did that night. Ever since then *ready up now* became our Bat Signal. With time, it was shortened to *R...U...N.*"

Understanding dawns on me, and my stomach drops. All at once, I'm sucked back into the memory of Elon's house that day. I can practically feel the pendulum in my hands as it moves across the scrying board first to *R*, then to *U*, and lastly to the *N*. I should have told Rogan what it said sooner instead of holding onto it like I did. I don't know if it would have made any difference, but the *could have* of it is going to eat at me.

"Hate me, Lennox," Rogan declares, pulling me from the memory. "I know I deserve it, but what would you have me do? If you could have saved your father, wouldn't you have done anything?"

"Don't," I warn, agony searing me and burning away any and all concern trickling through me. "Don't you fucking dare bring him up and try to manipulate me with it," I growl.

"I'm *not* trying to manipulate you—"

"Yes, you are!" I scream at him, irate. "Don't talk to me like we bonded over war stories, like we spent nights together showing each other our battle scars. That story wasn't yours to hear!"

We stare at each other, both of us breathing heavy, bleeding pain, and begging to be heard, to be understood. But he wants something I can't give, I couldn't offer it to my father, and I sure as hell don't know how to find it in my heart for him. Rogan's looking for forgiveness, but all he'll find here is a burning coal of *never again*.

His eyes fill with understanding, and I feel my own brokenness mirrored in his gaze. "I know I hurt you," he starts, slowly stepping closer as though he's afraid if he moves too fast, it will startle me and I'll run. "I wish I would have met you differently," he confesses, just barely above a whisper. "I would have found excuses to stop by your shop. I would have gotten to know you better. Made you laugh. Asked you out. Cherished you. I would have shown you who I was before the tragedy and the scars."

His eyes well with tears as he studies my face.

"But I don't have that luxury, Lennox. It was stripped from me a long time ago when everything became about survival, about protecting my brother. It doesn't matter how bad I want you, how much it consumes me. As long as Elon is out there, I *have* to do everything I can to find him. I have to save *him* at all costs."

Tears drip down Rogan's cheeks, his confession breaking me in new ways, not just for me, but for him too. For what's been done to him. For what's been done to his brother. I understand what he's saying. I get where he's coming from. But it changes nothing.

I'm a sacrifice he's willing to make.

I understand, even support, the reasons why, but it doesn't make anything hurt any less. I know where I stand. If the roles were reversed, maybe I'd do the same. But either way, things between us are done before they really had a chance to start, and I'm surprised by the loss I feel knowing that.

With a resigned breath, I shove the excess of magic I've been holding onto into the connection between Rogan and me. I watch him as I give back what I took, expecting to see relief in his gaze. Instead, I track tears as they spill from his eyes unchecked. A deep, permeating sadness fills my chest at the finality of this moment. We may still be tethered, but everything else between us is fractured now, and we both know there's no coming back from it.

My eyes prick at his naked emotion. We've known each other days, but it all feels so much more profound. When all of his magic is returned, I release the tether like it's molten hot and dangerous, and Rogan flinches in response. It's over. We stand quietly fragmented in each other's presence for a moment longer. He reaches up and twists one of my curls around his finger, and then just like that, he leaves.

There's no *sorrys* in his wake, no promises waiting to be broken, or hope left to hold on to. Like he said, it's about Elon and nothing more.

I wrap my arms around myself and work not to fall apart. When my dad died, when I found his note and all the evidence of his betrayal, something shifted in me and I shut down. I lost a piece of myself that day. I wait for the same thing to happen now, but all I feel is deep and profound sadness. No matter how hard I try, I can't shut it out. I can't figure out how to turn it off. It ripples through me, refusing to abate or to be ignored. So I do the only thing I can do...I surrender to it, and it destroys the heart I've worked so hard to keep safe.

5

"What do you mean I can't go see the missing Osteomancers' apartments?" I ask Marx, his dark chocolate gaze filled with apology and his blond hair combed to the side in a perfect wave. "How am I supposed to read them if I'm not in their space?" I add, frustrated with the house arrest it seems I've been placed on.

Aggravatedly I run my fingers through my hair, which will probably frizz the crap out of my curls, but I give no fucks at this point. I feel trapped, and I hate it. All talk of me being able to return home went right out the window as soon as the use of demon magic was confirmed—not that I really believed they'd let me go before.

No, they still think my dead Grammy Ruby is behind all of this somehow. It doesn't matter how much I assure them that couldn't be the case, I'm just some biased witchling no one wants to listen to. I feel the weight of eyes on me, and I know without looking around that the stare belongs to Rogan. I've barely seen him since our talk a couple of days ago, but that doesn't keep me from being painfully aware of his presence. It's as though telling myself that it is never going to happen only made me hyper aware of every breath he pulls into his lungs and dispels, or every time he steps into a room I already occupy.

I could even feel him behind the mirrored glass, watching, the two other times I've been interrogated, the same questions lobbed at me over and over again. I feel like I'm going to go crazy in this place, and I'm starting to wonder if that's the Order's goal. My Grammy was right to keep her distance. I feel as though I've been caught up in some kind of web, and I'm never going to be able to break free or rid myself of the sticky residue or the feeling of being hunted by spiders.

My association with Rogan has painted me as suspicious. No one in the Order can understand why a good witch would be associating with a renounced one. Add to that their nonsense theory about my grandmother, and there isn't anyone around me offering friendly smiles or support.

"I'm sorry, Lennox, I tried to convince them, but the Order has deemed it too risky. A team will go and procure anything they think you could read and bring it back here for you. That's the best I could do," he reassures me, and I huff out an irritated breath.

"It isn't just about their things, it's about being in their space," I argue. "It's about their energy affecting a reading and possibly helping us home in on clues we wouldn't get anywhere else." I can already see I'm not going to get anywhere with this, and I growl vexed.

Members of Prek's team stand casually around my quarters, everyone listening and watching but pretending not to. I wish I could say they've faded to the background with their constant presence and need to follow me everywhere I go, but they haven't.

I've been slowly trying to learn their names, not that

they're any help with that. Apparently, Prek is the only one allowed to speak directly to me unless I'm being given an order to *wait* while they sweep a room and then catch a passing *all clear* before they go back to the silent treatment. And because all of this isn't torture enough, I've been moved to a different floor where Prek, his team, Rogan, and lucky little ol' me now cohabitate...for safety, of course.

"I know, Love. I argued for you," Marx assures me. "But they're not having it. Until they catch who they think is behind all of this, they're not going to let up," he adds, and I throw my hands up, exasperated as I sit down in a chair, setting my pouch of bones on my knee.

"This is stupid, the person they're looking for is dead. She would never hurt me in this life or any other, but no one wants to hear that. I could be doing more than just sitting around answering the same useless questions. Can't we just sneak out or something?" I press, feeling like a petulant teenager who's been grounded unfairly.

Marx chuckles and pushes a few stray strands of his blond hair back from his face. "Suuurrreee, but *if* we survive the shit that inevitably will hit the fan while we're out in the world unprotected, you'll be right back here without any of the freedoms you have now. Don't think you didn't get special approval to walk in the park when you want. They warded the shit out of that place before giving you the okay to spend any amount of time there. And what about that coffee shop you like to sit in after your walks?"

I roll my eyes. "The *park* is right next to this building and is sandwiched between four Order outposts on a block that's witch-owned. Oh, and so is the coffee shop. Is the Order *really* doing me any special favors? Or are they just making it seem that way so I don't demand more freedom or access to this case than I already am," I challenge, grabbing the purple velvet bag I had set on my knee and feeling for the pieces of bone inside.

Touching the bones, even through the material of the pouch, has a calming effect, and I send out a silent apology that they won't be used today to read the missing witches' residences like I thought they were. I was really looking forward to getting out of this place for a bit. An image zings through my mind, cutting off my thoughts. It's of an analog clock, like one I used to see hung up in every classroom I've ever sat in. The time reads five p.m. A man opens the door located right under the clock, and then suddenly he disappears. The image of the clock and the man are replaced by a woman hugging the same man, a feeling of peace and excitement permeating the vision.

I blink and the hugging couple are gone. Once again, the familiar scenery of my quarters appears before my eyes. I get a subtle itch just under my skin, telling me that what just happened is a message meant for someone else, and I look around the room, trying to deduce who is meant to have it. I stare at each individual here, trying to place what just happened with who the message is for, but nothing resonates. I let go of the bone I'm holding through the velvety fabric of the bag, and the itchy sensation immediately disappears. I reach out to clutch the bone piece again to see if the feeling will come back, but nothing happens.

Weird.

I sit like that for a moment, lost in thought, grabbing and releasing the piece of bone in my bag expectantly, but the vision and the drive to find who it belongs to is gone.

I look up, and my eyes connect with Rogan's. He watches me constantly, but I never look long enough to try and decipher what's in his stare. I tell myself it doesn't matter. What's hidden in those moss-colored depths isn't for me, but the magical tether that connects us sings in my chest like a plucked harp string, intent on proving me wrong.

I ignore the magical call, pulling my hand from my pouch of bones, doing my best to disconnect from my magic all together. I don't want to do anything that will strengthen this connection or further twine our abilities together more than they already are. I know when we find the missing witches, we'll be back at his aunt's, severing this tie, and I'm going to do everything in my power to set up that separation for success.

"I'm going for a walk," I announce, jumping up from my chair, eagerly chasing the need to flee. I have to get away from those eyes and my jagged thoughts. Maybe I'll call Tad or Alpha Riggs again and check up on Hoot, fall into that distraction for a while. Hopefully, it will last until the team is back from the missing witches' apartments with something for me to read or do or examine.

My guards circle around me fluidly, all moving together like they're more flock than individual. I realize I still have my bones in my hand, but turning around to set them down means having to look at Rogan again, so I tie them to the belt loop on my jeans instead and hurry for the door. Prek silently falls into step next to me, and as soon as the door to the apartment closes behind me, I feel like I can breathe easier.

We load into the elevator, my mind doing what it has been since I woke up in this place, overanalyzing everything. I can't seem to turn it off. I just keep cycling through conversations with the Major, Prek, Rogan, the Order members they've sent to interrogate me.

"Any news on Eleanor?" I ask as the elevator doors close and we start to move down. I sense a palpable tensing in the guards all around me and snap my head toward Prek, my eyes demanding answers. "What happened? I thought they stopped the curse and had her stable?"

Prek clears his throat, and foreboding crawls through me. I can feel the bad news in his words before he even voices them. "She died early this morning," he announces, turning away from me to watch the descending numbers light up our descent to the lobby of the building.

I look up and watch the same countdown, not sure what to think or feel about this news. I didn't like the witch, but I also wouldn't have wished what happened to her on my worst enemy.

"Any news on the curse?" I question, trying to change the subject to something less helpless and depressing.

"They've concluded that what happened was definitely some kind of safeguard, and the magic had another purpose underneath the curse that attacked Eleanor. Unfortunately, they're still trying to isolate exactly what that purpose was. They're also working on what the triggering mechanism was supposed to be. The hypothesis is *you* would have set off a reaction just by being near it, but we'll have to wait to confirm those details," Prek tells me, his tone analytical and empty.

I try not to think about all the possibilities of what could have been waiting for me. I've discovered in the past couple of days I have a very active imagination, and that's most definitely not a good thing when it comes to supplying an endless and creative list of all the ways I could have been hurt or killed. Only Stephen King is into that level of morbid shit.

I'm angled toward one of the building's multitude of exits. So far, we've never exited the same one, and I've been warned that I won't be allowed to walk around the same time every day. It seems if my need for fresh air is sporadic and unpredictable, then it's okay. A cloudless blue sky welcomes me before the brittle wind Chicago is famous for executes its assault. I'm not even mad at it as I wrap my arms around myself in defense against the cool draft. I push curls out of my face and follow my guards to the entrance of the green space between high-rise buildings that's just barely big enough to call a park.

I tilt my head back to the sky and stand for a moment so the sun's rays can try to warm me a little. Birds chirp excitedly between the heavy sound of traffic and honking, and I find myself missing the quiet of Tennessee. Mentally, I slap that thought across its annoying face and force myself to replace Tennessee with Marblehead, Massachusetts. Home. A hollow feeling sits dead center in my gut, and I exhale deeply in an effort to dislodge it.

I want to scream, but I swallow it down. I've known Rogan for less than a week, and yet somehow, he's sunk his talons so deeply in me that I can't get away from him. I'm missing a place I only spent a couple of days in and trying not to mourn the loss of an asshole who's screwed up my life so epically I don't know how I'm going to come back from it.

It hits me that I've been an Osteomancer officially one week today, but I swear it feels like it's been years. So much has happened in the last seven days, and I haven't the foggiest clue how to process it all. I pull the city air deep into my lungs and start to follow the paved path that's surrounded by green grass and benches. There's the occasional tree here and there, and people scattered about in office wear, who look like they're out to enjoy the decent weather and their lunch.

I try to calm the whir of frenzied thoughts churning in my mind and focus on the world around me. As though it's something I've been doing my whole life, I reach out for the bones near me. I feel my guards and the skeletal structures of everything in the park. I sense the bone a dog's playing with across the green space, and the chicken legs someone has in their lunch box. I feel the animals above the ground and below, and discern the osteo-matter in some of the wards around the Order's strongholds.

My pouch of bones bounces against my leg as I stroll, a keen feeling of solace moving through me as though my ancestors are trying to tell me that everything is going to be okay. I make a plan to sit in the grass and see if I can commune with them, see if the ones who came before me can offer some guidance on what the hell I'm supposed to do with the hand I've been dealt. I pick out a spot in the sun that no one is sitting around, but just as I move in its direction, that telltale itch starts just under my skin.

A prickle of need tickles my consciousness, and I start searching for who the bones want me to help. My probing gaze lands on a woman walking toward me. Her bright red hair blows on the breeze, and her silver eyes are troubled and far away. I watch her as she moves obliviously closer, recognizing her from the strange vision I had earlier of the clock and the man.

I open myself up to the magic, welcoming it into my veins, and it merges seamlessly with my instincts. Peace crashes through me, and I close my eyes and revel in it for a moment. Everything else around me can be chaos and disaster, but *this* is right. I've missed it. Relief moves in and out of my lungs as I breathe in this feeling, and then I open my eyes and focus back on the witch who's just about to pass me and my surrounding protective barrier of Order guards.

She's so buried in concern and worry that the unusual display of overprotection doesn't even faze her. I reach for my bones, but they don't warm up or give off that odd feeling of excitement like they did for the other reading I've done, and then it dawns on me what they want me to do.

"You should tell him," I shout randomly after the distressed woman.

I felt earlier that the unusual vision was a message, and it seems the message is for her.

"What?" the woman asks, her stormy eyes glancing over her shoulder and landing on mine before looking around like she's expecting me to be talking to someone else. I'm a little surprised that she even heard me, but I fix a kind smile on my face and repeat myself.

"You should tell him," I offer again, a knowing glint in my eyes. I watch as she works through what the hell I'm on about, and a spark of surprise goes through her as she makes a connection.

"Wh-why do you say that?" she stammers, clearly taken aback by the out-of-nowhere exchange.

My smile grows wider, and I step closer to her. My babysitters step in my way and refuse to allow me to close the distance between myself and this stranger. I give a small huff of annoyance, and the woman's brow dips in concern as she finally takes in the contingent protectively surrounding me. I toss her a look that says *just ignore them, I do.*

"My bones told me," I explain, patting the purple pouch on my hip.

Her eyes widen with shock, and I'm reminded of something I figured out the other day. When it comes to magic, Osteomancers are few and far between. I've yet to figure out if there's a reason for that, but I let that thought go and focus on the message I've been asked to deliver.

"He'll be home at five," I tell her. "And he'll be happy when you tell him," I add, smiling even wider when I see the emotion well in her eyes at my declaration. She blinks it away and swallows down the relief I feel coming off of her in waves now.

"Thank you," she whispers to me, a beautiful smile overtaking her face as she cradles her abdomen protectively with her hands.

"He's going to be so excited," I reassure her, and she laughs sweetly and wipes a falling tear from her reddening cheek.

"We've only been dating a couple of months," she tells me, chagrin in her eyes but joy in her face.

I nod in understanding, the vision of the man and woman hugging floating before my eyes. "I know, but it will all work out exactly as it's supposed to."

"Thank you..."

"Lennox," I reply in answer to her searching pause.

"Thank you, Lennox," she offers, and with that, she turns to continue her walk, a sense of excited urgency now in her steps.

I smile and turn my attention back to my own stroll. I pick out the perfect spot of grass again and head for it when a voice behind me catches me by surprise, and I pause.

"Is that how it works? You just randomly tell someone what they need to hear?" the big brute of a guard behind me asks. I think they call him Preach, but I'm not sure if it's a nickname or an actual name—either first or last—that he has.

He looks a little flustered, shooting a look from me to Prek and then back again, like what he's doing might get him in trouble. Prek doesn't say anything, and I take that as a sign that this exchange is okay.

"Um, I'm honestly not sure," I admit with a shrug. "I've only been doing this a little while. The sensation that I needed to help her was the same as the ones I've felt before," I explain, thinking back to what I felt when I knew I needed to help Rogan or the time I was drawn to read for Paul.

Preach's lips flatten in thought, and he nods in understanding.

"I caught a glimpse of her message earlier today. I didn't know who it was for until I saw her just now though," I go on, not wanting the interaction to be over so quickly. "Do you want me to do a reading for you?" I ask curiously, a zing of excitement moving through me.

Preach's eyes widen, and he stammers a resounding, "No! I mean, no thank you. Wait. You would just do that? Read me just like that?" he asks, snapping his fingers and looking stunned. You'd think I just offered to drop to my knees and lick him like a lollipop with how flustered he suddenly got, and I recall Rogan being surprised when I casually offered to read for him too.

"Am I missing something?" I query, turning to Prek expectantly, like he's the weird-dude-whisperer or something.

Prek looks a little astonished by my offer too, but quickly gets a hold of himself. "Readings, or any kind of prophesying, is considered very sacred, and it isn't usually offered so...um...freely," he supplies, and my cheeks warm with embarrassment and confusion.

I feel like I've just committed some kind of witch faux pas, one that makes no sense to me. My Grammy Ruby talked about the bones and what they could do as though it was a gift the world needed and deserved. It was constantly hammered into me that it was our responsibility as Osteomancers to serve anyone the bones chose.

"I've watched my grandmother read strangers and friends alike with no reservations or need for anything more than a hug and a warm smile," I tell him, not sure if I'm defending myself or offering reassurance.

"I've heard that about her, but it was very much the

exception and not the rule when it comes to that offshoot of magic," Prek answers, and I'm flummoxed by that revelation.

I look from Prek to Preach and back again. "Then how do the others work? Do they not follow where the bones lead?"

Prek shrugs. "I don't know. I know what Osteomancers do in theory, but I've never seen one in action," he confesses, his eyes leaving mine to diligently scan our surroundings.

Rogan's voice fills my mind, and I'm lost in its depths for a moment. *There are four Osteomancers on the northern continent—know how many of them are missing? All of them except you.*

I wade through his words a couple more times before surfacing back to reality. I knew that number before. That when it comes to bone magic, there aren't many wielders, but I never really got what that meant in comparison to the rest of the witch race until now. I look around me, at the towers of Order buildings reaching up to the sky like raised hands ready to worship. There are thousands of witches buzzing around just these buildings alone, most of them Circummancers who control one or more of the elements. The disparity between the lines of magic is staggering, and I had no comprehension of just how much until I came here.

I scratch at my arm in an effort to relieve an itch, and then realize what the presence of that itch means. I look up at each of my guards, but once again the feeling doesn't select any of them.

"Well, you may not want me to read for any of you, but I'm pretty sure you're about to witness one," I announce as I search the people around me.

My probing gaze lands on a woman with a wistful look on her face as she stands and watches a dog bring a bone back to its owner. I take a deep breath and study her, confirming with the bones that she's the one. I feel the pouch heat against my leg, and I ready myself.

"I know you guys aren't allowed to go too far from me, but readings can be incredibly intimate, so please honor that as much as you can," I advise my surrounding wardens. "That is, if she even wants one anyway. Ask Rogan about the poor mom I accidentally pushed over the edge, if you want a good laugh sometime," I add, and then I make my way over to the woman who's now smiling as she watches the dog fetch the bone and wag its way back to its person.

I do my best to dismiss the twinge of anxiety I feel as I close the distance to this woman the bones have chosen. So far, the consensus here seems to be that me randomly offering to do what I do is met with shock and suspicion. I expect that reaction more out in the world of humans, with their varied beliefs and understandings of how the world works, but amongst witches, I didn't anticipate being rejected as much as I have been so far, first with Rogan and just now with Preach. I get their immediate hesitancy, as it's not something that's typically offered so freely and with no strings attached, but you'd think once they got past the initial shock of the offer, they'd be even more on board for those exact same reasons.

As my surrounding horde—dressed head to toe in black—approaches, the woman immediately notices and stiffens. She moves to stand at attention, offering Prek a stiff salute as he stalks closer. She's dressed in a less intense version of the uniform my guards are wearing, and if I had to guess, I would say she's a sentry somewhere around here.

"Captain," she barks out in greeting as we stop in front of her.

"At ease," Prek commands, and she relaxes a bit, dropping her salute and spreading her stance, but I can see her trying to work out why we've approached her.

"This is Osteomancer Osseous," Prek introduces, and she nods at me in greeting. "She has selected you for a reading. Would you like to commence with that here or somewhere more private?" he no-nonsense snaps at her, and she balks, clearly dumbfounded by the odd command.

I step in front of him, ignoring the warning growl he gives me as I do. I shoot Prek a *fuck off with that* glare and plaster a sweet *no need to run* smile on my face for the woman.

"What the captain *meant* to say is that *if* you would like a reading, I would be happy to offer you one. You don't have to though, there's no pressure. My bones chose you, but you're under absolutely no obligation to say yes. I won't be offended either way," I tell her, hoping it smoothes over what just happened. I shoot Prek another glare over my shoulder for good measure.

The sentry stares at me for a beat, shock swimming in her hazel eyes, which are bouncing from me to the dozen guards all around me and back again. "You...you want to spill your bones for *me*?" she hedges, looking around as though she expects this to be some kind of setup.

"Only if you want," I offer, trying to drown the uncertainty in my voice with warmth and kindness.

"Uh, okay," she agrees with a small shrug, still looking around as though she expects someone to jump from the bushes and shout *gotcha!*

"Really?" I squeak, half in shock and half in excitement. I clear my throat, hitting my chest with a closed fist. "I mean, excellent. Where would you feel comfortable getting a reading?"

We both look around at my question, and as though the fates are looking down on us with a warm smile, a group of witches stands up, abandoning a shade-drenched picnic table.

“How about there?” the witch wisely chooses, and I nod and gesture for her to lead the way.

Prek steps back in front of me with a look, and I concede to being ushered behind the woman, like a toddler who can’t be trusted to its own devices. I sigh quietly and release a silent plea that all of this need for protection will be over soon. Then I square my shoulders and get my head in the game.

I’m on the cusp of my second live reading, and I can only hope that I’ll be able to channel whatever it is that she needs to know.

Ready or not...here I come.

6

"I'm Colby," the witch introduces, extending her hand to me as we shuffle to opposite sides of the picnic bench and move to have a seat.

"Leni," I offer in return, reaching out and clasping her forearm in a witch handshake.

She looks around me and then at the guards, who move to encircle the table, some of them facing us while others face out, tension and anticipation ripe in the surrounding air. She doesn't say anything or ask what the hell this is all about as she sits down, but she does have a cautious look on her face.

I take my own seat across from her and drop my pouch of bones on the concrete table top. I debate offering her some kind of explanation for why I'm rolling twelve deep in Order guards, but I don't know if the missing witches is common knowledge, so instead I say nothing, choosing to ignore my contingency of babysitters and focus on Colby.

Instinctually, I want to say something that will assuage her obvious discomfort for this awkward situation, but as I open my mouth to tell her that *I'm sorry for this random encounter*, I stop myself. I'm not actually sorry that this is happening. I don't know the *why* of it all yet—and maybe I never will, maybe that's only for Colby to know—but I know the bones have their reasons, and I believe in them, regardless of whether or not those reasons are clear to me.

I shake off the *niceties* ingrained in me by culture and remind myself that words have power. I shouldn't speak nonsense out of politeness, no matter how much I want to smooth over an uncomfortable situation. I straighten my back a little more and give Colby a confident smile.

"Thank you for your faith in me, and in them," I add, patting the velvet pouch in front of me. "I'll do my best not to keep you too long, but you never know what the bones are going to say," I warn as I untie the strings at the top of the bag.

Colby nods and settles into her seat a little more. I sense excited curiosity mixing with the waves of trepidation I feel coming off of her.

"It helps me if I can get three items from you, things that have some kind of meaning. Do you have anything on you that might work?" I ask, looking over her to see what might fit the bill.

Her brow dips in thought, and she pats at herself for a moment before unzipping her light jacket and detaching a pin from her black shirt underneath. I recognize the gold pentagram lying on top of what could be mistaken for a circle but what I know is actually an *O* that represents the Order. I've seen other Order members with the same symbol embroidered on their collars or on patches attached to various parts of their uniform. I asked Prek once how they keep humans from storming the building with pitchforks, screaming *cult*, at seeing these pentagrams so proudly displayed on their uniforms. But all the cheeky fucker would tell me was, "*Magic*."

Colby sets the pin on the table between us, and then she

hesitantly reaches up and removes one of her earrings, setting it next to the pin. She pauses for a minute, and then her worried hazel eyes meet mine.

"I don't have anything else," she tells me with a clear apology in her voice.

"That's okay," I reassure her. "I can assign you a totem, that's no biggie at all." I turn my attention to my pouch and work to conjure something that Colby can use for this reading.

When I feel like a new item is in my bag, I reach in to pluck it out. I wrap my fingers around what feels like a bracelet. I pull it out of the bag, and sure enough, I'm holding a bone bangle with intricate carvings wrapped around the entire circumference of the exquisite piece. The carvings are delicate swirls and lines. They don't hold a recognizable pattern to me, but it's beautiful all the same. I hand Colby the bangle.

"Hold this for a moment," I instruct. "Push some of your magic into it, your essence. Think of any questions that you might want answered by the bones today," I tell her, and she nods and wraps both hands around the bracelet protectively.

She closes her eyes and then brings her hands and the bracelet up to her mouth, whispering something to it that I can't quite hear. I know right then and there, without the aid of the bones, that she's a Vox Witch, like Marx, and that she's sharing her magic with the item the best way she can, by speaking it directly into the bangle of bone. Hazel eyes meet mine once again, and she hands me back her borrowed totem.

With a warm smile, I drop it into the pouch, adding her pin and her earring, before tying the top closed and shaking the bones. I shake them for longer than I did with my first reading, and I feel more than just Colby's eyes on me as I do.

I fight the strong desire to yell out *Yahtzee* when I finally get the impression that the bones are ready, and I dump them on the table, eager to see what they have in store.

I feel a collective intake of breath as the bones scatter, group, and settle. It's obvious that more people are watching this—watching me—than just the witch this reading is intended for. I try not to let that added pressure settle into *my* bones and become timidity. I breathe in and out evenly as I look down at the spread and see what the bones have to say.

The first thing I notice is that the bangle, the one she bestowed her power and intention on, is lying on top of symbols that represent family, roots, upbringing. Mixed in with those symbols are others that show me darkness, rejection, judgment. I look for that grouping to be severed from the others, to indicate that this toxic, painful showing has been cut out like the cancer it is, but I follow a tether of little bone chips back to the other collections that represent this witch and her life.

Indignation swells in my soul at what I'm seeing, but I know I can't start there. I can't start with the darkness, it's better to ease into that. I need Colby to feel the light. Because everything about her spread is screaming *I'm lost*, and she needs someone to find her.

No.

Not someone.

She needs to find herself.

I meet Colby's curious gaze with one radiating warmth, acceptance, and belief. "You're strong," I start, offering her a genuine look of admiration and pride. "Tenacious. There isn't a thing on this earth that could stop you when you put your mind to something," I tell her, and a slight blush creeps into her cheeks as her eyes dart around to see who else might be listening to my declarations.

I shake my head and draw her attention back to me. "They don't matter," I whisper conspiratorially, dismissing the unwelcome audience of guards and other random passersby. "Fuck 'em," I joke with a cheeky smile and a wink.

A grin slowly spreads across her face, and she exhales a deep breath, her body relaxing slightly. "Fuck 'em," she repeats.

We both chuckle, and it works to strengthen her resolve. She leans in a little closer, and I give her an approving nod and continue.

"You've had to fight to get where you are in life. The road has not been easy, and as much as you might want me to tell you that it will get better, that things will become easier, the bones don't want me to do that," I tell her, cutting to the heart of things like a hot knife through butter.

I mean, who doesn't want to be told, sorry your life's been shit, but I see more shit in your future. Nice, Lennox, why don't you freak the witch out even more than she probably already is.

My eyes bounce back and forth between Colby's, looking for any sign that this information makes her want to bolt, but all I find is steadfast determination and oddly...hope.

Well, okay then, maybe I haven't fucked this up as badly as I thought.

I take a deep breath and survey the bones again. Symbols jump up at me, mixing together to create meaning and purpose. Shapes, fragments, and combinations guide my way, and I settle into the marvel of this magic. I study the bones connecting the pin and the earring and look up.

"You've been debating about something for a while now, a job maybe or some kind of task, although there's more to it than that," I hedge as I read the symbols hugging her Order pin and branching out from it. "I see that you're searching for something, but you're looking in the wrong places."

Colby's eyes shoot to the Order members all around us and then once again meet mine, her eyes probing for guidance. "Does it say where I *should* look?"

"Sure as fuck not anywhere near your family, it's a miracle you survived that pack of psychos," I blurt, and then my face immediately heats.

Shit. Way to ease into that.

"I mean, I'm sure they're *whatever* in their own right," I rush to add. "And it's clear you haven't cut them off...but maybe you should consider that, because everything I see around them, in relation to you, is bad. Sorry," I offer awkwardly, but Colby gives me a warm half smile.

"Don't be, you're not telling me anything I don't already know," she explains with a sigh. "It's a good reminder though. I use the last name Trapet here because I don't want any issues, but it's short for Trapetti," she reveals, her eyes searching mine for recognition.

There isn't any. I have no idea why it matters.

"Cool," I tell her casually, and she barks out a laugh and shakes her head.

"You really don't know?" she asks, her eyes alight with amusement.

A guard coughs, one hack leading into a full fit. I think his name is Timin. He pounds on his chest and gets a hold of himself after a moment, returning to his perusal of our surroundings like nothing happened. Colby and I look away from him, and she shoots me an eyeroll.

"Yeah, I'm actually relatively new to the whole witch thing, and I know fuck all about most things beyond these bones," I admit on a chuckle.

"The Trapetti coven is like the mob, I guess that's the best comparison. The mob with magic," she adds with an irritated huff and disapproving shake of her head.

"Oh, okay then, well, I guess that makes sense with what

the bones are saying," I declare, gesturing to the spread. I notice a couple of guards around us fidget, but I don't draw attention to it.

Colby rubs her cheek absently. "Yeah, things have been really tough for me for the last couple of months. I lost someone, and my mother has tried to reach out. I doubt she even knows anything has happened, but shitty people always seem to know when you're at your most vulnerable, don't they?" she asks, a humorless laugh escaping her as her eyes drop to the bones, and her face becomes sad.

"It's like a sixth sense," I agree. "I swear there's an alarm that goes off in my ex's head every time I'm lonely and horny," I add, and then internally roll my eyes at myself.

Right, Lennox, because that's the same thing.

Colby laughs and nods. "Exactly, it must be something we put off, wavelengths or pheromones or something. All I know is, if I ever figure out what it is, I'm breaking it."

"Well, be sure to tell me, because a girl can only take so much," I tell her, laughing. I focus back on the spread as she smiles and nods. "When things are hard and sad, it can be so easy to try and rewrite history with toxic people. We can convince ourselves that it was us, or that they can change, but don't do that," I tell her, my tone empathetic but matter-of-fact. I look down to her borrowed totem, the bangle sitting atop a pile that represents putrid roots and decayed familial connections. "Don't turn to people who were never capable of giving you what you needed, what you deserved in the first place. There's no coming back from that."

She sighs, but she nods. "Then where should I turn?" she asks, but the question sounds hollow, like she already knows there's no one.

"I'm going to sound like some spandex-wearing, protein-pumping, self-help freak, but have you ever thought to just turn to yourself?" I ask. "And before you roll your eyes and say, 'Thanks, but no thanks, witch, no one is buying your bullshit today,' hear me out," I plead, because I see in her demeanor that a wall just went up.

"You don't trust yourself, I get it. But why? When have your instincts or inner voice led you astray? You've relied on yourself most of your life, but you don't give yourself enough credit for that. You should," I implore, hoping that she hears me, because with what I can sense she'll be facing in her future, trusting herself is going to be the difference between life and death.

I try to shut myself off from the images and feelings that flood me from both Colby and the bones. The years of neglect and disinterest that Colby felt growing up. All the questions she battled as she tried to understand why her brothers and sister were loved but she was hated. I push away visions of the war inside of her that constantly tells her she's not good enough, not loveable, not worthy. I feel sick that these things were hammered into her by the people who should have loved her, valued her, treasured her. But family isn't always what they should be. Sometimes they're the poison, not the antidote.

"You've been looking for a sign, something to force your hand, well, here's your sign," I tell her, feeling like I'm doing a bad impression of Bill Engvall.

As though the heavens themselves got the joke, a ray of light drops through the clouds and falls on the bench next to me. I turn to take it in, only when I look, it's no longer a ray of sun peeking in on our reading, it's a woman. She's Colby's age, statuesque, with stunning golden blonde hair, hanging stick straight almost to the small of her back. Her bright blue eyes smile at me as she sits there like her presence is simply no big deal.

My eyes widen, and I freeze as I stare at her...as I stare through her. She's there, but not fully. There's no flesh or blood about her, and yet I feel her presence just as surely as I feel Colby's.

"Are you okay?" Colby asks, warm concern spilling out of her tone. "You're doing great," she reassures me, and I could just hug her for being so sweet, but that would mean I'd have to stop staring at the ghost who just copped a squat next to me.

I clear my throat and turn my shocked stare to Colby as a name rings clear as a bell in my mind.

"Do you know a Diem by chance?" I query, my voice a little more froggy with surprise than I'd like.

I feel like I'm experiencing an epic Osteomancer fail. Why was my first reading so smooth and amazing? But with this one, I'm tripping all over myself, blurty, and now a ghost has stepped in to get things on track. I'm totally shitting the bed.

Colby flinches as though the name just reached out and slapped her. "What did you just say?" she asks, every ounce of warmth gone from her tone. I can tell she thinks I'm fucking with her, and I really wish that were the case. I'm as lost as she is right now.

I want to scream *mayday* and quickly dive away from this whole situation, but she hasn't started screaming at me yet, so this is still not as bad as the mom in the diner was. I straighten my shoulders and try to pull my shit together. I can feel that Diem is here for Colby, that her presence is incredibly important, and I work to clear my mind so I can hear what the bones and Diem need for me to communicate.

"Diem is why you and I are here," I start, my eyes darting to the ghost on my left before settling on Colby's again.

Colby looks at the empty space next to me skeptically, and the sound of laughter fills my mind.

"She knew you wouldn't believe it. Which is silly

because you talk to her all the time. She hears you, and she tries to answer when she can, but you dismiss it or ignore it just like you've been doing to your instincts," I declare, but I can see that Colby's still not all the way on board.

"Gonna need more than that, Diem," I whisper to the ghost. "Time to bust out the secrets only you would know."

I smile and shake my head at the response that floats into my mind from the bones Diem points to. It's as though Diem can only communicate with the bones, and then the bones show me the message. It's a little weird and somewhat like having a translator filling you in on a conversation, but it's also humbling at the same time. I get the impression that what's happening is rare and that it's only happening now because Colby is special.

"Diem said that she would never reveal secrets even to prove that she's here with you, but she wants to tell you that Shadow is with her and that she's throwing his favorite ball for him."

Colby's eyes close in anguish at my words, and an audible hitch stalls her next inhale. I recall how she was watching the man with his dog when I first noticed her, and an ache starts in my chest for all that she's lost. First her best friend and then her dog.

I want to punch fate in the throat for what it's demanded of the witch sitting across from me. I know everyone in life has their own hurdles and hardships, but why do some people's paths never clear of obstacles? Just when they climb over one, there's another demanding to be conquered. Rogan's face pops into my mind unbidden, and I take a moment to want to punch fate on his behalf too. Then I take another second to daydream about punching Rogan himself in the face. It's an odd juxtaposition to feel severe empathy for someone but also want to hurt them for what they've done to you.

Colby's breaths pick up, and goose bumps crawl up both of our arms as she blinks just a little faster in an effort to collect her emotions and shove them back down. Her hazel gaze settles just to my left, and in a broken whisper, she asks, "Diem?"

Tears fill my eyes at the overwhelming loss pouring off of Colby, while another part of me wants to celebrate that she believes.

"The one and only," I confirm, my voice thick with emotion as the phrase is shoved into my mind and comes spilling out of my mouth almost involuntarily.

Colby chokes on a small laugh and brings her hands over her mouth in shock. Her hazel eyes are wide, and I get the distinct impression they're contacts and not her real color.

"She used to say that all the time," she tells me, longing sloughing off her words in thick cloying drops. "Does she know," she starts but has to stop to rein in her loss. "Does she know who murdered her?" she finally asks, her eyes watery but resolute.

I look down at the small moonstone earring and the marked bones it has all around it. It's the reason we're here. I close my eyes and take a moment to breathe. What the bones want her to know, to do, is not the happy-go-lucky message I hoped all readings would be. It's not the map to happiness that Colby deserves, or at least it won't start out that way. And yet, I know this kind of reading is just as important as the warm and fuzzy ones.

"She doesn't know who murdered her, but that's what you're meant to find out," I tell her solemnly.

Diem's presence feels oddly warm and comforting by my side, and it's clear she's as much a part of this reading as I am. It's an unusual sensation. With Paul, I knew about his wife, about the kind of spirit she had and the love and light she carried in this world, but I didn't see her, didn't feel *her*. Not like I do with the very present ghost next to me.

"I've been trying to find out what her assignments were, but I don't have clearance. I hit nothing but dead ends every time I try to find the truth," Colby defends, and I nod in understanding, not wanting her to feel like I'm saying what she's doing is not enough.

"I know...she knows, but there's more to all of this than the Order can help you uncover," I tell her, and Colby's brow furrows with confusion.

I quickly look around to make sure we have as much privacy as we can get, given the circumstances, and lower my voice to a whisper. "I wouldn't normally condone this message, but since it's coming from the bones and I trust them implicitly, I'm going to say it anyway. Maybe if you can't find things the right way, it's time to start looking at them the wrong way," I declare, trying and failing not to side-eye my bones just a little.

"Ookaaay, but I thought you said stay away from my family, so exactly what *wrong way* should I be taking then?" she asks, perplexed.

I look down at the bones with a raised eyebrow that says, *do tell, how much of a law breaker should this nice witch become?* I study the spread of the bones again, trying to interpret the answer. I take in the layout of the bangle and her family line, the pin in relation to her current job, and the path the bones want her to take. And lastly, I observe the moonstone earring, one half of a pair that Colby gave Diem for her eighteenth birthday, a gift Diem treasured in life and Colby treasures now because of Diem's death.

"You should find a new angle, but don't go as far as your family has," I tell her cryptically, but I see that Colby grasps what I'm saying. I point to the earring, and she follows my gesture. "See how the earring is sitting in the middle of these bones?" I ask, and she nods. "These markings resemble a journey, one that's essential and urgent. Your life and the truth of what happened to Diem is intertwined around this totem. Sometimes with readings, I'll see multiple paths and outcomes mixed with these bones, but for you, this is it. There's only one way you can move forward, and it's not going to be easy. But I think you already know that," I declare, and Colby studies the earring and the different symbols surrounding it as though she too can see what they mean.

She nods after a beat and seems to steel herself. "Did Diem feel any pain?" she asks, her gaze now hard and determined, but there's a fragile wobble in her lip showing just how much she's working to keep it together.

I wait for Diem to communicate with the bones and for the message to be relayed to me. "No, it was quick, and she didn't see it coming," I reassure her.

"They said it was fast, that she didn't suffer, but I figured that's what they say to everyone. I didn't believe..." Colby drops her head back, struggling to rein in the surge of acute emotion I see force its way to the surface.

Diem reaches out and sets her hand on her best friend's arm, and Colby's eyes immediately drop to survey the new goose bumps speckling her skin. She closes her eyes and places her own hand on top of the phantom hand of her soul's sister.

Her anguish hits me right in the chest like a kick from a horse, and I feel my own eyes sting from the impact of it. I can see the connection between these two women, feel that they are each other's family in ways neither of them ever had in their life. Their friendship was pure and beautiful, and what happened to Diem rocked Colby to her core. It threw her off her axis, and she hasn't been able to find her way since. She's hiding, and she doesn't even know from what anymore.

"I know you feel like the world and everything good in it has abandoned you, but you're not alone, Colby. You never will be. Diem is here, she's as stubborn as you are, and she's not going anywhere," I tell her, my eyes earnest, my heart hoping that she hears what I'm saying, that it sinks into her and holds her up in times where the darkness tries to drown her. Because it will. I hate that for her, but I can also see she's strong enough to handle it, to find her way no matter what.

Colby nods her head and offers me a watery smile as she wipes her eyes. "Thank you," she tells me, raw emotion and gratitude pouring out of her. "I've been floating in this abyss of fucked up shit since they found her body. The Order said it was a robbery but could never tell me what was stolen. Everything has felt off about her case from the beginning. I've been slowly sticking my nose where it doesn't belong, but then I thought maybe I need to let this go. It could be just a fluke horrible thing and I'm holding on for nothing," she admits.

I want to wrap her up in a hug, but that's not what she needs. It won't help her navigate the difficulties she's going to face.

"I get it," I start, my smile empathetic. "But here's the thing, Colby, if you don't learn to trust the voice inside of you, trust the things you feel, the instincts that scream for your attention, then this hunt for justice *will* get you killed. Diem never saw it coming, but you won't be so lucky. It will be vicious and painful unless you really trust yourself and let your heart guide you. It knows the way, but you have to be valiant enough to follow it," I warn, but the bones tell me more, and it seems my inner positive Pollyanna isn't quite done. "This will be dangerous and at times feel insurmountable. It will harden you, play on your mistrust, and occasionally bring you to your knees. But the answers you find will change everything for you. The life you deserve will fall into place because of this."

I fill each word with hard love and driven purpose, hoping it will work to help hold her together to drive home what she needs to do and the only way she'll succeed. Colby stares off in the distance for a moment, contemplating what I'm saying to her, and I can practically hear the debate in her heart as it settles into a fortified decision.

"Diem says to begin with her cases, that's where she would start. She wishes she could be of more help, but she has no idea why someone would want to kill her, just that they did and the reasons are important."

"Is she okay? You know, where she's at?" Colby asks me softly after a moment.

My smile turns sad, wistful, as Diem's reply fills my mind. "You know, she'll never be okay until you are," I answer honestly, touched by the bond these two witches have.

I expect Colby to break at some point with all these heavy revelations. I know I'd be a hot mess, crying and snotting all over the place if I were in her shoes. I can see how hard she's working to keep it together, but I've clearly underestimated her strength.

She hardens in front of me, wrapping herself up in her loss and pain until they're an impenetrable suit of armor. I know one day she'll take it off. That she'll breathe easier as the weight of all she's been through falls from her shoulders. But today isn't that day. Today isn't the end of this brutal journey of heartache and hurt. Today...is the start of it.

I lean back, letting everything I've said settle between us, giving her time to really think through our exchange and the messages I just shoved her way. I scan the bones again, looking for anything that I might have missed. There's no financial guides. Nothing pointing to relationships, other than small indicators that romantic love will come in time, and only then if she'll open herself up to it. But none of that feels relevant to the crossroads it seems she's at.

I know the bones and the path in front of Colby won't ease her suffering or help her find peace, at least not at first. Acceptance, understanding, solace, all of that will be a choice for her, one that will come much further down the road. It's not the *everything will get better, and this is how* kind of reading I've had before. And yet, as I study the witch across from me, I don't regret giving her this message. If she's brave enough to listen to her instincts, she'll find happiness, and it will be worth all the hardships she'll go through to find it.

A fragile tranquility rises up around me, keeping me from saying more to Colby. The silence stretching on between us tempts me to lay more information at her feet, but Diem and the bones reassure me that it's not needed, that this exchange was always meant to be brief but profound.

"How are you doing? Regret saying yes to a reading yet?" I ask with a concerned but teasing tone.

Colby offers me a large smile and shakes her head. "No, never. It's exactly what I needed," she assures me.

Relief washes through me, and I feel a little less awkward about the intensity of everything that just happened. "Do you have any questions? Anything you want me to look at more?" I ask, knowing I need to wrap things up but not knowing the best way to do that. I just chucked a lot at her and yelled catch. I can't just wish her luck with everything and duck out.

Colby studies the moonstone earring as though it's whispering things only she can hear. Or maybe she's just in shock; I doubt she expected an Osteomancer to approach her on her lunch break, declare the presence of her dead best friend, and then spew a bunch of meme-worthy Disney-level shit about trusting who you are and following your heart. That could take anyone for a ride to *what the fuck-ville.*

A couple blinks later, Colby's green-brown gaze meets mine again. "No. I don't know how to thank you for this," she starts, gesturing to the bones and us sitting together at the picnic table. I wave her away awkwardly, not really knowing what to say.

"I'm just a bone messenger," I reassure her and then cringe. "Well, that sounded dirtier than it did in my head," I admit with a chuckle.

Ugh, and I was doing so well. Bone messenger? That sounds like a creepy escort service.

Colby laughs, her smile is wide and her burden just a little lighter, and Diem gets brighter with appreciation. I reach over to the borrowed totem, rotating the bone bangle in my hand until it clicks into the right position for what I feel driven to do. I close my eyes, focusing on the bracelet, and call on my magic to braid protections into its very essence. This offering is different from the one I bestowed on Theresa in my aunt's damaged foyer. This isn't just my line of magic blessing her and offering its appreciation, this is all magic at its purest working to safeguard the wearer. I don't know how I know that or how I could have access to more than just my line, but I don't think twice as I create a shield for Colby, one that she desperately needs.

The bangle heats in my hands and starts to change. I open my eyes and witness as it goes from rare and priceless bone relic to simple, delicate, gold-chain bracelet. I blink a couple times as I stare down at the now innocuous looking piece of jewelry. In my hands, I can still feel the weight of the bone, still run my finger over the intricate carvings, but my eyes now tell me that none of that exists. The truth of it is camouflaged, and it feels like a perfect totem for what Colby's about to take on.

"This is for you," I offer, extending my hands and the tiny gold chain pinched between my fingers and thumbs. Colby looks surprised but doesn't hesitate to lift her arm and proffer her wrist. I slip the bone bracelet disguised as a chain down her hand, like I would a bangle, and her eyes widen as she feels the truth of the illusion now around her wrist. "When it's served its purpose, it will fall off," I tell her cryptically, handing her the pin and the moonstone earring too. Her reverent stare is filled with questions, but she simply nods once, closes her fist around her precious items, and then returns her hand to her lap.

I look over to see if Diem has anything else she'd like to communicate, but the ghost is gone. I look around for her, just in case she moved or something, but I don't see her anywhere.

"She just left, didn't she?" Colby asks me, an amused smile on her face. "She used to do that shit all the time, no goodbyes, just there one minute and gone the next. Worst wing-woman ever," she tells me playfully as she pushes up from the table.

I chuckle and stand up too. For a few seconds, we stand across from each other, two soldiers who have seen some shit and are forever bonded even though we're strangers. I don't know if I'll ever see her again or know the details of what she'll discover, but I'm okay with that. She holds her arm out, and I reach out and grab her forearm. Reassurance and peace move through me as we shake, and I can tell by the look on her face that she feels it too. I give her a nod of recognition and understanding, and she returns the gesture, hers filled with gratitude and respect. And then just like that, we drop our arms, and she walks away.

Her steps are quick and obdurate, and I send all the *you got this, girl* vibes I can, trailing after her in her wake. Just like with Paul, I know I'll never forget this moment, that it changed me for the better, and that I can learn from the messages meant for others too. I smile, a flicker of pride moving through me as I start to pick up bones and place them gently back in the pouch. I once again thank them for what they've done here today, and promise to honor each and every one of them until long after my magic has passed to the next in line.

No one says anything to me as I pack up the bones and head back toward the building, done with my outside adventure for the day. Silence wraps protectively around me, and I can feel a subtle change as my guards move assuredly to get me safely where I need to go. Somehow, I'm not as much of an outsider as I was before, like my nuisance factor has been severely reduced. It's an odd feeling that comes over me as we all walk in tandem, but I think it's the first time I've felt as though I've risen in their general estimation. That I'm less something they've been assigned to watch over and more someone deserving of protection.

I pat the bones once again tied to my hip and thank my ancestors for guiding the way. Maybe things here will start to feel a lot less lonely and I'll stop feeling like I don't belong. I look around at the men and women potentially putting themselves in harm's way for me. I could get on board with this whole *everything happens for a reason* theory. I just wish I could figure this one out.

7

Something shines in my eyes, and I shrink away from it. It's too damn early for someone to be fucking around with a flashlight. I attempt to shut my sudden awareness down and go back to sleep, but warning skitters its way up my spine, and suddenly I'm wide awake. I open my eyes, assessing silently what's setting me off, but it's pitch black in my room, and I can't make anything out.

My eyes adjust quickly, but there's still a haze to everything that makes me feel even more uneasy. I listen for any indication of movement around me, and when the scream comes, it's so loud and jarring that I scream myself in shock and fear. I slam a hand over my mouth, but it doesn't stop the smell of old, stale blood from assaulting my senses.

The scream trails off, the sound so visceral and raw. I couldn't tell you if it was from a man or a woman, but the urge to run is nipping at my every nerve as my heart hammers in my chest and I try to process where the hell I am. I can't see right, and the smell is wrong. There's no way I'm in the room I fell asleep in last night, but then where the hell am I and how did I get here?

Memories clamor in my mind of Prek blowing powder

into my face, Rogan holding me, and the feeling of a needle being shoved in my neck. Confusion pulses through me in time with my heart. Did that just happen? Did it happen again? My thoughts are fuzzy like they're floating in stagnant water with weeks' worth of mold growing on them.

The screaming starts again, and this time I bite down on my own panic. I call magic to me, try to blanket myself in its protection, but even when it comes, I don't feel better. Maybe it's because I can't see. I can't tell what's coming my way or what's making that person release such feral, soul-shattering pleas.

My name bursts out amidst the screams, and suddenly everything around me clicks into place. It doesn't matter that everything is black and hazy or that I can't smell anything beyond rotten blood and dust. I know who's screaming, and I have to get to him now.

"Tad!" I bellow, pained and desperate as more agonized wails reach wherever the hell I am. "Taaaad!" I scream again when silence crushes everything around me like a tidal wave, and nothing and nobody answers me.

I try to feel for what's around me, for what my eyes refuse to reveal, but I realize I can't move. I'm trapped somehow, and I know if I have to hear him screaming again, there will be no coming back. I will fracture into a million pieces and never be the same. Dread pools in my gut. Anticipation chokes me, and just when I'm about to scream from my inability to take it, I gasp and sit up in my bed.

Alarm strikes through me like a jackhammer. My room comes clearly into view, everything tucked in by shadows and kissed by night. I pull air in and rush to expel it, my lungs on the cusp of hyperventilation. Sweat drips down my brow, and I swallow the acrid taste of panic as once again an echo of a dream haunts me.

I have no fucking clue what's going on, but I ignore the

need to try and figure it out as I reach for the charging phone on my bedside table. Fingers shaking, I struggle to unlock it. I almost yelp with relief when my third attempt finally pays off and I pull up Tad's number. The line starts to ring, and I say a silent thank you to Prek for finally trusting me with this device. I bite at my cuticles as ring number three trills in my ear, and a silent plea of *come on, Tad, answer the damn phone* starts in my head.

"Hello?" a froggy, sleep-laced voice asks.

"Tad," I practically scream in relief, my eyes prickling with tears. "Are you okay?" I demand, pushing sweaty curls from my face as I lean back against the cushioned headboard in my room.

"Leni?" Tad asks drowsily, and I hear him sit up in his bed. "What happened?" he presses, his voice a little more alert and focused.

"Nothing, I'm fine, but are you okay? Is Aunt Hillen okay? Nobody that you know of currently being tortured?" I ask with a strained chuckle as I run a hand down my face. Adrenaline starts to abandon me, but when I close my eyes and rest my head against the tufted headboard, it's like I can hear Tad's screams all over again. I sit up with a jerk, shoving my tangle of covers away from me.

"Yeah, we're fine. Everybody is fine. Why? Are you sure you're okay?"

I release a deep, relieved breath and take a moment to collect myself. *What the hell is up with these nightmares?*

"I had a bad dream. It...it freaked me out, I'm sorry I woke you up," I offer, but I can't seem to shake the boulder of trepidation now sitting square on my chest.

I felt like the dream about Rogan was some kind of prophecy, maybe a warning, but I won't survive if this dream about Tad is one too.

"You wanna talk about it?" Tad asks, worry ringing in his

tone.

"No, not really, go back to bed, I'm sorry I woke you," I concede, but neither one of us is quick to hang up.

"Talk to me," he encourages simply, and the familiarity of his warmth opens the floodgates to my worries.

"I don't know, maybe it's this place that's fucking with me, but I just feel...hunted. I can't explain it, but it's like I'm watching a clock that's counting down, and I can't do anything to stop it. I don't even know what happens when it finally gets to zero, just that it feels bad, wrong somehow," I confess, dumping on my cousin and best friend a burden that's getting too heavy for me to carry.

"That makes sense," he reassures me, and I pull the phone away from my ear and stare at it, bewildered for a moment.

"It does?" I ask, chagrined.

"Well, yeah. I mean, you're up at witch central, working on a case about missing people," he tells me as though I need the reminder. "And come on, we've watched enough crime dramas to easily think of all the horrible things that could be happening to them. Of course you feel like you're racing against time. You're out of your element with all this. Not to mention, you just went through some shit with Tall-hot-and-untrustworthy. If you *weren't* freaking out a little, I'd be worried. We solve already-solved crimes from the safety of our couch, thank you, Netflix. But now you're there, actually trying to solve some real-life crap, and that's bound to take a toll."

His words work to comfort me a little. I mean, he's right. Nothing in all my massage school classes ever prepared me for this kind of shit.

"Stress does weird things to people, like give them nightmares, or finds them falling into bed with their enemies," he adds, innuendo drizzling all over his tone.

I snort out a laugh and roll my eyes. "You have got to let that one go," I chastise, my worry easing and the boulder on my chest lightening ever so slightly.

"Pshhhh, I refuse, and you can't make me," Tad teases, and I can't help but chuckle at his antics. "Any news on the missing witches?" he asks hesitantly, and I rub my eyes, hating my answer.

"No, nothing."

"Have you talked to *him*?" he asks after we're both quiet for a beat.

"No, not since the *I don't choose you, you don't complete me* talk. He just stares now," I admit, judging myself as a forlorn sigh punctuates that revelation.

I will not sigh over Rogan Kendrick.

"Did he ask for another chance?" Tad questions, a hopeful note in the question.

"No. He told me his *reasons*, but I think he just wanted to make himself feel better by explaining why he did what he did."

Tad hums in understanding, and I can practically see him nodding and thinking things through on his end of the line. "Would you give him another chance if he asked?"

I shrug even though Tad can't see me. "I don't even know what chance we had in the first place," I admit. "We don't know each other really. I think I found myself locked into his tractor beam of hotness, and that was about it," I joke, trying to lighten up the somber mood.

"The truth isn't going anywhere just because you want to pretend you can't see it," Tad chirps, and I make a face at the phone.

"You're taking this Spirit Guide thing too seriously. Don't Miyagi me," I grump.

"Miyagi? First of all, ain't no old man waxing anything over here, Lennox Marai Osseous, let's get that straight.

Second of all, I was clearly channeling my inner Cinna, because yes please to Lenny Kravitz. And third of all, truth is truth, Lennard, so there."

"Don't you *full-name* me and then follow it up with a *so there*," I playfully object as I laugh and shake my head in disapproval. "Cinna was the shit, though," I concede after a beat.

"You know it."

"Things just aren't that simple, Tad. And before you go lamenting that relationships never are or nothing good was ever easy, don't. I already know all that. It doesn't change what happened. No one should get away with taking your choices. He treated me like a passenger in my own life; that's never going to be okay. There's a pattern there, and I'd be an idiot to ignore it. No pretty face, nice body, or meddling cousin is going to change that," I mock, ignoring Tad's sigh. "Besides, I'm here to do a job, not get into Rogan's pants. So, subject change," I announce, closing the door on any more Rogan talk.

"Fine, but you liked him, Leni. You don't like anyone, and you liked *him*. Shouldn't that say something?"

"Yeah, that I have questionable taste," I counter playfully, even though it reeks of truth to my own nose. "Plus, I think magic is changing me," I admit. "I drooled over a couple lycans I first met, so I'm going to go bark up that tree if I need some fun."

"Please, that's just sex, I'm talking about feelings," he counters.

"Bye, Tad," I deadpan.

"You can't run from your feelings, Lennox!" he shouts into the phone.

"Love you. Miss you. Stay out of trouble," I coo as I go to hang up.

I hear a muffled, "I refuse, trouble is my middle name,"

before I end the call with a laugh.

I look back at my lumpy pillow and ruffled covers, debating if I can try to get back to sleep. Chills work their way down my arms at the thought of another nightmare, and I quickly dismiss more sleep for a hot cup of tea.

It's two in the morning, and I know the whole flat is sleeping aside from the guard at the door outside this apartment. I don't want to wake anyone up, but I also don't want to sit in here, reading too much into a dream and looking too hard at my anxieties. I get up, my bare feet feeling loud on the hardwood floor.

Why is it, whenever you're trying to be quiet, everything always feels ten times louder?

I sneak out into the hallway, my pulse too loud in my ears when the quiet I'm enveloped in triggers my alarms. I'm trying to be stealthy and considerate, but for some reason, I'm suddenly feeling like it's too quiet.

Did I shout out in my dream? I know I was sure as fuck freaking out inside of it. Why didn't anyone come check on me? I freeze mid-step, just before I'm about to round a corner. I try to listen to what's going on around me, but I can't hear anything past my own needy heart and pounding fear. I want to scream at my body to shut the fuck up; my pulse is making it very hard to detect if I'm about to die. Fear sinks into my limbs, and I'm stuck statue-like in the middle of the hallway.

Out of nowhere, a body comes speeding around the corner, but instead of screaming like I want to from the shock of its sudden appearance, I react. My elbow is cocked back, and I'm slamming my fist into a hard, chiseled jaw in no time.

"What the..." my attacker shouts, but his nose is crunching under the force of my follow-up fist before he can so much as utter his choice of a swear word.

Running steps fill my ears, and I ready myself for a fight. Lights blink on as someone flips the switch behind me, and I whirl and blink against the disorienting flood to my senses.

Prek comes running toward me, shirtless and exhausted looking. "What happened?" he asks, confused, a long knife in his grip as he looks around for the threat. Three more guards spill out from different rooms, and I spin to point at the intruder I surprised with my one-two combo.

Rogan straightens up from a semi bent position, hands cupping his face and blood seeping through the seams of his fingers.

Well, oopsie.

He glares at me, and I scrunch my face with chagrin.

"What did he do?" Prek demands, stepping up behind me protectively. I don't know if I should appreciate that he's not giving Rogan the benefit of the doubt in this scenario or roll my eyes at how deep the roots of their grudge grow.

"Nothing. I didn't expect anyone else to be up, I just reacted," I explain hurriedly, and the tense guards around us relax.

So much for not waking anyone up.

"I'm going back to bed," a woman named Stevie announces, and then with shuffled feet and grunts of agreement, everyone except Prek, me, and Rogan returns to their rooms.

"Are you okay?" Prek asks me quietly, and Rogan moves his glare from me to the Order member currently assigned as my guard.

I roll my eyes and step between them before they can start rehashing their history with their fists. "Yeah, I'm fine, he just surprised me, no harm no foul," I reassure Prek, and Rogan levels me with a look that says, *really, no harm?*

"*Bara,*" I call out with a wave of my hand, turning off the bloody spout formerly known as Rogan's nose.

He freezes, his eyes filling with warning before bouncing to Prek and then back to me. Realization dawns on me, and I try not to let raw panic show on my face.

Shit.

Why did I just do that? And in front of an Order member of all places. I don't even know why I tapped into blood magic like it was no big deal when I know all its going to do is mess with this damn tether.

Fuck up much, Lennox?

I'm afraid to look at Prek, as though one look into my eyes will give us away, but not looking at him could also be weird. So instead, I throw my head back and laugh. Because that makes sense and screams *not guilty.* I release a good chortle, doing everything in my power not to let it sound forced.

"Ummm, what's wrong with you?" Prek finally asks as I dive into round two of the weirdest belly-laugh ever.

"I've wanted to punch him for a while," I tell him, as though that's all the answer he needs. Prek eyes me for a moment before flicking his suspicious gaze at Rogan. We just stand there, Rogan covering his nose, me freaking out that I just gave us away, and Prek eyeing us.

"It felt better than I hoped," I add, crossing my fingers that the admission will trigger Prek's hate and cloud his skeptical and all too keen observational skills.

After a beat, Prek steps back from me. "Yeah, I know the feeling," he agrees, his russet stare moving from Rogan back to me before turning and heading back to his room. I'm about to breathe a sigh of relief when Prek calls over his shoulder, "I'm not an idiot, Osteomancer," and with that, he disappears into his bedroom, the door clicking shut behind him.

I stare after him, not exactly sure what that means. Does he suspect that we're tethered? That I beat Rogan in my free time? Does he think we're out here doing something we're not supposed to do? I look to Rogan for answers, but he's still cupping his nose, probably to keep what he bled into his hands from getting everywhere.

"Come on," I huff, waving him back toward the kitchen so he can clean up. I should probably feel bad for decking him, but the word *karma* keeps bouncing around in my mind, making it impossible for guilt to get too comfortable anywhere.

Flicking the switch for the light above the sink, I turn the faucet on and start opening drawers to look for towels. Rogan leans over the sink and dumps his cupped blood down the drain.

"I think you broke it," he declares, his voice pinched and more nasal than usual. I look over and see him gingerly touching the now misshapen bridge of his nose. I find a towel and move closer to inspect the damage.

Yep, definitely broke it.

The petty part of me wants to leave it like that, not that I think it would deter women, but more as a reminder of all my threats that he never took seriously. Then again, I don't want to give him any excuses to tap into my magic. Vanity and my immature urges are not worth strengthening our tether any more than it already has been.

"Well, I hope this will teach you not to laugh the next time a woman tells you that you will *rue the day*," I chide as I lift a hand to his nose and whisper, "*Aval.*"

The cartilage snaps back to the bone of his nose with an audible crunch, and he hisses in pain, making me cringe slightly too.

"Fuck," he snarls, cupping his hands over his nose protectively before bending over the sink—probably just in case it starts bleeding again.

Okay, maybe I feel a little bad.

"Lurking-hallway-assailant a new hobby of yours?" Rogan quips, delicately feeling his once again straight nose and then splashing water on his face.

I give a humorless snort and chuck the towel at him. He catches it, keeping me from the satisfaction of watching it smack him in the face.

"I was just going to make tea. You came at me in the hallway. Can't blame a girl for defending herself," I declare casually, pushing up on the counter until I'm sitting atop it as Rogan dries his face.

"Lying in wait for the perfect opportunity is more like it," he retorts, a hint of teasing in his voice.

I shoot him an unamused look. "That just shows how well you know me; I wait for no man."

We stare at each other for a moment, awkward silence seeping into the cracks and fractures between us. Tad's annoying warning sounds off in my head, and I do my best to ignore it. Rogan and I haven't known each other long, but despite how we met and what we've been up against, we've never had this stilted, uneasy tension between us. Not like there is now.

"Why are you really up this late?" he presses, threading the towel between his fingers.

I watch him as he fidgets, and if I didn't know any better, I'd say he was nervous. I debate feeding him some bullshit and then shutting myself back in my room, but the idea of being alone again with nothing but foreboding and worry for company ties my stomach in knots.

Rogan sighs and throws the towel on the counter. I see a hint of the Rogan I'm used to dealing with. The cocky, run headfirst into everything version, instead of this quiet, uncertain, sullen person who's been skulking around lately.

"I had a nightmare," I admit after a quick debate about whether he can use any of this against me somehow in the future. “I think all this craziness is finally catching up with me,” I add, gesturing to everything around us. The rest of the kitchen and living room is bathed in either shadows or moonlight, the recessed fixture above the sink barely illuminating the two of us.

“It’s a lot,” Rogan agrees, leaning back against the counter as he nods and crosses his arms over his chest.

“What have you been doing the past couple of days? I haven’t seen you,” I ask, reaching for something else to make this weirdness between us disappear just a little longer.

“You’ve been looking?” he solicits with a raised brow, and I huff out a small laugh and roll my eyes.

“No, but one grows accustomed to the temperature dropping every time a certain frigid asshole walks in the room. When it doesn’t happen, one takes notice.”

“Does one?” he taunts with a small smile.

“One does,” I reply, sounding like a bad impression of that assassin dude from *Game of Thrones*.

Rogan releases a deep exasperated breath, showing the fatigue and frustration that’s just under the surface of his playful mien. “I’ve been looking for information. Seeing if there are any other recorded prophecies that might serve as a key to the one your grandmother had. Other than that, I’ve been meeting with people who owe me favors, hoping they might have heard something or at least will keep their eyes and ears open for anything that could give us a break.”

He pauses and rubs his face with one hand. I study his movements and wonder who he talks to? Who does he have to unload all of his worries and stress on? There’s no doubt that he’d do anything for his brother and that they’re close, but the protective way Rogan talks about Elon, I doubt he lays any unnecessary worries at his brother’s feet. There’s Marx, but again I get the impression that there’s a wall there, that the catalyst for so much of their communication lately is this case and not a deep-rooted friendship.

"I've also had to sit down with some of my mother's upper council." The words out of Rogan's mouth are like a slap. I'm instantly pulled from my sympathetic musings and shoved right back into the stark reality of our situation.

"Why would you do that?" I demand, looking around to ensure no one is eavesdropping.

"It's how I got access to this," he tells me, circling his finger to indicate the Order building we're standing in. "I promised I'd cooperate to the best of my ability, if they granted unfettered access to their information and resources here."

I stare at him completely dumbfounded. He was willing to be cast out, to be renounced, hunted, and tortured to keep his secrets from falling into the wrong hands. Now, just like that, everything's changed? I know he said he'd do whatever it took to find Elon, but this...potentially giving shitty people the key to immortality—or at least access to surviving death *once*—it's too much. His parents and their council could be the ones behind all of this, in which case Rogan is just handing over exactly what they want. I get his intense level of devotion and responsibility toward Elon, but he has to see that some costs are too high.

"Rogan, you can't do that," I whisper, shocked.

Guilt bleeds into his gaze, and he drops his eyes from mine. "I'm being careful."

I give an indignant snort. "You said you and Elon barely made it out of this place. That you don't even know the extent or limitations of what happened to you. You're risking too much," I plead, but I can already see him starting to shut down and shut me out.

"Rogan, look at me," I snap, and his green eyes flick up

to mine, a flame of determination building in his hardening stare.

I feel the wall come up between us, and it's painfully obvious that anything I'm about to say is going to be a waste of breath. He's not going to hear me. He never has. He does whatever he wants, consequences be damned, and I curse the gods or fate or whatever the hell is out there that they gave someone like Rogan Kendrick such immense power. He doesn't care who he hands it off to, or how it might be corrupted. All he sees is what he wants, and he'll do anything to get it. Why am I even wasting my time thinking that what I have to say or my opinions on the matter will make a difference?

Shaking my head, I hop down from the counter. "Good night, Rogan," I lob at him before turning to head back to my room. I'll take the nightmares over wasting one more breath on this idiot.

Frustration fills my steps, anger making them even heavier, and when Rogan calls my name in an effort to lure me back, I ignore it, focusing instead on putting one foot in front of the other to get as far away from him as possible. My covers are a mess just like I left them, my room still dark and foreign feeling. I grab the door and move to slam it behind me, no longer caring which Order asshole gets jarred from their too peaceful sleep. The door bounces against something and doesn't close, and when I whirl to find out why, I discover Rogan's big frame stomping into my room behind me.

"Get out," I snarl, but all he does is quietly close the door behind his intrusion.

He stalks forward, fury radiating off of him, and it pisses me off even more. He has no right to be mad, I do.

"Let's hear it, Lennox. Lay on me everything you think I'm doing wrong and how *you* could do it better. Don't hold back, stop swallowing it down and thinking you're fooling anyone. I see it in your eyes when you bother to look at me, so let's hear it once and for all," he goads.

"Eat a dick," I snap indignantly.

He glares at me.

"What? You were hoping for pity? Poor ol' Rogan, fucked someone over and now they don't want anything to do with him. Poor guy probably cries himself to sleep, oh wait, he'd have to give a shit, he'd have to care for that to go down," I thunder. "What happens to the rest of us if your shitty relatives figure out how you and Elon came back?" I demand, outraged.

"Watch what you say," Rogan growls, prowling forward until my back hits the wall behind me. I didn't even realize I was retreating from him until his arms come up and box me in. "I do care," he snaps at me, his voice quiet, undiluted menace. "And I think the real issue is that you do too, and you hate it."

His breath brushes enticingly against my face, and I loathe the reaction I have to it. Goose bumps crawl up my arms, but I refuse to get lost in his presence, to cave to what he can make me feel. I don't care how he can coax my body into betraying my mind, I've had enough of this.

"Oh I care, Rogan, or I could have before you stomped all over me like I was nothing. Don't worry though, it'll pass."

Hurt flashes in his gaze, and this time he doesn't push it away, he doesn't shut me out. He just stares at me, his eyes hemorrhaging pain and begging for something he's no longer worthy of.

"Tell me how to fix it," he whispers brokenly, and I don't know if he's asking to fix what happened between us or the situation we're in now, maybe it's both.

I'm not sure what's changed since the last time we

talked. He was so resigned that there was no going back, so was I, but that's not what I'm seeing in his face right now. I want to soothe the anguish he's sharing with me in his troubled gaze, but he hasn't earned it. He doesn't deserve what I have to offer.

"You can work hard to save Elon, but you can't sacrifice everything for him," I start.

Rogan shakes his head, his lips readying an argument, but I cut him off.

"We don't know where he is or who could have him. You could be walking right into the High Council's trap, and for what? You think telling them what they want to know ends all of this for you? You're renounced, Rogan, there's no overturning that once it's happened," I remind him, my eyes begging him to see the truth in what I'm saying. "You and Elon—if we ever find him—won't be any safer than you were before. Do you think they'll let you live?" I ask, rolling my eyes and shaking my head at the thought.

"That will never happen. They'll test the limits of this *gift* you have, because once the powerful have what they want, they remove the threats. You're a threat, Rogan. They'll eliminate you if possible, and if not, they'll lock you up and throw away the key," I tell him, resisting the urge to run the back of my hand over the tic that's started in his jaw.

"You sold me out because you needed more resources and access to more information, but are we any closer to finding your brother than we were before?" I demand. "You're not thinking straight, and you're making choices that have long-lasting consequences not only for you, but for our entire race. I don't know how or why what happened with you and Elon happened, but grow the fuck up and stop playing like this information isn't a game changer. Yes, you have a responsibility to your brother, but you also have the responsibility of keeping what you know in here," I add, leaning into him and flicking his forehead.

He reaches up and catches my hand, pressing it against his cheek. He closes his eyes, leaning into the touch in a way that breaks my heart a little. I strengthen my resolve, tilting away from him...but I don't pull my hand away.

"I killed you," I blurt out of nowhere.

His lids open, and lost moss-green eyes find mine.

"I watched you bleed to death at my feet, and it felt good. But then I died too." I pause, silence stretching between us like the magical tether I'm not sure I'll ever be free of. "You bulldozed my life, Rogan. You've altered my magic, obliterated my choice, and traded me like you had the right to. There's no fixing that," I finally say, answering the other part of his complex question.

Pained, Rogan closes his eyes, reaching up and cupping my cheek. His presence overwhelms me. The need that flutters through my belly makes all of this harder. It reminds me of what could have been and shows me that I really wanted it. As annoying as Tad can be, he's right. I liked Rogan, and now all this fucked up shit is what I have to show for it.

"For what it's worth, Lennox, I am sorry. I know you think I'm irredeemable, but I'm trying not to be."

I breathe him in, feel his sincerity, and bask in the desire I sense billowing off of him. If only that were enough for me. I reach up and slowly pull his hand from my cheek. I look up into his stunning eyes, tracing the strong angles of his face greedily with my gaze. I settle my stare on the scar that's a small representation of the damage he holds inside. And then, with everything in me, I let go.

"And I wish your apology was worth more to me than it is," I tell him honestly, and then I duck under his arm and leave him standing, lost and forsaken, in my room.

8

I stare at the hair brush sitting on the table in front of me and groan. I look from it to my bag of bones, not even bothering to see if they will react to this useless item. Just like they haven't reacted to any of the other dumb shit the Order's team procured from the other two missing Osteomancers' homes. There's not one bone or anything containing even a speck of osteo matter in the pile of confiscated items, and honestly, I want to scream at someone about it.

The powers that be said it wasn't safe for me to go. They said they'd bring back any useful items they found and I could see what I could get from them. Well, what the hell is a Bone Witch supposed to do with an empty can of Coke, a hair brush, some dirty clothing and a brand new beeswax candle?

Fuck all is what I can do.

I grunt frustratedly at the useless collection and start to wonder—not for the first time—if the Order is incompetent or doing this shit on purpose. There's no way that they went to two separate Osteomancers' homes and didn't find one bone to bring back for me to try and read. I sit back in my chair with a sigh, taking in today's interrogation room of choice. This one is bigger than the others I've been in, with only one long half-wall-sized mirror to spy on me from. I turn around and stare at my reflection, wondering who's on the other side of it today.

The door slams open with a loud bang, and I jump from the sudden movement and noise. I'm on my feet just as two guards spill into the room, their uniforms nicer and slightly different from the crew that usually surrounds me. They stand at attention on either side of the door, making way for two men in suits to stroll in, derision and pellucid judgment written all over their faces. One is in a deep cranberry suit, with a dark chocolate shirt and no tie. His crisp shirt is unbuttoned a little too low for my taste, and even though his long hair is the exact same shade, the color coordination can't hide the signs of aging on his tan face. He's definitely closer to my parents' age than mine, although my guess is that he probably doesn't like being reminded of that fact.

His companion is in a midnight blue suit, clean white shirt and coordinating polka dot tie. His salt-and-pepper hair is shoulder-length and looks shiny and soft. His angled features have held up slightly better against the test of time, and there's something familiar about his face that has me throwing decorum and appropriate social graces right out the window while I stare at him in an effort to figure out where I know him from.

I'm still digging through my memories when a tall, lean woman finally steps through the door. Her cream floor-length dress is cinched at the waist with a chunky belt that looks like it was made from a poor albino alligator. Her outfit hugs every curve of her lithe body, making her look elegant and powerful. Her hair is dark as pitch, with a thick white streak framing her face and breaking up the black.

Green eyes quickly appraise me, and a kind smile decorates her full mouth.

I school my features, reining in the shock that catapults through me as who I'm dealing with registers. Sorrel Adair, the High Priestess of Witches, just walked into the room. The green of her eyes is more kelly-green as opposed to the moss color I've come to appreciate, but there's no denying how much Rogan takes after his mother. I look over to the man in the midnight blue suit and now easily recognize Rogan's father. The third man bears no family resemblance, and I figure he must be a trusted council member, maybe one of the witches Rogan said he's met with.

I immediately wonder if Rogan knows they're here, and then I set that thought aside to focus on *why* they might be here and how I want to play this. With a flick of her wrist, the door slams shut, the display of her elemental magic I'm sure meant to intimidate.

Dramatic entrance much?

She saunters into the room confidently, stopping on the other side of the table across from me. She looks over my head to the mirror behind me, but I don't turn around and follow her gaze. No, I'm too busy recognizing that someone just did something to the room. It doesn't impact my magic —nothing in this building ever has, although I've been working hard to keep that on the down low—but there's a change all the same. And I get the sinking suspicion that whatever devices, charms, spells, and runes used to spy, observe, and record what happens within these four walls just went dead.

The man in the cranberry-colored suit winks at me, and I'd bet good money that he's a Contegomancer. Corium Witches are almost as rare as my kind, but they specialize in protections, shields, and concealment among other things. They're the ancient palm readers of old, holding dominion over a person's skin—their protective shell so to speak—but that protective magic translates into so much more beyond simply reading the lines of someone's palm.

"I'm sorry we're meeting under such circumstances, but it's nice to meet you all the same, Lennox," the High Priestess tells me in lieu of a formal greeting, her eyes alight with kindness and her smile warm. Rogan's father moves forward to pull the seat out for her, and she sits down stiffly like she doesn't want to touch anything for fear of catching something.

She doesn't address me formally, which is the respectful thing to do, or attempt to introduce herself at all, clearly deciding that I should already know who she is. I do, but it's arrogant and rude all the same. She waves for me to have a seat, and since I'm not trying to start shit as of yet, I plop back down in my chair and wait. Her High Council side-pieces sit down after I do, but it feels less like a chivalrous move and more an effort to make me feel cornered by them.

The High Priestess and I study each other for a moment, her perusal shrewd despite the sweet mask that's fixed on her face. I try to calm my hammering heart, remembering that Rogan told me his father is a Soul Witch and is probably reading my body's reactions like a book. Then again, anyone in their right mind would be startled by the sudden appearance of the High Priestess of Witches. So maybe I'm okay on that front.

"Does your grandmother have my son?" Sorrel asks, forgoing the beating around the bush pleasantries and getting right to the point. I almost respect the move...almost.

"No," I answer just as frankly.

"You believe that despite the evidence?" she counters coolly, folding her hands demurely in her lap.

"And what evidence is that?" I ask. "I mean, despite the circumstantial and conjecture-based theories that have been spat at me, I've yet to see any evidence that supports this accusation."

"It doesn't seem like a logical conclusion to you based on the facts?" she asks, deflecting my question.

"It does not," I tell her simply. "And unless the Order is keeping vital information to themselves, there are far too few *facts* available to us to draw any accurate conclusions from."

"How do you know my son?" she pivots, once again dodging my point.

"I don't know him, I only know that he's missing."

"No, not Elon, Rogan?" she redirects.

"You know the answer to that question; I've been asked it repeatedly by the Order and have answered honestly and the same every time."

"I'd like to hear it for myself," she presses.

"He came to me, asking for help with finding his brother. I agreed to help him. Here I am," I tell her, offering the CliffsNotes version.

"Yes, here you are," she coos, the smile still in place on her lips, but her eyes now cooling from our exchange. "My sons were renounced for murdering their uncle in cold blood. Were you aware of that?" she asks with a little sniff.

"Yes."

"And that's not a concern for you?" she queries innocently, but the judgment in her green eyes gives her away.

"Honestly, it's none of my business," I counter, trying to calm the anger that starts to boil my blood as the High Priestess of Witches, Rogan and Elon's mother, tries to paint her own children with lies and disdain, all to further some ridiculous power grab. She can judge me all she wants, but I know what she's about, and it disgusts me.

A small voice in my head is begging me to stay calm, to play along and not fuck with the people who more or less rule my race. I could easily play the victim, make Rogan out to be the bad guy just like she's doing. He might even deserve it, but that's not who I am.

Maybe it's the flashes I saw of his life as a kid when Rogan and I first used magic together. Or the truth of what happened to them, and the people who stood by and allowed it. Perhaps it was the realization that nothing is what I thought and that there are far more gray areas in the world than my black and white upbringing would have ever had me believe. But as I feel the weight of High Council stares on me, sense the subtle disdain leaking out of the kelly-green eyes of the piece of shit witch across from me, I've hit my limit with playing small.

I'm done with all of it. The Order can shove this *for your protection* bullshit up their tight ass. Rogan can fuck off with his too late apology. This bitch can kick rocks, thinking she's better than me. And I can stop being a little bitch and pretending I'm anything other than what I am, a powerful as fuck, badass Bone Witch.

"How is murder and the safety of your fellow witches none of your business?" the High Council member in the cranberry suit demands.

I roll my eyes and direct my answer to the High Priestess. "If they're so dangerous, why renounce them instead of execute them? You want me to worry about their penchant for killing, but clearly you as High Council members weren't worried, because you let them loose on society. So yeah, it's none of my damn business. Besides, no one came to me and asked me to kill anyone. I was asked to help find missing witches. Witches, it seems, no one around *here* is actually interested in finding, and frankly, I'm *really* starting to wonder why that is."

"Careful, witchling," she warns, losing her cool.

"Heed your own warning, lady, you don't know shit

about who I am," I snap back, pushing out of my chair and onto my feet. I'm surprised when Sorrel Adair balks slightly before shoving her all-powerful mask back in place and matching my stance.

Rogan's father and the other witch rise, and then the High Priestess snaps her fingers. The guards still positioned on each side of the door immediately turn and leave. I narrow my eyes at the three remaining witches and call on backup in the form of a fuck ton of power. They'll probably slaughter me with three against one odds, but I'll take a bitch out as I go.

"Are you questioning the decisions of the High Council of Witches?" the High Priestess asks me, amusement flickering in her cold eyes.

"Like I said, it's none of my business, but since you asked, yes, and if you think other people haven't come to the same conclusion that I have, then you've highly underestimated the people you say you lead."

I see the exact moment that Rogan's mother begins to wonder what it is that I might know. Her eye color perfectly reflects the gleam of greed I see in her stare, and I know without a shadow of doubt that she's calculating my pawn-status, like this is some fucked up game and not people's lives she's messing with.

Her gaze dips down my body, like she's looking for physical evidence that I know more than I'm letting on. I tamp down on the shiver that climbs up my spine when her covetous stare rises and fixes on the mirror behind me before meeting my eyes once more.

"You're a beautiful witch, Lennox," she declares smugly, as though she has anything to do with it.

I shoot her a look. "I'm aware, but remind me what that has to do with the missing witches?" I ask, my tone saccharine.

I work hard to pull back my irritation. I need to redirect this encounter back to what's important and try to reduce the massive target I think I just put on my back. I don't know how she put it together that there might be a deeper connection between me and her son, but I'd be an idiot to trivialize the conniving wheels I can almost see turning in this witch's head.

Internally I start to berate myself, but I quickly shut it down. She might've come for me no matter what I did. Playing nice or telling her to piss off wouldn't have changed her desire to use me if she could. I suspect that's all this woman knows how to do.

"What's your endgame, Osteomancer?" Sorrel purrs at me, the sound more feral than soothing. Rogan's dad and the other suited council member move to stand behind her. The shape of their position means something, but I can't for the life of me remember what.

That'll teach me to zone out the next time someone is going on about sacred geometry.

"Solving this case and then living my best life sounds pretty good to me," I chirp in response.

A flame flickers to life in the High Priestess's hand. She caresses the small ball of fire lovingly, but I scoff, unimpressed.

I can wave my hand through the flame of a candle too, lady. Get better parlor tricks.

I feed my well of power, careful not to pull anything from Rogan in case somehow these elite witches can feel it, or in the event that Rogan is in a situation where he needs to defend himself against them. I'm still not clear exactly why they're even here talking to me, and I just hope wherever he is right now, he's okay.

Magic swells within me, and I'm shocked by just how much is building inside of me. I have that same full feeling I had when I syphoned from Rogan's source, only this time, I know for a fact that I haven't gone near our tether.

Rogan's dad tilts his head to the side and studies me. He mumbles something to his wife, and the High Priestess raises an eyebrow in reaction to whatever it is he says. I want to know what the Animamancer is picking up, but I keep my mouth shut.

"We don't have to be enemies," she tells me resolutely, the ball of fire she's conjured in her hand weaving itself in and out of her fingers playfully. I shake off the hypnotic way she wields her strongest element, and focus back on what she said.

"I didn't know we *were* enemies," I retort, playing dumb. "I'm simply here to help. I'm not sure how that puts us on opposing sides of what's happening," I add, to really hammer home the *sweet and innocent* thing I'm trying for.

"You're powerful, you could do great things in life," she continues, ignoring the valid points I'm making.

"Thank you, my Grammy always said so, but she was biased," I quip, dropping my *sweeter than honey* efforts when they clearly miss their mark.

With a flick of her fingers, the High Priestess launches her small fireball at me. I'm ready to yank the bones out of her body to protect myself, but the trajectory of the flames is off, and it goes flying past me. The sound of shattering glass fills the room. I flinch and spin to see the large mirror that takes up half the wall behind me crumbling in chunks to the ground. It reveals some kind of control room, but the only person standing in it is Rogan.

He stares at his mother, his gaze blazing with contempt and rage. No one utters a word as they survey one another, their unspoken conversation only interrupted by the sound of glass tinkling to the ground. A cruel smile tilts the High

Priestess's lips, and her insidious gaze slowly, purposefully moves to me.

I beg Rogan in my mind not to move. Not to flinch. Not to so much as glare at his mother and confirm what it's clear she suspects. I can feel the threat in her probing glance, sense that she's probing, that she's trying to gauge the possibilities. She wants to test what her son might feel for me, and I'm terrified of what that might do, what that could reveal not only to her but to me. I don't know if she'll outright attack me or maybe him to see what *I'll* do. Will anyone stop her? Will they just watch as, out of nowhere, the High Priestess attacks her renounced son and an innocent witch?

Adrenaline ravages my insides, and my magic reaches its distended peak. I feel like any minute I'm going to explode, and I don't know what will be left in my wake. Rogan's father's head snaps in my direction, but before he can give any warning, a door behind Rogan flies open, and a squat woman with thick glasses comes running in. She's waving a paper, her cheeks flushed from probably running over here.

"I found it!" she announces between gasps for air. "The curse was just a failsafe, but I figured out what the demon magic was supposed to do."

Everyone's attention moves to the woman, and she all at once seems to take in the shattered window and the standoff taking place on the other side. Her surprised eyes land on the High Priestess and grow even wider as she drops into a deep bow.

"Your eminence, I'm so sorry I interrupted," she squeaks nervously, her eyes darting to Rogan, then to the broken glass, and back to the ruler of the witches.

"Ah, finally, someone who knows how to behave in the presence of their Priestess," she points out, leveling me with a loaded look, demanding that I bow too.

"I don't recall ever swearing fealty to you," I tell her simply, stopping myself from flipping her off and telling her to *bow to this, bitch*.

She hums in disapproval, her green eyes shimmering with amusement. "Something to look forward to the next time we meet then," she declares sweetly, smoothing her dress and turning to leave.

"Yes, that and stabbing you with your own femurs sounds like a good time," I call to her, annoyed by the hoity dismissal.

A choking-cough-gasp sounds off behind me, and I look to find the bespectacled witch staring at me in complete horror. I also catch that Rogan is trying very hard not to smile. He's doing a shit job of it, and not even the hand he brings up to mask what's happening on his face is fooling anyone. I turn around, my unamused gaze landing back on scheming green eyes that radiate *this isn't over*.

So I send her a fiery *not by a long shot* glare, and then I stand there as my newest enemies, the High Priestess and her cronies, leave. The door slams shut behind them, knocking the last of the mirror from its frame to the floor. I'm sure the move is meant to remind me of where I am versus where they are, but honestly, all it does is pull the stopper in my chest and let all the tension filling my body drain out.

What in the name of the moon just happened?

My eyes find Rogan's, questions and worry swimming in my gaze. I expect to find the same trepidation and distress I'm feeling in his watchful stare, but instead there's something else there entirely: admiration and...need. I refuse to let myself react in any kind of way, instead turning from his intense regard and focusing on the woman who might have just inadvertently saved us from a serious magical ass kicking.

I want to hope that I could have held my own, but this is the High Priest and Priestess we're talking about, and at least one of their lieutenants. My confidence and ability is growing, but I'm not completely delusional that I would have come out of that unscathed.

"I'm sorry. What were you saying?" I ask the short witch, and she blinks at me, confused for a moment before she once again waves the paper in her hand.

"Right, yes, I was saying that I know what the demon magic was supposed to do. It wasn't a curse. I mean, there were protective curses put in place, which is what hit that witch and made most of her go poof, but those were just fail safes. The root magic was an inlet," she declares excitedly, and I can't help but cringe at her casual *poof* description of what happened to the Order member in the room that day.

"What's an inlet?" I query, not getting what she's saying. I make a note to read up on demon magic and try to prepare myself for what we might be up against.

"It's like a portal," Rogan explains, his eyes now looking the level of troubled I expected to see earlier. "It means when the target of the magic touched the paper, they would have been portaled to whatever end location was magically predetermined."

"Exactly," the plump witch agrees, impressed, a wide happy smile spread across her face.

"Let me guess," I huff wearily. "The target of the demon magic was me?"

"There's no way to confirm that since the fail safes were activated, but based on the contents of the note, it would be a safe guesstimation," the witch confirms, and I nod and stare at the ground as I try to take this all in.

"Is there any way to find where the inlet's final drop would have been?" Rogan presses, his tone heartbreakingly hopeful.

"We're working on that now. It's complicated magic, but if anyone can do it, it's my team," she declares cheerfully.

I shake my head, and a hollow laugh escapes me. I once joked that Rogan had a talent for making enemies, but man, I've got him beat in that department. I've been a witch for a week and a half, and they're just climbing out of the woodwork at this point. I mean, I'm so good that I don't even have to *meet* someone in order to make them want to hunt me down and do who-knows-what to me. I run my fingers through my curls, scratching at my scalp, sighing. At this rate, I'm going to need a list. It'll start with the angry mini-van-driving mom, and next I'll add High Priest and Priestess to the list, their cronies, and some random nameless demon.

Yep, what can I say, I've got skills. Mad skills...literally.

9

I stare into my head-sized coffee cup, lost in thought as I swirl the creamy goodness around and around. The smell of dark roast and baked goods wraps me up in a friendly hug as the bell above the door rings, indicating that someone is either entering or exiting the busy coffee shop I've commandeered a table at. Lucky for me, *Trouble Brewin* is witch-owned, and no one has said a word about me sitting alone at a table while my guards do the same all around me.

I'm probably cramping someone's access to free Wi-Fi and denying them their favorite coffee spot table. But so far everyone's keeping their opinions to themselves as I stare into my cup and try to find the meaning of life in its contents. I suppose that's one perk to having Order SWAT surrounding you twenty-four seven, it deters the shit starters.

I bring the magical, piping hot liquid to my lips and take a deep pull of the full-bodied and perfectly-sugared liquid. It's good, but I've had better. Visions of Rogan's exquisite coffee machine float to the surface of my mind, and I stare at them with unadulterated longing. *She was a snotty bitch, but she was the best.*

I dismiss my lusty yearnings for the coffee machine I most likely will never see again and redirect my thoughts to the task at hand. I know my Grammy Ruby is dead—and therefore not involved in what's happening with the missing witches and the demon shit—but I can't shake the feeling that I'm missing something. She knew Nikki Smelser, checked in on her, cared about her. Did something happen between them to trigger this?

Was the personal connection with Nikki the reason why she couldn't divine any more information from her dream or the bones? I keep swirling all of it around and around in my mind, trying to make sense of it all. But I can't get the picture of Nikki out of my head, I can't shake the idea that her being the big bad in the scenario just doesn't fit. Maybe I'm a fool for a pretty face? Fuck knows I'm where I am now because I didn't see past Rogan's *gorgeous* to the backstabber underneath.

My thoughts shift from Nikki to Rogan, and I wonder if he's made any progress on tracing the demon magic's final destination. He hasn't left the side of that team since they announced their big *inlet* breakthrough yesterday. I wanted to help too, but apparently my presence could create issues, so I'm not allowed. The only thing I am allowed to do is attempt to read the useless items they brought back from the missing witches' homes. That is just a waste of time, so now I've found a new way to waste time that involves over-caffeination and overanalyzing every second of my life in search of clues.

Two of my guards get up and then a couple seconds later sit back down. I don't look up to see why, too focused on trying to piece things together and figure out what I'm missing.

How do you see the unseen?

Someone clears their throat nearby, but I ignore the

sound, too preoccupied with staring into space. A large body stops at the edge of my table, and I can tell from the lack of black uniform that it's not one of my guards. I look up, naked irritation in my eyes. If someone wants to lecture me about table etiquette, I'm going to punch them in the throat. Well, at least in my head I'd do that; in reality, I'd probably just say sorry and then go sit with one of my guards.

My glimpse up shows me snug-fitting, worn, black jeans and a khaki-colored waffle Henley hugging muscles that are more a piece of art than a body. Interest piqued, I continue my perusal up to find long, thick strands of auburn hair draping around the man's shoulders, and the next thing I know, my eyes are meeting a familiar golden gaze.

"Saxon?" I question, surprised by the lycan's unexpected appearance.

He answers with a gorgeous wide smile. "Hey, fancy meeting you here," he teases, his nostrils flaring slightly as though he's scenting my reaction to his presence.

"Is Hoot okay? I just talked to Riggs this morning, he said everything was fine?" I start, worry pumping through me as I try to figure out why he's here.

"He's fine," Saxon hurries to reassure me. "Riggs said you sounded down when he spoke to you, that you could probably use a break. So I volunteered to come give you one," he explains, rubbing at the back of his neck sheepishly.

"Oh," I chirp, taken aback.

"I know that's presumptuous as hell, but I hope that's okay," he asks, searching my face while simultaneously smelling the air.

"Yeah, that's fine. That's...really nice of you actually," I assure him, gesturing to the chair next to me. "Have a seat," I encourage, moving a small stack of napkins to make room for him.

"Are you sure?" he questions hesitantly. "You look like you're having a pretty intense exchange with your coffee." His eyes light up, and I laugh at the teasing lilt in his tone.

"Only if you promise to be better conversation than this cup has been," I playfully counter, and Saxon pulls out the chair and sits his massive body down. I look over at my guards, expecting them to stop what's happening, but oddly, they don't.

"Sounds like stiff competition, but I'm down for a challenge," he jokes, his golden eyes taking me in.

Heat sinks into my cheeks, and I do my own discreet perusal. He looks just as good with a shirt on as he did that day on the stump with his shirt off. His hair is down and has that perfect man-wave to it that women spend hours achieving with tools, and men get from simply letting their hair air dry. His skin is sun-kissed, the golden tone complimenting his golden eyes, and...*shit,* am I drooling?

Saxon sets his to-go cup of coffee on the table, and I offer him a warm smile, inwardly panicking because I have no idea what to say, or ask, or do. I try to cover my awkwardness with a large sip of java, and then I take another because I've still got nothing.

"Riggs said you were up here working on finding Elon Kendrick. How's that going?" he asks casually before taking his own sip of coffee, and I realize that Saxon might be nervous too.

"Um, I mean, it's *not* going really. We still don't know where he is or what happened. Time is ticking, and things are tense," I blurt, thoughts of what happened with Rogan's mother the day before coming to mind.

"I'm sorry to hear that, I'll check in with the Major and

see if there's anything the pack can do to help," he offers, his eyes serious and filled with concern.

"Have you been up here before?" I question, not expecting him to be so familiar with the powers that be in the Order. I add in my guards' non-reaction to his presence to the equation and—surprise, surprise—feel like I'm missing something.

"I have actually. I'm here pretty often. I called the Major on my way up and told her I'd be here to see you, it was all cleared. I'm a liaison for the pack business, so I've worked with the Order and some of the other witch corporations for quite some time."

I raise an impressed brow. "Wow, that's...cool, how'd you get into that?"

Saxon smiles and relaxes slightly. "I more or less fell into it pretty naturally. I've always been interested in the pack's dealings. I like getting out and meeting different kinds of people and figuring out how to box out the competition," he explains on a chuckle.

"Competition? I thought what Riggs did was one of a kind?"

"In the beginning maybe, but with time, competitors popped up. We're still the best..."

"Naturally," I playfully agree, and he chuckles.

"Are you recovered from your accident?" he asks, giving me a quick once over.

"Yeah, it wasn't anything major," I lie dismissively. "I didn't get a chance to say thank you for dropping off the bones," I add, taking another sip of my coffee.

"As you can see, I'll use any excuse to get to know you better," he tells me, keen interest shining in his eyes.

Caterpillars wriggle in my stomach, creating an airy, slightly weird sensation. It's not full-blown butterflies wreaking havoc on my insides, not like I've felt with... I shut that line of thinking down. Rogan Kendrick is a non-factor, I tell myself. Besides, butterflies are cute in theory, but when you look closely, they're really just creepy looking bugs.

I direct my thoughts back to the attractive lycan sitting kitty-corner from me. The one who's a teachably good kisser and has made an effort not once, but twice now to get to know me. Maybe this is what I need. A healthy distraction from all the chaos I've been submerged in since the day the bones found me. It's been a while since my inner fiend was satiated, which is probably why I'm having trouble letting go of an asshole. But if I introduce her to a nice guy...

"So, Saxon, what do you enjoy doing aside from wrestling people half-naked on a tree stump?" I ask, a flirty smile flitting across my face. "I would also like to know how that even became a thing," I add with a chuckle.

He laughs and leans back in his chair. "I had that one in the bag until you showed up," he taunts alluringly, and I lean into his calm and captivating vibe. "Nora almost lost it for a minute until Riggs stepped in and declared the outcome."

"Nora?" I ask, confused, my smile faltering slightly.

Saxon's eyebrows drop with uncertainty, and his golden eyes study me in earnest. "Yeah, Nora, the prize," he explains, his tone suggesting that this is information he thought I knew already.

I growl internally. *Do not tell me this dude has a girlfriend or, worse, a wife.*

My smile becomes a fraction more brittle as I work to keep it plastered on my face. "Um, prize?"

Saxon's features crumple with concern, and he leans toward me. "I'm taking the look on your face to mean that you didn't understand how the competition worked, what was at stake?"

I shrug, thinking back to what Rogan said to me about it.

The purpose was to knock the person on the stump off. You couldn't use magic, and the winner gets something. Longing filters through me as I visualize the coveted jackalope antler that was almost mine.

So close.

And then I realize what Saxon is saying. "Wait. Nora? Like, as in a person...named Nora? *That's* what was at stake? You were competing for a woman?" I ask, my voice getting fractionally higher with each word spoken.

Saxon cringes infinitesimally, and I try to bring my tone back down to a decibel not offensive to lycans or nearby dogs. My heart slams against my ribcage like it wants to escape. I can't even blame it for trying to fly the coop, this last week and a half has been a serious test of our cardiac health.

"It's not what you think," Saxon defends, and my stomach drops.

Men should just never utter that statement. It sends every woman's bullshit meter right off the charts. I lean away from Saxon, my expression teeming with *I've heard that before*.

He shakes his head adamantly, holding his hands up in a placating gesture. "I know what it sounds like, but let me explain," he pleads.

Lassitude tugs at my soul, and I try not to sigh or feel fed up with the opposite sex all together. I want to spend a night working off a little stress with a decent dude; is that too much to ask? I resist the urge to throw my head back and demand answers from the universe, and instead address Saxon. "I'm listening," I encourage, but I'm not holding my breath that what he's about to say is going to make the warning bells stop ringing in my head.

He surveys my face and then nods. "My *friend*," he starts, really hammering home the emphasis on the word *friend*,

"Nora, was getting a lot of pressure from her family to settle down. She thought they'd back off after a while, but the more she stalled, the worse it got. So she came up with a plan. She pitched the idea to her family about having a competition at the next solstice gathering under the pretense that she'd find the strongest candidate that way. And then she asked if I would buy her a little more time by winning."

I wait for a beat for him to continue, but it seems that's the explanation in its entirety, and I can't help but feel like he's ignored some vital and concerning points. "Okaaay," I hedge, sorting through the flood of questions streaming through my mind. "So you were going to marry her? Was that what was going to *buy her a little more time*? Also, why couldn't she just say no, that she wasn't ready to settle down, and that's that? Why all the hoops to climb through or should I say stumps to stand on?"

I almost chuckle at my own joke, and then horror seizes me as understanding seeps into my bones. "Oh shit! I knocked you off the stump, so does that mean she had to marry someone else?" My eyes get even wider. "By stump law, am *I* that someone else?" I add, panic making my eye start to twitch and my mouth grow dry.

Did I just accidentally throw some girl to the wolves all because I wanted a jackalope antler?

Saxon chuckles, and I shoot him an unnerved look. "Lycan culture can be a bit archaic. Not all families are like that," he reassures me, "but there are some that believe strongly in alliances through marriage. Males outnumber females four to one, and some families believe that a female's most important duty is to make a prosperous match and breed stronger lycans. Nora's family is pretty old school."

"Okay, so does that mean same-sex marriage is out? Was I automatically disqualified then?"

"Well, technically you didn't knock me off the stump," he declares, a saucy glint in his eyes.

I open my mouth to defend that I pretty much did when I realize what he's getting at.

Rogan.

He technically was the reason Saxon stepped off the stump. I cover my mouth with my hands, shocked. "Does that mean Rogan is engaged and doesn't know it?" I ask through my cupped palms, ignoring the swirl of anger that spins through me with the question.

Saxon's nostrils flare, but I'm too stunned to call him out about this whole smelling me thing. "Riggs declared Rogan the last man standing, so to speak, but since he didn't stay to continue the contest until every lycan had a fair chance, the competition was put on hold."

"So what happens now?" I demand nervously as I tamp down the swirl of conflicting emotions running amuck inside of me. I shouldn't care. I know I shouldn't. And yet, there's no ignoring the flicker of emotion that wants a Nora-the-Lycan beatdown.

"Well, Rogan will be required to come to the next gathering and defend his claim. If he doesn't show up, then he'll be open to challenge by any lycan, anytime, anywhere."

Amusement trickles through me at the thought of random lycans picking fights with Rogan while he's grocery shopping or trying to go to work. Some might call that poetic justice. Now, if I can just keep him in the dark so he doesn't see any of this coming, then we'd have a real knee-slapper on our hands.

"So, I guess one way or another, Nora bought herself some more time," I point out with a laugh as I digest everything he just told me.

He chuckles, a brazen gleam in his golden eyes. "She's very satisfied with the outcome. She now has the extra time to implement the second phase of her plan," Saxon agrees.

The bell over the cafe door rings, and it pulls me from our focused conversation. I look over to see colors painting the sky as the sun starts to tuck in for the night. *When did it get so late?*

"So, does that mean, if you had won anyway, that you'd be a taken man right now?" I query, my gaze returning to Saxon's, the question once again hanging between us.

I watch him and realize that I'm not sure what I want the answer to be, or maybe the real issue I'm having is that I don't know if I care. I wouldn't pursue anything with him if he's with someone, that's not my style. But as I wait for his answer, I realize that there's no apprehension speeding my heart, no unease or lurking threat of disappointment at the possibility that nothing might happen between us.

Saxon is gorgeous, confident, interested and—if I'm reading this situation with his friend right—kind. But for whatever reason, everything that he is isn't sparking anything major in me.

"I'd never be just a man, Leni, but yes, in the eyes of my pack, if I had won, I'd be taken." The cocky smile on his handsome face doesn't distract me from the impression that he likes this exchange.

I think he's reading my questions as a sign of jealousy or deeper interest, but we're not there yet. He's still firmly in *hit it and quit it* territory, not in *I like you, so stop talking to other girls* land. I'm just trying to understand the dynamics that were in play that day at the stump and ensure I'm not stepping on anyone's toes or inviting any more drama into my life than I'm already dealing with. I'm not over the moon for him or feeling some profound connection, but that doesn't mean we can't have some fun. I just need to make sure we're on the same page with that before this goes anywhere else.

"So, if you had won, you'd be there playing house, but you didn't, and now you're here," I recap, taking a sip of my coffee and watching him from under my lashes.

"Yes, I suspect a sneaky witch ensorcelled me, and I've had no choice but to pursue her in hopes of relief," he teases, his voice a little lower, a hint of growl and delicious innuendo snaking through his words.

My inner fiend rises with a clear *that'll do*, and I do nothing to stop a cheeky smile from playing at my lips. "Ensorcelled, you say?" I exclaim with faux concern. "How ever do you know?"

I'm not sure why my flirting has taken on a Steel Magnolias*-esque quality, but I do declare, it's working for me.*

Saxon laughs and I let the rich sound resonate through me. I recall what it was like to kiss him, to nip at his lips and feel him respond to me. The memories work to heat my blood, but out of nowhere, my thoughts shift to a different set of lips on mine, on the feel of different hands as they cupped my face and kissed me until I felt like I was home. My body comes alive at the new reel playing in my mind, and the contrast in my physical response is jarring.

What is wrong with me?

I shove the memory of kissing Rogan away, hard, but the damage is done. Saxon purposefully breathes me in, and I see the second he picks up on my hesitation, on the frustration and confusion tainting my interest and arousal. His brow furrows, and the heat banked in his eyes cools ever so slightly.

"What just happened?" he asks me gently.

I close my eyes for a moment and sigh, because as much as I want to answer nothing, we both know that's bullshit.

"Witch emergency," I tell him lamely, and after a

moment, I see his eyes light up with understanding.

"Hmmmm, I suspected there might be something there. He was eyeing me pretty hard when I dropped your package off," Saxon divulges, and I can imagine the sour lemons that would have been written all over Rogan's face at seeing Saxon again so soon. "So were the two of you a thing? Are you still?"

"No," I answer simply, hating the twinge the truth of that sends through me. "But it's...complicated," I add, knowing it's accurate but not helpful.

I laugh at the absurdity of it all. A girl never wants to hear *it's not what you think*, and I'm sure men could live without hearing *it's complicated* out of the mouth of someone they're interested in. Saxon smiles and sits back in his chair. He runs a hand through his long auburn waves and considers me.

"Tell me about why it's complicated," he asks out of nowhere, and a rush of heat climbs up my neck as I stare at him, wide-eyed and floored.

"No!" I exclaim quickly, shaking my head and finishing the last of my witch's brew. I debate for a moment going to get a refill just so I can escape the weirdness of this moment. But I have a feeling even if I made a break for the door, he'd come after me, damn persistent lycan.

"I am not talking to a guy I want to sleep with about another guy I wish I didn't want to sleep with. Nope. I draw the line at being *that girl*," I blurt and then immediately wish I hadn't.

I look over at my guards, who are all scanning the place, looking vigilant but bored. Dammit. Why didn't I think to come up with a *get me out of here* signal until now?

Note to self: immediately come up with a signal as soon as I get home.

"I mean, I'm on board with the guy you want to sleep

with part of that statement in case you had any doubts," Saxon teases, and I chuckle and wish it were that easy.

"I normally would be too," I confess. "And I'm trying, trust me..."

"I sense a *but* coming," he supplies with a warm smile, and I instantly want to smack some sense into myself.

Seriously. What. Is. Wrong. With. Me?

I could be in the bathroom right now with this dude, riding what I'm sure is a sizable dick, while judging the cleanliness of the facilities and chasing that O. But no, instead, I have the female version of a limp dick because Rogan Kendrick has fucked with my head. Limp clit? Is that a thing? Because it feels like a thing, and I have to say I am *not* a fan.

I scrub my face with both of my palms, beyond fed up with my own crap. I'm going to get that betraying bastard out of my head if it's the last thing I do. But tonight is not the night.

"I'm sorry," I tell Saxon, my gaze contrite. "Honestly, I'm saving you a lot of trouble here, because my life right now is a mess." I throw my hands up in exasperation, wishing that what I'm saying weren't true, but it is. "It was a mess before the missing witches, and now it's so beyond fucked that it's unrecognizable. You should run. Like, right now. You should bolt and never look back before my atom bomb of a life annihilates you," I warn with a hollow laugh, completely serious. "Full disclosure, if you don't run for the hills, I'm going to completely judge you. You should care more about yourself than getting entangled in my nightmare," I tell him, and he laughs.

Saxon takes me in, his eyes alight with amusement and curiosity, his smile sexy and still not doing a damn thing for me.

Ugh.

He frees a deep exhale from his chest and gives a conceding nod. "Okay, Leni, I'll run. I'll save myself," he teases. "But let me walk you home first," he tells me.

I eye him suspiciously, which earns me another rich chuckle and him raising his hands in a gesture of innocence.

"Promise I won't try a thing, I just don't want you walking back in the dark alone."

An incredulous snort sneaks out as I once again scan my guards. "You may not have noticed, but I have a lovely set of shadows that were gifted to me by the Order," I point out, waving at where said shadows are seated all around me.

"Oh, I'm aware," Saxon declares with a sly look on his face. "But one lycan is worth a whole team of witches, you can trust me on that."

With a wink that I'm sure is laden with implication, Saxon rises to his feet and offers me his hand. I smile despite myself, allowing him to help me up and ignoring the hostile grumblings of my guards, who clearly don't like the dig he just took. He tucks my arm in his as my shadows surround us, and then we're on our way.

The sun is lost behind the high-rises all around me, but dusk kisses the sky goodnight as a chilling breeze winds its way between the buildings. A shiver climbs up my back, and I pick up my pace. Saxon doesn't say anything as we go, he seems just as intent on watching everything around us as my guards are.

"Thank you for coming and trying to give me a break, it really was amazingly thoughtful of you," I tell him, my arm still tucked in the crook of his.

"It was my pleasure," he assures me. "I hope it helped you forget all the pressure on your shoulders, for a little while anyway."

I smile and try to fight the blush creeping into my cheeks at his words. He really is so incredibly decent, and I berate myself all through the security checks to get into the building and the ride up in the elevator to my floor. How am I not getting all over that?

Stupid, stupid, stupid.

The elevator dings, opening its doors to the floor I'm staying on, and Saxon and I hang back as my guards check everything out. Nerves skitter in my stomach as we meander to a stop at the door to my suite, my guards making themselves scarce for a moment. I'm wrestling with my thoughts when Saxon surprises me and pulls me in for a hug.

"If things change, call me," he offers casually, stepping back and giving me a stunning smile. "Until otherwise decreed, friends?" he asks.

I laugh. "Friends," I agree, my own wide smile fixed on my face as he waves and moves to leave.

"Saxon?" I call out, and he pauses. "Can I kiss you?" I query, parroting what I asked him the first time we met. He surveys me curiously for a moment, and then in two strides he's in front of me. I laugh, not able to help it as I tell myself that the world has it wrong, curiosity didn't kill the cat, it killed the lycan.

Before I can talk myself out of it or let things like emotions get in the way, I press my lips to Saxon's. Unlike the first time this happened, there's not an ounce of hesitation on his end, and he absolutely took notes on what I showed him I liked. He wraps one hand around the back of my neck, and the other presses in on the small of my back. He pulls me into him, his mouth taking and giving in turn. I meet him nip for nip and stroke for stroke, trying to get lost in the feel of him.

He tastes like coffee and desire. Feels like a warm fire on a cold night, comforting, and safe. But the kiss is just a kiss, there's no building, no inferno. As much as I want to dive into Saxon to escape Rogan, the oblivion I'm so desperately seeking isn't there. Maybe it could be, someday, but someday is too far and filled with too many unknowns for me to bank on.

Our lips slow, the failed crescendo of our exchange all I can taste now, as Saxon's hold on me loosens and he relinquishes me. I can see in his eyes that he feels what I feel, but there's no frustration in his golden gaze, only understanding. His nostrils flare, and I chuckle at the odd response that makes him so much other than I'm used to. His smile grows wider, and he gives me a quick peck, whispering, "And now we've come full circle," against my lips before stepping back.

I'm confused at first by his declaration, but as Saxon puts more distance between us, my stare lands on a pair of infuriated green eyes. Rogan stands in the hallway, stiff and radiating wrath.

"Call me whenever," Saxon reminds me, moving around Rogan with a wave goodbye and pressing the call button for the elevator. I stare at Rogan, who looks enraged and like he's actively working to control his breathing.

Part of me feels bad, but another part of me knows this needs to happen. That we need to sever as much of our emotions as we can until we can sever the bond and go our separate ways. I hear the elevator ding, but I don't watch Saxon get on. The doors close, leaving me and Rogan tensely standing and staring at one another.

His eyes flash with heat, with questions, and sadly with resignation. I don't know what I want him to say or do, but when he walks by me without a word, entering our quarters and shutting the door behind him, everything in me screams *that's not it*.

I close my eyes against the onslaught of pain. I try to get the rational side of me to override the emotional, but I'm fighting a losing battle. I want to hate him. I *should* hate him, and I don't know what it says about me that I can't.

10

I trace the veins of texture on the ceiling with my eyes. I conjure shapes and images from the random lines and peaks, the shadows in my room adding depth and darkness to my jumbled thoughts. I reach for the phone again, waking the device to check the time. It's 1:22 in the morning. Four minutes since the last time I checked it.

I groan in frustration and turn on my side, fluffing the pillow underneath my head punishingly. I close my eyes and try to convince my body to succumb to sleep, but I can't turn my brain off. I can't stop seeing Rogan's angry eyes or, worse, remembering what it felt like to kiss him instead of Saxon. I keep replaying what happened tonight, picking things apart and attempting to rearrange them into a structure that makes sense. One where everything isn't so confusing and I haven't gotten in too deep with someone who I know won't choose me in the end.

But try as I might to change the picture I'm looking at, as soon as I stop messing with it, everything snaps back to where it was, and I'm left overthinking and trying not to stare truth in the face. I flop onto my back again with a sigh and accept that it's going to be a long night. I'm tempted to call Tad, but he's bitchy when he's tired, and I already know what he'll say. That's part of the problem. I know what I need to do, but I'm stalling.

I sit up and decide it's time for a pep-talk. It's time to stop kidding myself and just woman up. I shouldn't be hiding away, acting like some timid weakling who can't face the truth. I'm the motherfucking Bone Witch. I was made for this shit. With clenched fists, I hype myself up and get myself ready. Rogan and I need to sort some things out, and now is as good a time as any, well, for me anyway. He's probably sleeping, but not for much longer. It's time to pay the piper.

I push out of bed and pull in a massive fortifying breath as I stride to my bedroom door. I open it, intent on maintaining this kickass momentum all the way to Rogan's room, but what I don't expect is for someone to be standing right there. I let out a surprised squeal and aim a fist at whoever it is. A large hand catches mine, and a deep familiar voice tells me, "Not this time," as he wraps a palm around my fist and backs me into my bedroom until I'm pressed firmly against a wall.

"Moon shits, you scared the crap out of me," I whisper yell, one hand caught in Rogan's grip while I press the other to my chest and try to talk my adrenaline down.

"Moon shits?" he repeats haughtily, an eyebrow raised in question.

"Yes, moon shits," I defend as my fight-or-flight reflex tries to walk it off. "What are you doing?" I hiss at him, irritated that he just jump-scared me again.

"I need to talk to you. I was just about to knock when the door flew open. Where were you going?"

My inner hype girl squeals shyly and abandons me. Suddenly I don't want to tell him that I was coming to talk to him.

Maturity at its finest.

"Um, I had to pee," I blurt, and then Rogan's judgy eyebrow gets even higher as he looks over to the door that leads into an ensuite bathroom. He knows this because every bedroom in this place has an attached bathroom.

Internally I facepalm. *I wonder what it's like to go through life and not be a raging idiot.* Guess I'll never know.

"What do you want, Rogan?" I ask instead, embracing my cowardice and flipping the script on him.

"I haven't had a chance to see if you were okay after everything with my mother."

I'm tempted to ask him what the hell that was about, but I'm pretty sure I already know. She was looking for leverage. I suspect she thinks she found it, which is laughable and dangerous for me. She'll be very disappointed if she tries to use me to force Rogan's hand. I'm painfully aware of how much I wouldn't win that showdown.

"Did you know she was coming?" I press, surveying him as he looks around my room awkwardly.

"No. One of your guards tipped me off when I noticed that they weren't where they were supposed to be. I asked why, and that's when they told me that the High Priestess's personal guard was with you. I got there about a minute before she broke the glass."

I run my hand over the texture of the wall at my back, still pinned against it by Rogan's arms. I should move away from him. I don't.

"Were you going to see Saxon?" he asks me out of nowhere.

"Wh-what?" I stammer, thrown off guard. "No, he's back in Tennessee."

Rogan's eyes study mine like he's looking for something. I'm not sure what it is, but I just stare at him until he stops.

"He's two floors down in a guest suite," he informs me, and I'm taken aback by that revelation.

Why is he still here?

"You weren't sneaking out to go see him?" Rogan accuses, and I balk at his insinuation.

I narrow my eyes at him. "Were you waiting outside to see if I was going to meet up with Saxon?" I ask incredulously.

A sheepish look overtakes Rogan's face, and I have to stop my mouth from dropping open. "Holy shit, you were," I accuse, shocked.

He doesn't say anything.

"News flash, Rogan, if I wanted to fuck Saxon, I wouldn't have to sneak out in the middle of the night to do it. What was your plan, anyway, order me back to my room?" I ask, shaking my head at how ridiculous he is.

"I didn't have a plan," he admits, leaning into me just a fraction more.

I stop breathing for a beat, searching his face for something that will tell me what all of this means. My body responds to his close proximity just like it always has, and I yearn to be tipped over the precarious edge I'm balancing on. Do I go with my mind, shut Rogan out, sever the bond, and flip him a pair of deuces as I leave him in my wake? Or do I trust my gut, give my body what it's aching for, knowing that it's going to burn hot and fast and probably scar me in the end?

I know there's no happily ever after here, and yet I still can't convince myself to walk away.

"What are you doing, Rogan?" I ask, and I'm not sure if I'm simply questioning what he's doing right now, with his life, or if my question is really about us.

It's clear he's feeling some kind of way about things, but I have no idea what that is or if I really even want to know.

Who am I kidding, I want to know.

He breathes me in, his gaze tracing my features and then lifting back to meet my flustered stare. "I don't know," he admits quietly, like if he talks too loudly, it will scare whatever is happening away.

"Why are you here?" I press, just as quietly, unsure of what I want him to say.

I should tell him to leave. Tell him that he can't come barging in here like this. I need to make it clear that it doesn't matter what he wants, he ruined things, and now he has to deal with the consequences of those actions. But the issue with all of that is I'm not thinking about him right now.

I mean, I'm definitely thinking about him and what I'd like to do and have done to me. But it's not about him. It's not about giving into the desire I see in the depths of his eyes right now. It's about giving into *my* desire. It's what's kept me up tonight, caused me to toss and turn with thoughts of my lips on his. My hands exploring that body, taking what I need from him like he's taken from me.

The problem though is that I know it won't stop there, at least not for me. As much as I love the idea of a solid night of revenge-fucking Rogan right out of my head, I can't do that when *he's* the one I want to fuck. He's burrowed into my soul despite my efforts to keep him out, and I don't know how to combat that.

I can pretend that I'm capable of a no-strings-attached situation that allows both of us to let off some steam, but the truth is I'm not capable of doing that with him. I know that I can't be safe *and* vulnerable in the same space when it comes to him, and I need both of those things in my life to be whole.

So where does that leave me?

I stare up into Rogan's sweltering gaze, my eyes slowly

dipping down his face and pausing on his full lips. It means that from here on out, whatever hurt or disloyalty he sends my way, it's on me. I'll have no one to blame but myself. I know what he's capable of, what he's done. He's told me himself that if push comes to shove, I won't be the one he's saving, that I'm not the one he'll choose. But here I am anyway, silently begging for him to close the distance between our mouths.

This has risk and danger written all over it in bright flashing neon letters, but I don't care. There's no going back for me now.

"Rogan," I start, his name half plea, half chastisement, as my eyes lift back up to his. But I don't get to utter another word, to tell him that just this once, I'll choose vulnerability over safety, that I'll choose him. Because suddenly his mouth is on mine, and I'm lost in him.

He cups my face, tilting my head back and pressing in against me. Our kiss is feverish and hungry, desperate and unapologetic. I moan into his mouth when his tongue teases mine, and he rolls his hips against me, igniting every nerve inside of me. It's so right it's fucked up. Someone destined to hurt you shouldn't feel so good, but he does, and all I want is *more*.

"Lennox," he whispers against my lips as he pulls away and takes me in.

"No," I whisper back, dropping my hands to the hem of his shirt and lifting it up his chest. "Unless you're telling me how you like it, asking how I like it, or moaning how amazing I am, I don't want to hear it," I tell him, and he lifts his shirt up and over his head.

"Lennox..." He tries again.

I pull my own loose tank top off. "No," I declare more adamantly, my naked breasts doing more to shut him up than my objections. "I've made up my mind, I want at least five orgasms, and I heard you loud and clear, Elon wins no matter what, I got it," I tell him, grabbing his hand and lifting it to my boob.

I hide my worry behind a breathy, nervous laugh, begging in my mind for him to shut up and give me this, let me take what I want from him. Just for tonight. I don't know why it feels so pressing, like a looming need to kick the wedge out from between us and see what we could be if we both just let our guard down. Maybe it's guilt for what happened in the hallway earlier, or maybe this is just me taking back some of the choice and power he stole from me, but I don't want to question it. I've spent too much time in my head since I woke up here, and all I want to do is not think, not overanalyze. I just want to feel.

His eyes flit back and forth between mine. "Five orgasms?" he teases, pinching my nipple between his thumb and forefinger.

Delicious sensations zing from my breast straight down to my clit, and I moan softly. "Yep," I answer breathily. "You have some solid fucking to do to make up for all the fucking-over that's been going down."

He chuckles and it morphs into a hiss when I reach down and palm his length through his pajama pants. His lips are on mine in less time than it takes to say, *speaking of going down*, and it's the kind of kiss that takes no prisoners and leaves no panties dry. He grabs my ass with both hands and lifts me so I can wrap my legs around his waist. He sucks on my bottom lip as my center aligns perfectly with his cock, and he rolls his hips, pressing his hardness against me in just the right way, and it makes me pant.

My hard nipples tease the planes of his chest, and his skin is warm against mine. I grind against him, deepening the kiss and threading my fingers through his hair. He moans into my mouth as I work my hips against his, and I drink down his pleasure like the heady elixir it is. Heat builds between us as our mouths and tongues and bodies come together, more untamed and frenetic with each passing second.

"Pinch me," I demand, pulling away and kissing the spot just below his ear.

"What?" he asks huskily, tilting his head so I can have better access to the side of his throat.

"Pinch me," I repeat. "I need to know that I'm awake."

Rogan doesn't argue, and he also doesn't pinch me. Instead, he pushes me back against the wall and nips hard at my neck. The pleasure and pain that shoots through me at the contact has me writhing against him, and I swear if he's not underneath me and then inside of me in the next minute, I'm going to spontaneously combust.

I try to push off from the wall, which only serves to send us bumping into the dresser. It teeters and something falls off of it with a loud thunk. Rogan and I both go still, waiting to see if anyone will come check on what the noise was. I hold my breath, listening intently, and then letting air out slowly when it seems like the coast is clear.

I unwrap myself from Rogan and slide sensually down his body. "Pants off and you on the bed, now," I order, and he chuckles quietly, the deep rumble of his laugh doing all kinds of naughty and welcome things to my body.

"Bossy, bossy," he teases, tilting my head back and planting a languid, thorough kiss on my lips before backing away from me with a salacious smile.

He starts to untie the drawstring of his pants, and I look down to see what fell off the dresser really quick so I don't trip over it and break something on my way to break in Rogan's cock.

A small, perfectly intact bird skull is lying next to my abandoned tank top on the floor. I'm surprised I've never noticed the perfectly white bones and beak before, and I lean down and pluck it and my shirt from the ground. I smile at what I think is an owl skull, but I'll have to geek out over it later; I have a gorgeous witch in my bed that needs riding.

I look up, intent on setting my shirt and the owl skull on the dresser, when everything suddenly goes wrong. Rogan's eyes are banked with heat as he tucks his thumbs in the waist of his pants and pushes them down. But I can't focus on him because it feels like someone just pulled a hook through my stomach and now they're yanking on it...hard. The room around me morphs, like I'm in some fucked up hall of mirrors making everything wider and longer than it should be.

Fear wells in my chest, and Rogan's eyes grow confused as he takes me in. I open my mouth to warn him, but out of nowhere, I'm sucked back violently like the wall is a drain and I'm being dragged through it by some invisible force. Rogan's face contorts with dread, and I hear him bellow my name before suddenly he's just...gone.

I hiss against the pain, whiplash cracking through my body as I'm yanked away into cold and bleak nothingness. My chest tightens, and my stomach drops like I'm bungee jumping into hell and the cord that's supposed to save me just won't catch. I can't scream or breathe or barely even think, and then all at once I slam against the ground with a pained *oomph*. Magic maliciously deposits me back into the real world, only this isn't my room in the Order, and Rogan is nowhere in sight.

I lie unmoving for a moment so I can breathe through the terror and pain radiating from every inch of me.

What the hell just happened?

I spot the owl skull still clutched in my hand, and I throw it away from me with a horrified croak that would probably be a squeal if I didn't feel like my lungs were broken. I quickly pull my tank top on, grateful that I hadn't lost it in whatever just happened, and wrap my arms around my torso protectively as I sit up and look around.

Pews are stacked and pushed against a stone wall on the other side of the room from where I'm huddled. The floor I'm sitting on is the same gray stone as the walls, only the floor has black symbols that look like they were first carved and then burned into the surface of the rock. The ceiling above me is vaulted with massive cobweb-streaked beams supporting it. And there's dirty stained glass windows spread evenly on the wall behind me and across from me as well as one massive round window behind the dais at the front of this church.

There are piles of what look like ash scattered around the front of the church, as though someone let fires burn down to nothing all over the place, but there's no black soot, so that's clearly not what they are. Huge double doors are sealed closed on my left, and the air I'm breathing feels heavy and tastes stale. There's an underlying scent to my surroundings, but I decide making a break for it is more important than going full bloodhound and trying to figure out what's tainting the air.

Worry swirls around in my mind, mixing with questions about how the owl skull got in my room and why the inlet that I just unknowingly fell victim to dropped me in a church? I file all of it away as I get up and sprint for the doors. Dread nips at my heels as the stone floor digs into the soft pads of my feet. I make it less than four strides and then slam up against an invisible barrier.

I bounce off of it, testing the limits of my ass when I fall hard to the ground. I skid back, scraping up my legs as my body absorbs the force from slamming into a wall I still can't see. I whimper feebly as I once again push to my feet and look for a way out. I inch my way toward whatever I just thwacked into, and as I close the distance inch by inch, I spot a line of engraved and blackened stones. I follow the soot-covered symbols in the stones and discover they cage me in on three sides, butting up against the wall at my back.

The stained glass window set in the wall behind me is too high for me to reach, and my search for anything nearby that I might be able to stand on produces nothing. I sit and listen for signs that anyone knows I'm here. There's no approaching footsteps or the faint muffle of voices. In fact, I don't hear any traffic or the typical animal sounds like an occasional dog barking or farm animals bleating that would hint at a more rural area. There's no crickets chirping or birdsong on the wind, there's just...nothing, like I've fallen into a soundless void.

I debate calling out for help but quickly shut the thought down. There's no point bringing myself to anyone's attention. Someone clearly set a trap, and I can put off meeting who for forever. Well, maybe not forever, starving to death sounds like a horrible way to go. Then again, even if I meet whoever forced me here, there's no guarantee they'll feed me.

I roll my eyes at myself and shove all thoughts of food away. I can worry about that later. I need to focus on trying to get out of here before someone comes along and makes my situation worse.

I immediately call on my magic in search of bones. It looks like I've been trapped in an old, long-forgotten church, which means there's probably a graveyard, burial site, or crypt I can work with. I push magic out of me in search of salvation, but when my power comes in contact with the symbols on the ground, a searing agony slams into me.

I scream and fall to my knees, begging the punishing assault to stop. My magic retracts immediately, working to soothe my abused body, but all I can do is try to climb inside of myself while the torment slowly wanes. I pant through the pain, lying fetal on the cold stone floor long after the hurt is just a ghost of an echo. I trace the mortar in the seams between the stones and drown in the terror of knowing that I'm trapped.

Rogan's face pops up in my mind, then Tad's, Hillen's, Hoot's, and down the line it goes until I've thought of each and every person I've ever cared about and hope to see again. Thoughts of them fortify me, and I get back on my feet.

Come on, Lennox, find the way out, find the loophole.

I look around warily, my gaze skipping over the piles of dead leaves that have been blown around and have now settled in the nooks and crannies of this place. The light from the big circle of stained glass at the front of the church falls on a stone altar. There are melted candles clustered about, some of them spotted with a dark substance that makes alarm skitter up my spine. I spot other scorch-marked patterns on the ground, and I suspect they're other magical cages, but there's no one else here.

My heart squeezes painfully with that realization. I look up at the light streaking through the filthy windows, and it dawns on me that it should be dark. If I'm still somewhere in America—no matter where that is—it should be dark.

Unease blooms in my chest as I track the shaft of light that falls from the window behind me to kiss the stony floor in front of me. It's hard to tell, but it looks like it's morning wherever the hell I am. I assure myself that they can still find me even if I'm oceans away. It's the Order we're talking about. But then flashes of interrogations about my grandmother rise to the surfaces of my thoughts, rattling the reassurance I'm trying to cocoon myself in.

Who am I kidding, they haven't found the others yet,

and I'm assuming I've been taken by Nikki or whoever she's working with. I look around me again, surveying my old and dingy surroundings. Why would someone go through the trouble of pulling me here just to leave me here to rot like the piles of leaves scattered about the floor? Unless somehow we misunderstood the end goal. The Order thought that it was to get to me, but what if that wasn't the case at all, what if someone was simply trying to get me out of the way?

The grandmother angle never sat right with me. I've been thinking this has something to do with her strange dream, but what if her dream was just that? A dream. I've had some weird ones myself lately. I blame stress, but perhaps I've been giving that aspect of this case too much clout. This could easily be about Rogan and his secrets, and we've been barking up the wrong tree.

Worry curdles inside of me. What if Rogan isn't okay? I mean, it's not farfetched to think that whatever pulled me away could have also let someone into the Order too. I fight the need to tug on our tether to check the response on the other end. What if he's fighting for his life as I sit here waiting for some big bad that might never come? No, I'll wait. I don't want to do anything that could distract him or fuck up whatever might be happening on his end. I cross my legs in front of me and start working on the new puzzle I'm up against. How do I escape an abandoned church when I have no tools and no access to magic?

Slowly the shaft of light that was in front of me moves further and further away. I'm not sure how much time has passed, but I'm picking at my cuticles, and I'm on *fifty bottles of beer on the wall*—for the third time—when a booming sound resonates all around me. I duck, putting my hands over my head as dust and pebbles sprinkle down from the upper structure of the church. A crack rents the air, and my head snaps in the direction of the entryway to the church as the doors slam open. Light floods the building, and I'm temporarily blinded by the glow. I try to block the light with a hand and squint away from the luminous assault.

Three shadowed silhouettes silently step through the now open doors. Terrified, I watch as they enter. My eyes slowly adjust to the light slicing through the center of the gloomy, dirty church, and my scared stare lands on a pair of green eyes that are hauntingly familiar. It takes me a second to place him, having only seen his face in pictures, but when I do, my heart hammers even harder in my chest.

Elon.

His stare is placid and cold as he takes me in. Two other figures walk behind him, but I can't bring myself to look away from Rogan's brother just yet. I'm too enthralled by the witch that unknowingly has altered the trajectory of my life in unimaginable ways.

He's here.

He's alive.

But judging by the look of things, *I* might not be able to say the same for much longer.

11

Elon is pushed from behind, and he stumbles forward. His hands stretch out to catch his fall, and I realize that a magical rope binds his wrist. My brow furrows in confusion, and my panic abates slightly. I thought for a split second that he was in on whatever is happening, but as I take in the state of him, I realize how wrong I was to jump to that conclusion.

He's lost a little weight, and he's dirty and exhausted looking. Elon manages to keep his balance and stay on his feet after being pushed again. But the woman walking a step behind him isn't so lucky. She hits the ground hard, a painful groan escaping her lips, and dark blue eyes look over at me pleadingly as she struggles to get back on her feet.

I look at the third person, the one roughing them up, and I have to swallow down my shock as I take her in. She's older than me by a handful of years, and it's clear she was once beautiful. It's also clear that things took a turn for the worse somewhere along the way. Her light teal eyes are a unique color, but they're lacking light and happiness in their depths, instead they glint flat and cruel as she looks down at the older woman on the ground like she's vermin. Her hair is a rich strawberry blonde, but it's not lustrous and healthy, it's dry straw and brittle. She has pale porcelain skin, but none of this is what's making my stomach churn and my pulse race uncontrollably with fear. What's doing that is the fact that she's marred with more demon marks than I knew one person could ever acquire.

The marks look raw and painful. A circle with some kind of symbol I can't identify is practically branded all over her. She has a mark on each cheek, one in the center of her forehead, and a trail of brands down the front of her throat. Her clothes cover up the rest of her skin, and I can only wonder how many barters and vows she carries all over her flesh.

I stop myself from looking down at Rogan's mark on my wrist, knowing there's nothing similar between them. I wear this vow as a reminder that I'm owed something. But demon marks work differently. I don't know a ton about their race, but I do know that when you wear a demon brand, it's because you owe *them* something. Horror fills me as I take the woman in. She's scarred so heavily, and I can't even imagine what she's traded to earn so many markings, or begin to comprehend why a demon would have bargained with her so much.

"*Fweto,*" the marked woman snarls, and with a scream, the witch on the floor goes careening across the stone and rolls into the cage of symbols that have been carved into the ground. She screams as she crosses the threshold of engravings, and I can only imagine she's experiencing that awful burning I did when I tried to use my magic inside this barrier.

The branded woman's marks light up like lava is flowing within them. A pained hiss escapes her mouth, and she closes her eyes until the marks deaden, the fire burning in them subsiding. When she peels her lids back, her eerie teal eyes land on me. Her gaze widens with surprise, like she hadn't noticed me until now, and it makes me wonder how dull her senses are from the pain she must constantly be in with all those demon-forged wounds covering her.

"Finally," she sighs, relieved, rubbing a finger over the symbol burned into the middle of her forehead. "I thought I was going to have to rip that building open and pull you out myself. But I'm glad you finally came to your senses," she tells me as though I'm somehow here voluntarily.

I'm not sure what to make of that statement, so I stay quiet.

"*Nahdugh,*" she snaps, and Elon steps into his own cage of symbols, only they don't seem to burn him like they did the other woman. When he crosses them, the red-hot-looking binds on his wrists disappear, and he rubs at his arms before moving over to where the wall meets the floor. He sits down, his back pressed against the stone blocks behind him and watches the scarred woman as she once again bites back what looks like pain. Does it hurt her to use magic?

I'm bothered by how resigned Elon is. There's no fight in him. He seems more like a beaten dog who's trying to go unnoticed. Maybe it's an act, but I worry that it's not.

I stop myself from instinctually reaching out with magic to get a sense of this woman, witch to witch. I want to gauge exactly what I'm up against, but I'm not going to do anything that makes the symbols all around me bitch-slap me with pain again. Not yet, anyway. It's obvious that using her abilities is brutal for her, but I'm not sure exactly why that is. Did someone do this to her?

"My apologies for not being here to greet you," she offers, stepping closer to the line of symbols separating me from possible freedom. "But someone had to pee, and then she tried to make a run for it," she half shouts, half snarls, her ruthless gaze flashing over to the woman she threw in her cage. "Didn't even bat an eye at leaving Prince Kendrick behind, did she?" she points out, eyeing Elon with a taunting smirk. "But we caught her, didn't we? I've gotten good at the hunt these days; stupid bitch should know that by now," she grumbles, and I get the impression she's talking more to herself than to anyone else.

"Worse than puppies, I tell you," she jokes, a vicious giggle punctuating her mocking words. "Now you'll all get buckets," she declares as though she's speaking to a bigger audience than just the three of us. "And if you don't like it, blame that one," she growls, gesturing to the witch who's huddled on the floor, shaking.

The odd woman's creepy eyes seem to fix on nothing for a moment too long before she blinks and seems to come back to the here and now, a sadistic smile spread across her demon-marked face.

Oh yeah, this one's a few fries short of a Happy Meal.

"But where are my manners?" she playfully chastises, as though we're acquaintances and niceties are required. "I'm Jamie, Jamie Smelser," she announces, her smile now beaming and making the skin around her demon marks crack. "Welcome, Lennox—or should I call you Leni like you prefer?" she asks, cupping her hand against her mouth like she's telling me a secret. The giggle that escapes her is far past unhinged and bouncing around certifiably psycho territory.

"Are you related to Nikki Smelser? Is she here?" I ask, interrupting the mind-humping she's doing to her thoughts. I probably shouldn't interject on the crazy person's thought-gasm, but it doesn't sound like I'm working with a lot of time here, and I'd love some answers before this mental case does whatever she's planning on doing.

"Nikki's my cousin, and she's outside with the others," Jamie informs me casually as she looks around the inside of the church like she's making a to-do list.

My stomach falls with the news that there are others. I liked the odds of a mano-a-mano type of situation; *others* complicates things.

"Why am I here?" I ask, grateful that my tone is even and strong and not reflecting just how scared I really am.

"Well, Leni...I'd like to welcome you to the death of your magic as you know it," she declares enthusiastically, arms flinging out at her sides and spinning as though she's the ringmaster introducing an exciting new show to a crowd of eager spectators.

I watch her spin, head back, eyes closed, with a wide happy smile on her face like she's dancing in the rain and embracing the downpour. Trepidation bubbles up inside of me as I observe her. There's no question about it, I'm not dealing with someone who's all there. This is a level of crazy I have no idea how to navigate.

I wish—not for the first time—that I had my phone. One, to call for help. And two, because I'd already be sending a picture of this psycho to the Order, accompanied by a message that says: *still think my dead grandmother is behind this, dumbasses?* I knew they were wrong, felt it in my bones the entire time. And if I ever get out of here, the vindication is going to be sweet. I'm going to make them send me an apology card every year on the anniversary of Grammy Ruby's death, saying: *Sorry we're dumb and didn't listen. Osteomancers rule, and the Order drools.*

"Ahh, I feel the moon. Do you feel the moon, Leni?" Jamie asks me, pulling me from my internal *told you so* celebrations to discover her staring at me with a disturbingly serene look on her face. I feel like I just made her year.

Sure as fuck wish I could say the same about meeting her.

Despite it still being daytime, I look up at the ceiling as though I can see the celestial body she's cooing about, but of course, all I see is old dirty beams and the roof.

"You came at the *perfect* time, Osteomancer. The harvest moon is just a day away, and finally...finally," she repeats reverently, "what was taken will be mine again."

I open my mouth to ask where I am, but Jamie turns on her heel and walks out of the church without another word. I hear her growl an incantation, and the next thing I know, the doors leading into the church slam closed with a bone jarring boom. Dust rains down on me again from above, and I cover my head and do my best to protect myself from anything more damaging that might come loose from the precariously old structure all around me.

I stare at where Jamie was just standing for a moment before turning to the two other witches now trapped in this hell hole with me.

"What is going on?" I ask no one in particular, dropping my raised arms and wrapping them securely around my bent knees.

Faint sobbing reaches me from the woman who was thrown into her magical cage at the front of the church. The small broken sounds tug at my heart, and I scoot over to the side of my cell that's closest to her.

"Are you okay?" I ask and then groan at the stupidity of that question. "Sorry, I'm a dumbass. Of course you're not okay," I correct, internally facepalming. "Are you hurt?" I try again, hating even more that I'm trapped and can't get to her.

I have no idea what they've been through since unhinged Barbie took them, but it's clear it's been a lot.

"She doesn't like it when we talk," Elon informs me, his voice low and filled with warning.

I look over at him on the other side of the church, opposite me, and my insides both leap with the fact that he's alive and then crash land because I don't know if this will be the case by the time Rogan or the Order finds us.

If they find us.

I drop-kick my morbid thoughts as far away from me as I can. I'm not going to give up. This situation isn't hopeless. I can find a way. If I can talk to Nikki, maybe I can tap into the nice girl I saw radiating out of her photo. I can try to convince her how wrong all of this is and that we're people who just want to go home to our loved ones. It's possible even that some of the others that fruit loop, Jamie, mentioned are having second thoughts and might be willing to help. And if playing to their humanity doesn't work, I'll figure something else out. I don't know what, but I do know that I'm not going to quit.

"Do you know where we are?" I ask, taking in our surroundings once again.

"I think Ireland, but honestly, I have no idea. It's really green outside, but we could be anywhere."

Ireland.

I ponder the possibility, feeling like the look of this church fits that guess. Like he said, though, who knows? I don't think we're in the US, but that doesn't exactly narrow things down. We only have the rest of the world as options to contend with. The woman's sobs pierce my thoughts, and I can only imagine what's happened to them since they were taken.

"They're looking for us, the Order is looking for us," I tell her, hoping it will offer some small spark of hope, but she doesn't show any sign that she's listening, she just makes herself as small as possible on the cold hard floor and cries softly.

"What happened?" I ask Elon, hoping he'll ignore his own warning and talk to me whether or not Jamie likes it.

He studies me for a moment and releases a deep enervated sigh. "That lunatic you just met, Jamie, well, she just murdered *her* husband," he tells me, jutting his chin in the direction of the woman who starts to quietly keen at his words.

Abhorrence cools my blood, and my heart breaks for the quietly grieving woman. I watch her fragile frame shake with grief, her blonde hair matted and dirty and her clothes stained and torn. Wait a minute...Nina, one of the other Osteomancers that went missing when Elon did, had dark hair, not blonde. I stared at the brush the Order brought me from her apartment long enough to have that fact cemented in my mind. A sliver of confusion pierces the sympathy I feel for what she's going through.

"But that's not Nina," I blurt flatly as I survey the woman, more intensely wondering who she is.

Elon's brow furrows with bewilderment. "No, Nina and Bernard, the other Bone Witches who were abducted with me, were killed days after they were taken," he informs me. "That's Brianne, she's one of Europe's Osteomancers. Her husband, David, was a Soul Witch," he explains, and I stare at him blankly as I try to understand what he's saying.

Bernard and Nina are dead?

What?

Brianne is another Bone Witch?

Did the Order lie? They said that none of the missing Osteomancers' magic had transferred to anyone else in their line. But if they're dead...

"How?" I ask, my voice suddenly thick and dry. "Their magic..." I start, trailing off as confusion stalls my voice.

"Their magic is what Jamie keeps trying to take," Elon explains, like he's talking to someone who doesn't get the plot of a movie or the punchline of a joke. Only there's absolutely nothing funny about any of this.

"Trying?" I query, homing in on the sliver of hope in that devastating sentence.

"Yeah, *trying*," he confirms. "Things haven't exactly gone as planned for our kidnapping crackpot. She has a ritual that's supposed to allow her to take magic from someone else, only it hasn't worked like she thought. When she killed Nina, nothing happened. But when she went to see if the magic had moved on to the next in her line, apparently that hadn't happened either."

"Where did it go then?" I ask, puzzled.

"*That's* the mystery that fucked up fruitcake has been attempting to figure out," Elon tells me with a scowl. "When I first woke up here, she would rant about restoring fragments of a line of magic back to one person. I guess her ritual is supposed to do that. But she thought those fragments would be given to *her* when she took the lives of the witches who possessed them. That didn't happen though. She's been working her way through our kind now, trying to find the source line. That's where she thinks the others' magic is reverting back to. Once she figures that out, she can kill the source line and take all of that carrier's magic for herself. Or at least that's what she keeps saying."

Information knots itself in my mind, and I struggle to untangle it all. *Grammy was right.* Someone is trying to restore the fragmented branches of magic back to one.

I survey Elon's face as his statement, *working through our kind,* ominously settles into my understanding like sand settles in water. If Jamie is killing Osteomancers...

"How many of us are left?" I ask Elon, taking in his dirt-streaked face, tired pine-green eyes, and the frown pulling the corners of his lips down. He looks like Rogan. There's no denying they're related even though Elon has black hair instead of Rogan's deep brown, and he's naturally leaner—even more so since he went missing.

Elon shakes his head wearily at my question and looks over at the whimpering woman and then back to me. "You're looking at what's left," he declares, a hollow ache in his tone that feels like a cannonball to the gut.

I put my hands over my mouth and silently plead with the universe that he's wrong, that what he's saying is impossible. But I can see the truth of it in the haggard planes of Elon's face and the bitter torment glistening in his eyes.

In all the magic in this world, we're the only Bone Witches left.

Horror assaults me, and I feel dizzy with the implications of what this means.

"What?" sneaks out of my appalled lips, but Elon doesn't answer.

How the hell did we let this happen? How did this whack job destroy so much completely unhindered?

I stare at Elon, completely unnerved. I hate myself for asking this question, but I need to understand what's at play.

"Why hasn't she killed you like she has the others?" I ask quietly, shame sloughing off of each syllable. What an awful thing to ask someone, like I'm insinuating he doesn't deserve to be alive, but there has to be a specific reason the others are gone and he's not, and I need to know what it is.

Elon scoffs incredulously and looks down at his hands as though he doesn't quite get it himself. "She likes to taunt me because of Nikki. She also gets a kick out of fucking with me because of who my family is," he confesses. "Story of my fucking life," he grumbles almost inaudibly, but I catch it all the same.

He extends his legs, crossing them at the ankle as though this conversation is simply casual and he's been forced to have it far too many times. "She's looking for the witch who has the source line for our magic; I think she assumes because of who my uncle was, who my family is, that I'm that source. She keeps saying she'll pour everyone's magic into me *and then* take it, like it will hurt worse and I'll suffer more because of that," he offers with a shrug. "That's why I'm still here when the others aren't. Trust me, if I could have changed that, I would have."

Understanding and pity hit me like a semi. The torture and pain he's being put through *again* in his short but scarred life makes me steep with rage. No wonder he's shut down. She's saving him for last. What an awful fucking feeling that must be. I watch him for a moment. His body language communicates *no big deal*, but the pain in his gaze is so intense and raw that I have to look away. It's one of those messed up situations where you wish you could do something, say something, that would make all the hurt and suffering go away, but you know you can't. There isn't a magical word or incantation to combat suffering, no matter how much I wish there was.

"How long does she usually leave for?" I ask, gesturing toward the doors to the church and offering him some reprieve in the form of a change of subject. "Is there a way to stop these symbols all around us from working? Is there a way to override them?" I look down at the soot-stained marks in the ground and then over to the same lines of symbols that have Elon and Brianne trapped.

"Don't bother," Elon dismisses. "There's no way out of these unless Jamie wants you out. They're tailored to fuck with our magic and to listen only to hers. Save your energy for what happens when she pulls you out of that cage," he warns, and it causes a shiver to flick up my spine.

I stare at the foreign markings for a moment longer and then return my eyes to Elon's, not sure what to say to that or to his clear surrender.

"Don't look at me like that," he growls. "You think you're

the only one to try and escape? Everything you're probably thinking of doing has been tried before by witches who are now dead. I've watched as other Osteomancers broke their own bones and tried to use them as weapons. None of them succeeded."

He shakes his head, his eyes hard.

"I fought at first. I tried everything I could to get out of here, to save the others as they showed up one by one. Nothing I did made a difference. I discovered that it pisses her off more when I don't react, so that's what I do now," he explains adamantly, as though he needs me to understand why he is the way he is, like he needs to defend against the judgment I must have let bleed out of my eyes.

The doors to the church slam open again. The boom they create from hitting the stone walls is a little less sonorous, like even they're done with this overdramatic type of entrance. I still jump, surprised, and let out a frightened squeal. I clutch my chest as Jamie stomps in, once again alone, one arm threaded through the handles of three buckets, and in the crook of her other arm are three small packages of something.

She chucks a bucket at me, and it goes careening just past where I'm sitting, hits the wall behind me, and then rolls, stopping just before the symbols trapping me in from the right side. Something else hits my foot, and I look down to see a package of original flavored digestives, or at least that's what the package says. I have no idea what that is, but it looks like gingerbread cookies or something, based on the packaging's picture.

I side-eye the *biscuits*, not nearly close enough to starvation-mode to risk eating anything someone this crazy is offering so freely. What I really want is water, but I'm not about to ask for it. I'm not going to give the woman anything more that she can lord over me.

Elon's bucket and crackers are tossed his way, and Jamie tromps toward Brianne, who is still huddled on the floor, her chest shuddering with grief, even though I can't hear her crying anymore. Jamie looks as though she's just about to toss Brianne's bucket and food her way when suddenly she stops herself. Her head tilts to the side like a dog who's staring at someone quizzically. She sets the bucket down on the wrong side of the scorched marks and slowly opens the packet of cookies or crackers or whatever they are.

One by one, Jamie removes a wafer from the package and crushes it in her hand. A small pile of crumbs starts at her feet as she destroys Brianne's food. The look in her eyes is malicious. She stands there as though she's daring the broken witch to look up and beg Jamie to stop, but she doesn't.

"You can't run from me," Jamie snarls at Brianne as she crushes another cracker. "There's nowhere you can hide that I won't find you."

Goose bumps crawl up my arms as fire licks through my veins. I've never been good at keeping my mouth shut when it comes to bullies. Jamie crushes another cracker, and I start to see red. How much more broken could she want this witch to be? She's literally crumpled into a ball of grief in the middle of a magical cage she can't get out of at the mercy of a woman who just killed her husband.

It makes me want to rip Jamie's head off and shove all those wasted morsels of nutrients down her throat. The carved marks in the ground all around me make it impossible, so I do the only thing I can to show her just what I think of what she's doing. I figure Jamie threw these crackers at me with no issue from the demonic symbols that comprise my cage; hopefully, I can do the same.

I grab the mysterious red and blue package of digestives at my feet and cock my arm back. I give my biscuits a good throw and watch them sail through the air, past the line of onyx symbols of my cage, arcing into Brianne's cage with a spiral that would make Tom Brady proud. They fall to the ground and skid just past Brianne's feet, coming to a stop where she'll be able to see them when she comes out of her current state of shock and emotional agony.

Jamie's head snaps in my direction, her features painted with rage. Defiantly, I stare at her, wondering if she'll breach the symbols on the ground and go retrieve the sleeve of cookies so Brianne can't have them. She doesn't. Instead, she walks over to my cage, and as mutinous as I feel, I also can't help feeling like I'm swimming in a pond and was just spotted by a crocodile. I have no idea what I might have just unleashed, but I guess it's time to find out.

"Awwww, the little Bone Witch has balls," she coos at me, like I'm some baby animal at the zoo. "You're willing to starve for her, but would she do the same for you, Leni?" she tsks, as though she's genuinely disappointed in me. "I know you're new to this whole witch thing, but let me fill you in on a little something. There isn't a more selfish species in existence than witches. One minute they're your friends, and the next they'll stab you in the back if it means keeping themselves safe or taking something they want."

Unbidden, Rogan's face pops up in my mind and slowly fades away just to be replaced by Major Griego's face, then the faces of every Order member who's interrogated me. Lastly, the image of the High Priestess of Witches and her two council members waves into focus in my head. My thoughts silently concur with the venom spilling out of Jamie's lips, and I hate it almost as much as I hate that I'm here, staring into the cruel eyes of this demon-tainted abomination.

"Your grandmother was friends with my aunt, even looked out for Nikki when the magic passed to her, but did the great Osteomancer ever check in on me? Did she even once ask how I was doing after my line was stripped of the same magic running in her veins? No, she treated us like the pariahs everyone else did. If only she could see me now, see what's going to happen to her line of magic when I take it from your very marrow," she practically snarls at me.

I open my mouth to snap that Grammy did see it coming, but something else Jamie just said makes me pause.

The great Osteomancer...

For some reason, these three taunting words send my mind reeling.

The strange dreams.

The overfull feeling of magic.

My ability to wield power so easily when it takes others years to master.

The feeling I had at my last reading, where I had access to more magic than I technically should have...

I thought what I was experiencing was normal—not that I would really know what normal feels like when it comes to magic. It's not as though I've had previous experience to compare it to. But I've never given what I felt and could do much thought until now.

Elon's flat tone starts in my head, *she's looking for the witch who has the source line for our magic.*

I don't know why that didn't resonate with me before, but...

Fuck.

I'm pretty sure I'm the source line Jamie is looking for.

The great Osteomancer.

Shock rings through my mind like a gong that's been hit too hard and now the noise is overwhelmingly loud. My body practically vibrates with understanding. Is this what's been happening to me, what's been making me feel so powerful? I mean, my line has always been strong. Jamie just brought it up like it was common knowledge. Even Rogan mentioned it when we first met. He was trying to magic-shame me by pointing out that my grandmother was powerful and probably one of the most gifted Osteomancers left. I never thought much about that fact before, but in this context, the truth feels blinding.

I do everything to school my face as Jamie rants. I struggle to tune into what she's saying over the sound of my too fast pulse in my ears. Maybe I'm wrong and Elon is the source like Jamie thinks he is, but in my gut, I don't truly believe that's the case.

"You think you're saving her, Leni? Well, newsflash: you don't decide who lives and dies here, I do, and your kindness just killed her, like her cowardice killed her husband," Jamie spits at me, and then she trudges out of the church, once again slamming the doors behind her.

I stare after her, finally understanding why some parents remove doors in their house to prevent this same, very annoying behavior from their children. Terror climbs up the back of my throat, and anger floods my every thought. It's all I can do not to scream as I think about her words and being trapped here. I don't want to wrap my mind around what's happened to all the witches who came before me. To think about how many stood in this very cell, hoping someone would find them, that something would stop this madwoman from stealing what she has no right to take.

But understanding is pulling me under against my will, and impotent fury is an ever growing spark inside of me, one I have no fucking outlet for. I look all around me, desperate to find something that might temper my rage. My frenzied search lands on the owl skull. The reason I'm now in a demon-marked cell, staring death right in its bleak and miserable eyes. How could I have been so blind?

Why didn't I see these corrupted bones for what they were?

I would have noticed an animal skull in my room before. I don't care how distracted I was by dick, I should have known better than to pick that thing up.

I stand up and stomp over to the skull. Apparently, I didn't throw it hard enough the first time to knock it out of my cell. I pluck it from the ground, and with an agonized bellow, chuck it as hard as I can against the wall. A fissure forms in the bone, but it doesn't splinter the way I want, so I pick it up from the seam of two stone blocks and throw it again like I'm a pitcher in the major leagues. Skull fragments explode against the wall, and I immediately sweep them into a pile with my hands. I pick through the remnants, looking for the sharpest, most lethal looking options and setting them aside.

If a crazy bitch wants to use these bones to trap me here, then I'll go ahead and use them to open her throat. This loon messed with the wrong witch.

Time to get to work.

12

I clench my teeth so hard against the inferno threatening to melt my bones, that I swear my teeth are going to crumble to nothing any minute now. Fire burns through my veins, and I fight against its desire to melt me from the inside out and push the bone dust to try and find a crack or a hole in the mortar cementing the stones of the church wall in front of me.

Sweat pours off my brow as I swallow down a scream, my throat raw and abused from fighting the demon magic of this cell for too long. I feel drained, exhausted, but I know I have to do this now, have to try and find a way, before Jamie comes back and does who knows what.

If I can just find the smallest weakness in the wall, then I can shove the bone powder through and see if I can destabilize it even more. The only problem is, agony doesn't even begin to describe what this cell is doing to me for trying to use my magic. In between passing out for the past handful of hours, I've already placed the sharp skull fragments I set aside around my cell so I can grab and use one if the opportunity presents itself. But the rest of the bones could be of some use, or would be, if using my magic didn't give me the excruciating understanding of what it feels like to live inside a volcano.

Black dots start to form threateningly in my vision, and I let go of the magic before I'm forced to pass out again. The bone dust floats to the ground, and I let out a frustrated exhale. I've still only been able to make it travel halfway up the wall. I need to focus, but I don't know how much more physically I can take. With a disgruntled growl, I slap the stones of the wall and then slide down it to rest for a bit before I try again.

"Feel better?" Elon asks, a critical eyebrow raised as though he just witnessed some ridiculous tantrum. "Finally come to terms with the fact that there's no getting out of here?"

Damn, and I thought Rogan was a judgy fucker, but the award for haughty prick definitely goes to his brother.

He hasn't said a word to me since Jamie left the last time. No *I told you fighting would get you nowhere*, not even a *should have kept your crackers to yourself.* Nope, he's just sat there and watched me as I've wrecked myself trying to find a way out. I mean, what the hell else do I have to do while being held captive? It's either *try to figure out how to escape* or *I spy*, and I get the feeling Elon will pretend he's too good for that game. I suppose it's good that he's kept his mouth shut. If he had tried to offer me a *don't bother*, I would have told him to shove it up his ass. Who's going to listen to shit advice like that? Certainly not me.

I shoot him a glare.

"You can choke on that *there's no getting out of here* crap, Elon Kendrick. I don't take that shit from Rogan, and I sure as hell am not going to take it from you. It wouldn't be a waste of your time to stop judging me and instead help me come up with a plan. Even if it doesn't work, at least we tried," I snap at him, annoyed while simultaneously feeling bad at being bitchy with everything that's happened to him.

He's just far too resigned and apathetic for my liking. I've been so focused on venting my futile anger and trying to do what I could to help myself, but it's time to really talk to Elon, to light a fire under his ass and figure out how the hell we're going to flip things on little miss demon-stained and her crew. I know I'm not the first witch to try and escape. I'm certain he's watched far too many try—and die anyway—but I'm not them. I'm Lennox Osseous, and I will figure shit out with or without his help.

The arrogant gleam in Elon's gaze falters, and I register shock sparking to life in his green eyes. He pushes up from where he's sitting against the wall and stops at the barrier of demon symbols trapping him in.

Yes! There it is, there's the fight we need. I should have stopped trying to figure out escape contingencies and name-dropped earlier.

"What do you know about my brother?" he challenges, the dispassionate and lethargic countenance he's draped around him like an invisible coat of armor gone. Now there's worry and hopeful longing in his arduous stare.

"Oh, you know," I offer casually, my body aching from everything I just put it through. "He's a dick, definitely an *ask for forgiveness instead of permission* kind of guy. Loves *you* more than anything, and is currently raising hell and doing everything he can to find you."

He eyes me as though he's unconvinced.

I clear my throat and adopt the thickest Texas accent I can manage. "*Ready up now, partner,*" I tell him as I mime riding a bucking bronco while sitting. "*Y'all better, R...U...N,*" I add for good measure, and Elon's face pinches with pain, and his eyes well with tears. "We got your message. You have a beautiful house by the way. I'm mighty jealous, I don't mind admittin'." I side-eye the lingering accent permeating what's now supposed to be my normal speech.

Elon tilts his head back and breathes deeply through what I can only imagine is a rush of anguish. I know he and Rogan have been through it together, and I sense that Elon had given up hope on ever seeing his brother again, let alone hearing an update about what's been happening while he's been gone.

I rub at my arms, massively underdressed for the chill that's crept into this place. I don't know how long I've been going at it, but the light coming through the windows feels like evening instead of morning now. This will teach me to wear light clothes to bed. It's going to be chastity belts and sweats from here on out if I make it out of here. I should also look into sleeping with a sword at all times. Maybe I can get a special holster designed that will keep it from getting stabby as I toss and turn.

"Your brother tracked me down first thing," I tell Elon, who's now wiping at his eyes. "Let's just say he wouldn't take no for an answer, and we've been looking for you ever since. What happened? How did you end up here?" I ask softly, hoping that Elon won't shut down like he looks like he wants to do and will fill me in.

He doesn't answer me right away, and I look from him to the now quiet witch who's still lying on the cold floor. The slow rise and fall of her chest tells me she's asleep, and I hope she finds some semblance of peace in her dreams as she escapes this waking nightmare for a little while.

"Nikki Smelser is what happened," Elon declares, and there's an angry bite to his tone, but I can't tell if the anger is directed at himself or her or maybe both.

"Are they doing this together, Nikki and Jamie?" I press, gesturing around at the church.

"Not anymore," Elon tells me cryptically, rubbing at his

face and smudging the dirt and tear tracks on his cheeks. He sits down crisscross applesauce on the ground just shy of the barrier, and I mirror his movement, sensing a detailed explanation coming.

"I met Nikki at a shop. I was there stocking up on some herbs and other things I needed that week. She was nice and pretty. She hit on me, and it had been so long since someone hadn't looked at me like I was a..."

"Murderer?" I supply quietly when he trails off.

Elon snorts indignantly and then nods. "Yeah, like the evil spawn they all think I am. She didn't see me that way, and I got a little more lost in that than I should have," he confesses, and I can't help but see a hint of the little boy that was never loved the way he should have been, peeking out in his eyes. It makes me so incredibly sad for him, and in that moment, it's easy for me to understand why Rogan would do everything in his power to make sure Elon didn't live his whole life feeling that way.

Elon sighs and straightens his back like he's pulling from some inner reserve of strength. "She said her cousin was after her. That she'd been trying to hurt her since Nikki came into her powers a couple years before." He looks over at me imploringly. "I know that probably sounds dumb and that I'm stupid for trusting her, but with everything that Rogan and I had been through with our families and being renounced, it wasn't a farfetched, impossible thing for me to believe."

I nod, understanding where he's coming from, because I know the truth about what happened to them. But I don't say anything or attempt to clue him in. This doesn't feel like a safe place to expose such a vulnerable secret, not with other witch ears listening—even though it appears Brianne is passed out. I'm also unsure of how he'll feel, knowing that I'm aware of the horrors he survived.

"It doesn't sound dumb," I assure him. "It sounds like you're a kind person."

Elon pauses for a moment, surveying me like I just spewed venom at him instead of paying him a compliment. I can see that he doesn't trust my words and he's looking for my angle. I hate that this is what he's been forced to do to survive, but I don't take it personally.

"I wanted to help Nikki with her cousin," he starts somewhat hesitantly, and I make a note to zip my lips before I freak him out and he stops talking. "I thought if I showed her cousin that Nikki wasn't alone and an easy target, she'd back off. Jamie was a Lesser, and I assumed she'd be easy to scare away.

"We came up with this plan to kind of disappear for a bit, cover our tracks so that Jamie couldn't find Nikki, and then do what we could to make her back off. If it didn't work, I'd help Nikki to actually disappear, using my reputation, and then I'd set her up somewhere safe. I was going to call Rogan and explain what was happening from the road, but everything went to shit before that could happen."

The image of Elon walking away from his home with a pack and his familiar in tow pops up in my mind. I don't see any sign of his familiar, but I'm hesitant to ask him about her and have him shut down. "But why the weird stuff you had in your house? The rowanberries and the ashes from the grill?" I ask instead.

"It was part of the backup plan if Nikki needed to disappear. Most witches think I'm some crazed killer. Some power-hungry psycho that's unhinged and could lose it any minute. The ashes and stuff were for Jamie in case she broke in looking for Nikki. We set up the impression that I lost my shit and killed Nikki, her familiar, and my familiar. Nikki told me to do the rowanberry thing, she said it would mean something to Jamie if she ever saw it. I figured, what would people do if they thought I killed again? It would be out of the Lessers' hands, and the High Council wouldn't care. If they didn't end me for what happened with my uncle, why would they care about a random Soul Witch?" he asks, the *I'm a murderer* lie rolling right off his tongue.

He shrugs, his eyes far away, his head shaking like he's looking back on it all now and seeing how stupid the plan was.

"So what went wrong?" I press, needing him to keep going and not to fall back into the impassive state he was in before.

"I discovered that Nikki lied to me about everything and that I'm a fucking idiot. That's what went wrong."

His words sink in, dragging his despair along with them. I study the Bone Witch across from me, who's been through entirely too much in his short life. He's wearing the same army green cargos and long-sleeve black T-shirt that was in my vision of him leaving his house that day. They're dirty and wrinkled beyond hope now, the sad state of them almost as pitiful as the broken state Elon is in. He seems to be teetering back and forth between hopeless and determined, and I'm worried one wrong word from me will send him careening into the darkness, and then we'll really be screwed, because I'm going to need his help to try and get us the hell out of here.

"Well, I'll beat Nikki's ass for you when we get out," I reassure him.

His brow furrows with confusion, and he sighs, looking at me like I've clearly missed something. I'm ready to lecture him about how he can't still want to save her after everything she's done, but he cuts me off.

"Didn't you hear Jamie? Nikki's dead. She's outside with all the others."

Understanding comes at me like Evander Holyfield. It

decks me so hard I see stars like some cartoon character version of myself. I look up at the grimy windows all around us, and all I can picture is bodies littering the ground of this church. My head spins, and I work to make sense of what he's saying.

"But why?" I ask, not able to piece it all together. If Nikki was lying, and she and Jamie were working together—which is what I'm assuming happened—why kill her?

"Because the cunt tried to betray me," an unhinged voice declares from the entryway of the church, and in walks Tall, Lean and Loony.

Well, shit, she's back.

Jamie strolls into the church, a bag hitched over one shoulder and the distinct smell of fresh blood trailing in her wake. Chills climb up my legs, skitter across my torso, and dance down my arms. I rub my hands over my extremities in an effort to banish the feeling, but try as I might, a sense of foreboding wraps itself around me like a shawl made of ice.

You think you're saving her, Leni? Well, newsflash: you don't decide who lives and dies here, I do, and your kindness just killed her.

Am I about to find out if this is true?

I try not to look too hard at Jamie as she passes me. I know it's stupid, but I'm terrified that if she looks too hard at me, she'll see the truth of what I am as clearly as I'm seeing it now. If she knows I'm the source line, then what does that mean for Elon?

I don't want to find out.

Jamie scoffs as she strides by. "Nikki was supposed to be there for me. She knew what my side went through when the High Whore in charge stripped my line of our magic. She knew how it destroyed us. But some silver spoon, pretty boy bats his lashes at her, and all that loyalty went right out the window," she snaps frustratedly, setting the bag on the altar at the front of the church.

Dusky light falls on her through the filthy stained glass window like some sickly spotlight. It highlights her pallor and the raw wounds on her face that look worse than when I saw them before. I wonder what she's been doing while she was gone. It's clear whatever it was, it's taken a toll. She starts to unpack things from the bag, but I can't make out exactly what without being able to get closer, and everything inside of me is screaming *do not get closer.*

"She tried to ruin it for me. Years of planning and putting things together for the benefit of our magic, and she decided none of it was worth it because she wanted to save *him*," she sneers, her deranged stare settling dangerously on Elon. "*Him!*" she shouts, as though she just can't fathom it. "She chose a cold-blooded murderer over her own blood! So I took her rotten blood and made it useful. And may the rest of her rot in hell with the others."

Jamie spits on the ground as though she's spitting on Nikki's grave, and although Elon says nothing, I can see pent up, barely contained rage brewing inside of him.

First, Nikki betrayed him, and then she tried to save him.

My heart grows even heavier for Elon. I can tell, despite his efforts not to, he cared for the Soul Witch.

"Why'd they strip your magic?" I ask accusatorily.

I thought that was almost impossible and wasn't something witches even tried to do anymore. Then again, I also thought death was unbeatable, so what the hell do I know about anything anymore?

"*Stole* our magic is the truth of it. Stole it because they don't want strong Bone Witches to contest their rule," she exclaims fervently.

"More like your ancestors were a bunch of con artists, growing rich off the misfortunes of others, just to find out that your coven was the reason for their misfortunes in the first place. You deserved to lose your gift!" Elon snarls at Jamie, obviously hitting his limit with all the bullshit.

"Our magic was ours to do what we wanted with. The High Council had no right to take what wasn't theirs!" Jamie screams back, all sense gone from her gaze.

"If that was so wrong, then what the hell are *you* doing?" Elon counters, but before he can say another word, he's slammed against the ground and writhing in pain. He bites down on a scream, and I squeeze my fists and clench my jaw to keep from screaming myself. I didn't hear Jamie utter an incantation, but it's clear she's doing something to him.

All her demon marks suddenly make sense as they start to glow like they're lit from inside. She's borrowing demon powers. Her line's magic is no longer viable, so she's bargained heavily with a demon for the ability to do what once would have come natural to her. That is *if* she were the chosen witch of her line. There's always the possibility it wouldn't have been her, and I wonder if this would have been her response to that possible outcome too.

I picture my own aunt and cousin and the lengths they were willing to go for power that didn't belong to them. A sick feeling settles in my stomach. Are they future Jamies lying in wait?

I shove that thought aside and get my scattered head in the game. I need to figure out exactly how the hell Jamie's robbing Osteomancers of their power, and then I need to do everything I can to keep that from happening to me.

"So how does it work?" I ask in a desperate attempt to figure all of this out without someone having to die for it.

My question pulls Jamie's sick attention from Elon to me. He stops seizing, foam dripping from his mouth as soon as her eerie teal glare is turned in my direction, but I shutter any relief I feel and put a stopper on all of my emotions.

I stand at the barrier to my cage, my entire body tense, wishing I could check and see if Elon is okay. I clench my fists, trying and failing not to show my distress.

"Your grandmother was chatty too. Pretty sure she saw me coming, but by the time I realized that, it was too late," she tells me cryptically, her head canted to the side as she examines me like I'm a specimen under a microscope. "I'm too smart to fall for it again," she adds and then returns to whatever she's setting up around the altar.

So much for the get her talking *effort.*

Dammit, didn't Oprah do a show about what to do if someone abducts you? I'm pretty sure *never let them take you to the second location* was definitely a big one she preached, but that ship has sailed, crashed, and sunk to the deepest depths of the vast and frigid ocean. No diamond-dropping old lady is going to be the heroine of this story—or at least I'm ninety-six percent sure that's not going to happen.

I know there's more that I've been taught from one article or season of *SVU* over the years, like *make them look at you like you're a person*, but the bitch is already calling me by my name, so I don't know how else to do that. I could maybe try and be her friend, but I doubt that's going to make her want my magic any less. She killed her cousin, for fuck's sake, I don't think being in the *friend* category is going to make me any safer than her *family* category was.

I watch Jamie silently as I try to figure out my next move, darting looks at Elon to make sure he's still breathing. Jamie said everything was going to go down on the harvest moon, so I'm not sure if she's just getting ready for that or if she's doing something else, but I watch her every move as though it will reveal the countermove to undo it all.

"Do you know we come from elves and fairies?" Jamie declares randomly, and I cross my fingers that there's some major evil-monologuing coming my way, anything to try to distract and prolong whatever is about to happen.

"I mean, not directly, but we have our magic because of them. Their wars were pissing off other races of magical creatures, so they brought humans into the mix, gave them abilities, and asked them to take out the fae and the elves so everyone could live their lives without all the bullshit. I never knew that," she admits. "I found it in an old ass forgotten book when I was looking for ways to get my magic back," she declares as she wipes down the altar with a rag and some substance in a bottle that she pulled out of her bag.

I wait for the astringent scent of cleaner to hit me, but instead I catch an earthy smell that makes me think she's using oil or something on her rag and not a detergent of any kind.

"Apparently, the first witches had all kinds of magic, but when we got tired of serving others and turned on the powers that be, they all got together and tried to take what we had away, but when that didn't work, they fucked up *our* magic by breaking it into pieces. That's where the separate branches come from, and then those branches broke into even more lines over time, and here we fucking are, shadows of what we once were," she announces, gesturing all around her. "The little bitches shut their world off from ours, but I'll change that when I make everything right again," she mumbles matter-of-factly.

Jamie looks over at me as she pulls a lighter from her back pocket and checks to make sure it's working. She moves around the dais, lighting candles one by one, and the smell of blood in the room grows stronger. My stomach churns uneasily, and I rub at my legs to try to combat the cold trying to settle in them.

"It's amazing what you can find in books. The information that people forget is important or the pieces you can put together if you just look hard enough. Fate has guided us all to this. It wants the branches returned to one," Jamie purrs, as though fate's scratching behind her ears and telling her she's a *good girl.*

I roll my eyes.

Jamie itches one of her demon marks on her cheek like it's calling her out by drawing attention to it. Fate didn't guide shit for this nutjob, but a demon sure as fuck might have traded the information she was looking for, or where to find it, for the right price.

"Mmmmmm, it's time," she announces, and the declaration makes my blood run cold, and my heart leaps from relatively calm to *oh shit* in a millisecond.

Time for what?

I look around, my gaze a silent plea.

Please don't tell me it's time for me to die.

13

I look at Elon as though he'll tell me what's happening with a glance, but he's not looking anywhere other than at his feet.

Shit. That's probably a bad sign.

With a smile that could give *any* version of the Joker a run for his money, Jamie reaches into the bag and pulls out something brown, furry, and squirming. I barely have time to identify it as a hare before Jamie twists its head, the sickening crack of bones reverberating through me, the sound making me feel sick. The poor animal immediately goes slack in her cruel grip, and I look away when she holds its lifeless body above her and starts to chant as blood drips down onto her face from the carcass.

It all happens so fast that I stand there as shock ricochets through me. How is she talking about books and elves one minute and then emotionlessly killing the next? It's a dichotomy I can't wrap my mind around or make any sense of. Is this how it starts, is this the ritual she uses to kill us and rip our magic away? My heart hammers in my chest, and I debate arming myself with a bone and giving my little skull weapons away or waiting and trying to keep them a surprise.

I don't recognize the language she's speaking as any form of Mancer I've ever heard or magically recognize. It's not Latin either, but something more guttural and brutish. The flames of the candles she lit earlier flicker, but I don't see or feel a breeze anywhere. With each growled word, the light in the church grows dimmer and dimmer as though the sun has gone down and the moon has forgotten to rise.

It all feels unnatural and alarming, every hair on my body standing on end in rejection of this atmosphere creeping in all around me. Jamie drops the hare, the body even more collateral damage that's been used and now forgotten in her madness. Her chanting grows more animated. I can hear the plea in it, and I realize what she's doing. She's summoning. Every mark on her body starts to glow red hot. I can even see the ones that are supposed to be hidden beneath clothing as they begin to singe the fabric covering them. She's more demon marks than skin, and I'm horrified by what I see.

Dread climbs up my body as a black mist starts to amass around her. The stupidity of what she's doing is next level, but it's clear she's beyond giving any fucks. I grit through the pain that strikes through me when I magically reach out to the bone powder I abandoned in my cell earlier. I call it to circle around me and infuse it with as much protection as I can before my body succumbs to the pain. Panting from exertion, I kneel down within my circle before my weak legs can give out on me.

I look over at Elon, hoping he has some way to protect himself from whatever Jamie's pulling here. He's huddled in the corner between his wall and the demon marks trapping him, his eyes fixed on nothing as though he knows what's coming and has zero interest in seeing it. I should have taken that as my cue to look away, but instead I make the mistake of looking back at the woman holding us captive. Shock flashes through me as the black cloud billowing around her has taken on more of a shape.

I don't know what I expect, horns, wings, just a regular looking human-esque being, but I'm not really prepared for what looks like the fully formed smog monster from *Fern-Gully*. Well, if that smog monster made you freeze in fear and fight not to piss your pants. The thick, acrid smoke-being pushes its way into Jamie's mouth, shoving her head back with unforgiving brutality and forcing her to endure what looks like a painful invasion. It pours down her throat, and I watch as she gags and chokes on the presence. Tears spill down her cheeks as she inhales evil, and I'm sickened by the relief I see on her face when the thing is fully consumed by her.

She writhes and moans and begins to rub up on herself as more thick smoke starts to move over her, touching and testing and making her demon marks burn like solar flares. I look away when the darkness dips into her pants, not wanting any more of this fucked up shit burned into my mind than there already is. The symbols on the ground around me start to glow eerily, and I watch them like they're a snake about to strike at any moment. Jamie's moans start to morph into whimpers, and then her whimpers become screams. I trace the almost invisible line of bone dust around me and try to think of happier times to block out the sound of her pain.

Maybe we'll get lucky and whatever demon she's making a deal with will finish her off once and for all.

There's a surge of tainted power that flashes out from the front of the church, and then suddenly it's quiet. I look up against my better judgment, but there's nothing there. Jamie and whatever the hell she invited here are gone. The candles still burn, and the bag she carried in remains on the altar, but Jamie, the smoke, and the dead hare are gone.

I'm silent for a while, looking around as though the psychopath will wander out of a shadowed corner or something. Nothing happens. The light in the church brightens slightly, and the symbols scorched into the ground dim and fade until they're once again black. Relief washes through me. I'm not dead. I haven't been tortured yet, but what just happened makes me feel uneasy as fuck.

"What the hell was that?" I ask, even though I'm pretty sure I already know.

I never thought *that* would be something I would witness. I was always taught that you don't mess with some entities in the magical world, and demons are one of them. Obviously, no one taught Jamie that lesson, because the idiot just summoned a demon and then went somewhere with it. Seems Jamie missed Oprah's *never let them take you to a second location* lesson too. There's no way that's a good thing for her, which means this can't be a good thing for us.

"That was Jamie getting her batteries recharged," Elon offers, his tone haunted.

"Was it doing what I think it was doing to her?" I ask and then suddenly wish I hadn't. There are some things I just don't want to know.

Elon thankfully doesn't answer.

The room reeks of foul magic, desperation, and sulfur. I bury my nose in the crook of my arm to try and block the smell, wishing I could crack a window. I stew silently and try to understand what would drive a person to this.

"What'll happen now?" I ask, my voice barely above a whisper. I hate the hint of hopelessness I hear in it. I tell myself I need to fight, to stay strong, but I'm beyond spent physically and magically, and I haven't even been here a day. How has Elon survived this long without losing his mind?

It's silent for so long I don't think he'll answer.

"She'll come back," he tells me, shattering the heavy silence. "And when she does, we'll all wish she hadn't," he adds cryptically, but it's not hard to figure out what he means.

When she comes back, one or all of us are going to die.

My heart starts to hammer in my chest. I can tell myself I'll fight, that I won't give up, but what if it's not enough? Who knows how strong she'll be when she returns or what she'll be capable of? Yeah, I'm an Osseous, but who knows what the fuck Jamie is anymore? How do I fight that?

I pull my knees to my chest and rest my head on the bony peaks. Internally I fight the despair that's trying to sink into me. I think of my Aunt Hillen and how she would hold me as a little kid. She would cuddle me and smooth my hair with her hand. She would sing to me one of her favorite songs, and then I would beg her to sing me my favorite until she tickled me and finally relented. I fall into the memory like it's a pile of warm blankets, letting it comfort and soothe me in all the ways I so desperately need right now.

I start to quietly hum "Savage Daughter," the lyrics rising out of my soul and fortifying my will. I think about my ancestors and the trials and tribulation they experienced and survived. I feel so brutally lonely, but as I hum, resonating with the message of the haunting song that was my favorite lullaby as a kid, I know that I'll never truly be alone. Not when the love of my family—both here and gone—is there to guide me.

I open my eyes to find Elon watching me. I offer him a half smile while I continue to hum my tune, each verse and chorus a soothing balm to my battered hope.

Something hits my foot, and I flinch away from it. If there are fucking rats in here on top of demons and batshit crazy witches, I think I will officially lose my shit. A girl really can only take so much. I look to find an opened red and blue package of digestives teetering at my feet. I look up to find Elon close to the edge of his cage, watching me.

"They taste like graham crackers," he informs me awkwardly. "She doesn't do anything to them, I've been eating them since I've been here and I haven't been poisoned yet by anything other than too much fiber."

I pick up the package and look at the nutrition facts. "These cookies have fiber?" I ask absently, and Elon chuckles and shakes his head.

"I don't know, I was just trying to get you to stop singing. The promise of death by demon spawn is one thing, but I refuse to be tortured by a tone deaf tune. Even I have my limits," he deadpans, but there's a cheeky glint to his eyes.

"Sit on it and spin, I have a beautiful voice," I counter, faux offended but grateful for the gesture he's making nonetheless.

"Tone deaf *and* humble too! Well, if I didn't just win the fellow abductee lottery," he teases, and I shake my head and pick up the half package of crackers.

"Pshhh, you know it," I declare. "You're going to be singing a different tune when I figure out how to get us out of here," I tease him right back, biting into the brown cookie-cracker hybrid thing that someone decided to name a digestive. Yeah, that's never going to make sense to me.

I look at the biscuit in my hand quizzically as the taste spreads across my tongue. He's right. Tastes like a graham cracker...so weird, but good. I shove the rest of it in my mouth like a squirrel preparing for winter, and I hear Elon chuckle quietly and then sit down.

"I'll sing whatever tune you want for the rest of our lives if you can get us out of here," he counters, the declaration joking but with an underlying foundation of sadness.

"Holding you to that," I tell him, pointing the package of

food at him as though it's serving as witness to this conversation.

I didn't think I was that hungry, especially not after watching Jamie kill an innocent animal and then practically fuck a foggy demon in front of me, but as soon as I swallow down the first cracker, I inhale the rest, suddenly starving. I feel bad for eating half of Elon's portion, the stars know he needs it more than I do, but I eat it all the same, grateful for his kindness.

I look over at the biscuits I threw to Brianne, but they're still just there, untouched and possibly unseen. Part of me wants to try and help her snap out of what she's going through, and another part of me feels like she's earned the right to deal with all of this however she wants to.

"Will the lunatic bring us water?" I ask as I swallow down a thick bite that feels like it gets stuck in my esophagus.

Elon shrugs and lets out a deep breath. "She has brought us bottles before, but who knows what she'll do now? If she really is planning on killing us all tomorrow night, she probably won't bother."

His words make me even thirstier, and I work hard not to think about it. I mime drinking a glass of water, as though it will somehow trick my brain, but apparently I don't give my brain enough credit, because it's not fooled.

"Do you think you're the source line?" I ask, somewhat out of nowhere. I'm pretty sure he's not, but I suddenly want to know what he thinks. Maybe he feels like a special snowflake too, and what I've experienced really is just normal. Maybe I'm reading things all wrong.

My instincts roll their eyes and throw out words like *denial* and *weren't you that witch who was just telling someone to always trust their gut*. I ignore my instincts' very valid points and survey Elon as I wait for him to answer.

"Could be," he states casually, punctuating his words with a half shrug. "How would any of us know if we are?" he poses, and I respond with my own shrug even though my insides are eagerly raising their hand and shouting *Oh, I know, I know!*

I look down at the now empty digestives wrapper. I study it for a moment, wondering if there's a way to turn it into some kind of weapon. I was killer at origami back in my middle school note-folding days, but somehow, turning this wrapper into a heart or a flower isn't exactly what I'm going for.

"Do you by chance know how to fold a ninja star?" I query, holding the wrapper up and pointing at it.

Elon looks at me dubiously. "Even if I did, what's your plan, slice her to death with plastic?" he taunts.

"No, asshole, I thought we could play a game with it, but if you're going to be like that, I'll just entertain myself," I snark, shooting him a glare.

"You just don't give up, do you? You really think you're going to make it out of this despite all evidence to the contrary?"

"I mean, I really was just trying to pass the time, but yes. I do think I'll figure something out. I'm discovering I'm quite the optimistic witch. What can I say, I'm plucky and shit. Don't worry though, it'll grow on you," I tell him confidently. "Besides, we can't all sit around wallowing in misery, shooting down everyone's hope like it's one of those balloon games at the local fair," I counter with a look that says, *totally just nailed your vibe and you know it.*

"Ah yes, the glass half full dolt who can't see what's happening until she's on the altar, covered in blood while the ex-witch cuts her magic out of her. To be so free," Elon gibes, but there's no real venom in it.

"Please don't talk about glasses, full or otherwise, I'm too thirsty to be held accountable for what I might do," I warn him.

He holds his hands up in surrender, and I nod my approval.

I wonder what the phrase is for someone who's so *thirsty* they're angry?

Thangry?

Thirstgruntled?

A sipbitch?

I snort, I sound like a lush, but I just want some fucking water!

The doors to the church crash open. I pat myself on the back for not jumping out of my skin this time. It still came out of nowhere, but I held it together. Go me. I am shocked to see Jamie already. I thought she'd be gone for way longer, you know, with all the hell-fog-fucking. Guess even demons can be two-pump chumps.

I track Jamie as she stomps back into the church, and wonder if she has any other settings besides stomp and trudge. She doesn't look my way as she passes me, and I get an unobstructed glimpse of her newest demon mark. My stomach roils at the sight of the encircled symbol burned into the side of her head. The parched strands of her tresses are now gone on the side of her newest demonic adornment. Melted clumps of hair stick to the oozing wound, and I cringe as she passes me.

"Are you ready, Leni?" she taunts, her voice brittle and mad.

I don't know exactly what happened to her while she was gone, but it's obvious that she needs to take some anger out on someone else, and it looks like that someone is going to be me. Fear swarms through me like a deadly hive of bees. My adrenaline kicks in to counteract it, and my hands start to shake. I barely have time to think of a plan before Jamie snarls, "*Delio*."

I flinch, waiting for the demon magic to wrap itself around me and force me to do Jamie's bidding, but it doesn't come. Instead, Brianne is yanked from her cage near the front of the church and dragged savagely up the stairs of the dais and fixed to the surface of the altar. The Osteomancer doesn't make a sound, doesn't scream or release a single noise of objection, and I don't know what's more traumatizing to watch, someone who fights and loses or someone who gives up from the start.

I want to look away, but I don't know if I can. What if I miss something and it was the difference between life or death when it's my turn to be dragged up there? Jamie strolls confidently to the dais and begins to root around in the bag she brought and then left while she was off doing who knows what to bargain for more power.

A silver glint of metal catches my eye, and I watch Jamie pull a gun from the bag and tuck it into the back of her jeans. Next, she pulls out a large gold bowl and a viciously sharp looking knife. What looks like a large Ziploc bag is pulled from inside the pack, and when Jamie opens it and dumps the contents into the bowl, I suddenly feel sick.

How is this happening? I feel like I'm experiencing life on fast forward. All I want to do is hit stop, but I'm careening toward *trauma you just don't recover from* at a breakneck speed, and there's nothing I can do about it.

Jamie's gaze sparkles darkly, and I wonder if she purged the demon that forced its way inside of her or if it's here, watching the show from her eyes. Brianne doesn't move or fight in any way, and I can't tell if she's being forced not to react by tainted magic that's holding her down or if she really is that far past caring. I'm going to go with the latter, because judging by the nasty look on Jamie's face, she is not a fan of the lack of reaction.

She leans closer to Brianne and asks her, "Do you know what I have in the bowl for you? I kept it special just for this moment. Aren't you curious?" she asks eagerly, like a predator taunting its prey. "This is your husband's heart," Jamie provokes barbarically, sloshing the contents of the bowl, the look on her face malevolent.

I want to scream at her, but I also don't want to make it worse for Brianne somehow, or for me. I cover my mouth with my hands and close my eyes against the sight of the witch's deadened gaze. I'm under no illusion that Brianne doesn't hear every word or that somehow her psyche has fractured enough to allow her to escape this torture. No. The tears streaming down her face are a dead giveaway that she's still in there. I want to rage, beg her to fight, do everything I can to make this stop, but when I call on my magic, the pain knocks me viciously to the floor. Panting through the shock and demanding my body give me more, I try again as Jamie starts to chant.

14

I scream with impotent fury as she reaches for the knife she pulled out of her bag. But when no one storms into the church to stop this, when the fates refuse to intervene, I beg them to make it quick, to spare the shell of a witch any more suffering than she's already been through. But then the screaming starts.

I look away, not able to stomach any more of the brutality. Rage curdles my blood, and I wish I could rip my ears off. Despite Brianne's efforts to give up, her body takes over, forcing her to try and survive even though it's clear she doesn't stand a chance. Her soul is scarred and shattered beyond repair, and yet the demon-bitch draws the pain out and revels in the suffering.

Tears pour down my face as sounds and smells assault me. I beg the world to make it stop. I don't know what I expected with all of her ranting and crazy delusions. I saw proof of how far she is willing to go branded all over her face, and yet my stupid ass didn't see coming the inhuman savagery that's happening right now. Light is sucked out of the room, and the screaming finally stops. I realize I'm huddled on the ground with my hands over my ears, crying and trying not to hear any more.

But the silence...the silence is almost worse.

I know what it means, and I hate myself for just sitting here and letting it happen. I didn't fight hard enough, didn't find the loophole, or attempt to talk Jamie out of what she was doing.

How did I get here? Oh right, I fucked up and now I'll forever pay the price for my own stupidity.

Shadows coalesce menacingly all around me, rushing to the front of the church like they're eager to be the first in line for something, but I don't dare look to see what's happening. A chanting murmur starts to build, the sound bouncing off the stone surfaces of the inside of this cursed church. Heat is stolen from my very bones, and then out of nowhere, in a flash of light and pain, something slams into me from behind.

I'm struck by a force powerful enough to bow my back and lift me off the ground as it fires through my every cell, destroying and rebuilding all that I am simultaneously. The pain is searing and overwhelming, and I'm incapable of breathing or screaming or even thinking the word *why* or *stop*. Cold burns through me, and disembodied voices sound off from every direction around me. Images flash through my mind, faces I don't recognize, readings I've never done. Bones. So many sacred bones turning to dust in my hands. Power reinforces my every atom. Then just as quickly as the power came to burn through everything I am with its frigid touch, it's gone.

I fall back to the stone floor, my body cracking from the impact. I catch a glimpse of Elon as I go, staring at me wide-eyed and filled with horror and knowing. My labored breaths are a cloud of frost, puffing in and out with each inhale and subsequent exhale. My cheek is plastered to the dirty stone floor, and I'm reminded of another time I lay just like this. Only it was on the floor of my apartment right after I first sealed the bones to me. I thought it was my ancestors bitch-slapping my ungrateful ass, but now I know it was so much more than that.

Reverence and dread pool in my gut in equal measure. I can feel the strength of the now fortified branches of bone magic in my veins, but I can also feel the hungry gaze of the deranged psycho who wants to cleave it from my body.

A pained whimper escapes me, and I'm going to have to talk to my body about the noises it's allowed to make in the face of danger. We really need to figure out far more intimidating and badass sounds to express when we're in pain.

An excited squeal comes from somewhere behind me. "Oh, Elon, and here I was thinking it was going to be you. You cunning little coward. Typical of a Kendrick to claim to be top shit when really they're the maggots feeding on the steamy piles." Jamie laughs as though this news is the best she's ever gotten. You'd think she just won a Powerball with the hooting and excitement she now exudes.

I'm still literally frozen in place and unable to see where Jamie is. I'm forced to wait for my body to thaw from the rush of power that just hit it, and I try very hard not to think about where all that power just came from. All this time, I've been wondering what the kidnapper wanted with both Soul Witches and Bone Witches. I hate that I know the answer to that question now. Brianne's husband was a Soul Witch, and Jamie just used his heart and his blood to take Brianne's magic. I'm sure the other missing Soul Witch's heart and blood met the same fate. How many of them has she killed to destroy all the Bone Witches she has? I'm revolted by the knowledge that one witch's blood makes the other witch's magical violation possible, but what really makes me sick is that I can feel how much stronger I am because of it.

I don't know how I'll ever get rid of this feeling that's whispering to me that I'm tainted inside, that I'm dirty because of what Jamie's done. How can I live with this power, knowing what happened to the witches it was stolen from? Tears spill down my cheeks, and a sob starts in my chest.

Jamie's laughter drowns out the sounds of my overwhelming sorrow, her mirth pouring salt in my fresh and painful wounds. "So you're the one. You're the source," she purrs, viciously amused from somewhere above me. "I was convinced it'd be our Prince Kendrick, but no, he's just an imposter, glass walking around like he's a diamond.

My finger twitches involuntarily, signaling that the feeling in my extremities is coming back. I focus all my attention on the building inferno boiling through my soul.

"I should have known it was you. Why give it all to a glass Prince when a Queen was in our midst the whole time? The way your grandmother fought should have tipped me off, but now we know, don't we, Lennox?" she declares, her voice closer to my ear than it was before.

Alarms are sounding off inside of my head, not from her sickening proximity, but from her words. This is the second time she's referenced my grandmother, as if she were there when... I withdraw from the direction of my thoughts. No. That's not possible. The necros said it was natural causes, this bitch is just trying to fuck with me, to get in my head.

"You know, come to think of it, she looked a little like this when I stood over her and watched her die," Jamie tells me, and I close my eyes and try to block out her words.

She's lying. There's no way she was there, they would have sensed it.

"She had that same angry fire in her eyes, but her body just couldn't keep up. She just laid there, clutching her chest and gasping for air, her eyes promising a vengeance that her body would never let her mete out. Getting old sucks." She tsks, and I feel like someone is taking an ice pick to my heart.

Agony starts to burrow in my soul at her words. Truth seeps into the cracks and fractures she's creating, and I want to turn it all off. I want to stop feeling. To not picture this heinous nightmare standing over my incredible, loving grandmother as her heart failed her.

A sob bubbles up out of my chest, but I silence it.

No, not just her heart...I failed her.

Jamie's voice digs into me like razor wire, the joy she's getting from this revelation like acid to my heart.

"Put a real wrench in my plan, I must say. If the old battle axe's heart hadn't given out, I'd already have what I wanted, what I'm owed, but no, I had to wait to see who the next in line would be. I almost took your cousin, you know, the prissy one with the pretty hair. When she showed up and took things from the apartment, I *almost* jumped the gun. Good thing she was complaining loudly about the unworthy piece of shit who *did* get the bones, or I would have wasted my time killing them. It was still tempting though."

My hand twitches involuntarily, and more and more with each passing second, I can feel the stone floor against my skin. Something is stabbing uncomfortably into my side, and I hope I'm lying on a bird skull fragment and not something worse like my broken ribs. I don't feel pooling warmth around my torso or anything that would make me think I'm bleeding. I want to pull a deep breath into my lungs to test for injuries, but I don't want to give away that I might be recovering faster than she expects. I just need her to keep talking.

"I almost had you. I was seconds away from following you into your store, but that one's brother had to stick his nose where it doesn't belong." I can't see her, but I can feel her crouched over my prone body, and I can imagine she's gesturing toward Elon as she talks about Rogan showing up at the shop that day.

He was right. I was next.

Rogan's face rises to the surface of my mind, as does the way I felt the first time I set eyes on him. He told me that he was pulled into my orbit, but really I think the opposite is true. I was sucked in by his gravitational pull from the get go, I just didn't know I was a goner until that morning in the kitchen when his lips touched mine and we became *more*, whether either one of us wanted to admit it or not.

Jamie keeps talking, but I'm not hearing her anymore. I don't need to listen to how she hunted me, how the hex that almost killed Tad was her handy work, or how close I came to being in these cells long before now. Instead, I focus on the plan. I focus on the fact that this murderous bitch is in my cell. She's right, I do have the same fire in my eyes as my Grammy Ruby, but my body...is just fucking fine.

Inconspicuously, I reach under me and wrap a fist around the sharp piece of skull I'm lying on. Jamie's still talking, and I can feel that she's still close. I don't turn my head to gauge exactly where though, I'll have to do this blind so I don't tip her off.

"Oh, this is going to be beautiful. First, I play with Elon, and then it'll be you and me Queen Osseous," she exclaims eagerly.

Yeah? Play with this, you stupid cunt.

Not wanting to waste a second more, I slam my hand back and up. I feel the shard of bone sinking into her, and I can only hope that I got her in the neck and I can end all of this quicker than it began. But when I look back, I discover that it's not in her throat, I've shoved the bone into her eye. Before she can so much as scream, I slam her with a surge of power. I want to crush her bones and boil her blood until there's nothing of her left. Magic collides with her so hard that a thundering crack explodes all around me. Jamie screams as my magic begins to eviscerate her, but the force of it throws her out of my cell and slams her into the opposing wall.

As soon as my pulse of magic hits the demon engravings, it's torn away from Jamie and shoved back at me in a searing flash of pain. It hurts, every cell feels as though it's on fire, but I won't bow down to it anymore. I can force myself to endure this.

Jamie collapses on top of the stacked dirty pews, and I can't tell if she's out or too hurt to move. As much as I want to, I can't let myself believe that she's dead yet, despite everything inside of me hoping it was that easy. I try to stride over to her, but when I attempt to step past the symbols in the ground, I'm thrown back and viciously hammered with pain just like the first time I tried to cross them. I grit my teeth through it, knowing it won't last. I taste blood from where I've accidentally clamped down on my tongue, and I work to unclench my jaw before I bite anything off.

The agony subsides, and I turn to see Jamie moving shakily. Her arm is definitely broken and hangs misshapen at her side. Blood spills from the bone still lodged in her eye socket, and she screams and whimpers as she tries to get to her feet.

I growl in frustration, livid with myself for not doing more damage. I hit her too hard and with too much power. Instead of the magic sinking into her like it should have, it blew her out of my cell where the fucking markings tore the magic from her. I test my theory by shoving another pulse of magic out, and sure enough, the barrier all around me stops it from going anywhere.

Fuck!

I just screwed up the best shot I'm probably going to get. She won't come back in my cell again, she won't risk me hitting my mark next time. What's worse is that this damage probably won't even last. A couple more demon marks and she'll be right as rain. Fury builds inside of me, and I just want to scream and rage and bring the walls of this nightmare down all around me.

"You stupid whore!" Jamie bellows, enraged, her cruel teal eye filled with fire and vitriol. She spits out a demonic word I'm sure meant to bring me to heel, but instead of her borrowed magic coming for me, she starts screaming in agony and drops to the ground.

I stare at her like some wild animal, biding my time until I can get close enough again to take a swipe. She whimpers and shakily pushes up from the ground with her good hand.

"Come here, Jamie, let me fix that for you," I taunt, my predatory gaze homed on the wrong angles of her arm. "Or are you too much of a little bitch to go head-to-head with one of us?" I goad, hoping I can piss her off enough to make another mistake. "Come here, let me show you what a Bone Witch is really capable of."

She glares daggers at me as she finally gets to her feet.

"How many times can one useless piece of shit sell their soul, huh, Jamie?" I demand. "Aren't they getting tired of bankrolling nothing but a cum dumpster?" I yell ruthlessly, and she grows more and more livid. "Did you tell your demon that you'd be all powerful one day? That your soul would be worth the trouble? Bet they're rethinking that useless trade, probably laughing their asses off as they watch you fuck up over and over again and come begging for them to fix it."

"Shut your fucking mouth," she snarls at me, but wisely she doesn't close the distance between us. "You think you're such hot shit, but who's in the cage, Osteomancer? Who put you there?" she screams at me.

"Your demon did," I scream back. "This isn't you," I bark at her as I gesture to the ground. "None of this is your magic. You sold yourself for it, who's the fucking whore here? It sure as hell isn't me, you stupid bitch. You think you can take what isn't yours? Well, fuck you. I'd sooner die than give you what you don't deserve."

Jamie laughs, and it bounces around the inside of the church like out of tune bells. "Be a selfish bitch. Please take yourself out. I'd love nothing more than to hunt down the rest of your fucking family and bleed them all until I get what I'm owed."

I growl with frustration and slam my hands against the barrier separating us. Pain refracts through my body, but I stand in place, staring at Jamie, a vow to kill her alight in my unwavering gaze.

Her smile doesn't falter. Despite her injuries and the blood dripping steadily down her face, the insanity flowing in her veins makes her certain she's going to win. I guess we'll find out soon which one of us is right.

Jamie struggles to make her way to the dais. I watch her shove the gold bowl and bloody knife in the bag and then, one by one, limp to every candle to blow them out. I can tell the pain she's in is excruciating, but it doesn't make me any less trapped here or feel any better. She tries to use an incantation, but it only ends up in her screams of agony as the magic somehow works against her.

I watch her every move and wonder if it has something to do with her marks, like maybe they're acting like the engravings that won't let us tap into our magic. She tries three more times, and the last screamed word causes a blue fire to erupt all over Brianne's lifeless body. In less than a minute, the remains of the Osteomancer and all of the blood and parts on the altar turn to ash.

The smell is nauseating, and I'm certain it will haunt my nightmares if I ever make it out of here. I bring the neck of my shirt to cover my nose and mouth to help dilute the smell, and when I look over at Elon, he's back to leaning against the wall, with his shirt wrapped around his face too.

Jamie does nothing to fix her wounds, she doesn't even try to pull the owl bone out of her socket. She does wrap a dirty handkerchief around it to soak up the blood, and I silently hope she'll get an infection and die from it in the next twenty-four hours. I don't hold my breath that Elon and I will get that lucky though. I silently observe the mad woman as she hobbles around until the altar is free of the atrocities committed on it, and Jamie's bag is once again packed. She drags it behind her as she limps out of the church, the double doors left open as she goes. I exhale a frustrated and anxious breath. Tomorrow, it will be Elon and me on that altar, and as much as I'd like to think I can overpower this psycho, I can't be stupid and underestimate her. I need to come up with some way to stop or stall her. It's time to stop messing around and do what it takes to survive.

Whatever it takes to survive.

15

I mirror Elon, sitting back against the stone wall, one leg up, with an elbow resting on my knee. Neither one of us has said a word to each other. What can we say?

Sure hope we don't die tomorrow.

Instead of figuring out what might make this entire shit show a skosh less depressing, I focus on that annoying little piece of me that's connected to someone who isn't currently trapped in a cage and counting down the hours until it all might be over.

Night has settled in all around me, and with it came more soul-tiring cold. Luckily, I figured out how to make my bones warm, and so far, the magic hasn't offended the demon symbols all around me and caused me to get shocked. Now, if only I could conjure up some more food or, better yet, some water. Although maybe it's better that I don't. I'm sure pissing and shitting in a bucket in front of a practical stranger is considered a bonding ritual somewhere in the world, but this isn't an episode of *Naked and Afraid*, or at least not yet—thank fuck for that.

I close my eyes, shutting Elon and this shitty church out, and focus on the tether. I take a deep breath, knowing that what I'm about to do could fuck with my magic for eternity. Then again, it's not just my magic anymore. Plus, being permanently tied to Rogan has to be a hell of a lot better than being tied to an altar and murdered. I'm aware that once I do this, there's probably no going back, because I'm about to make this tether as strong as I possibly can from my end. I'm going to make this connection as clear and herculean as I can, because I don't want to die and I don't want Elon to either.

I don't know if it will work like I'm hoping, but it's the only thing I can think to do outside of getting out of this cell and hunting a crazy bitch down. I cross everything I have to cross that Rogan will feel me. That he can somehow figure out how to find us.

I've debated the best way to go about this, gone back and forth with whether or not it's possible to use this connection like a can and string telephone. I really hope that wherever he is right now, he can pay attention to this and that it won't be a distraction that could get him hurt or killed.

Here goes nothing.

Softly, I wrap my intention around the tether, and then I give it a solid yank. I pull on the connection, hard, and work to syphon Rogan's magic to me. I don't take it all, not like I did that day when the Order first interrogated me, but I take enough to get his attention. After a moment, I then *push* on the tether instead of pull, feeding Rogan's magic back into him and adding an extra boost of some of my own.

Slowly, methodically, I repeat the process two more times, and then I wait.

I lean my head back against the cold wall and think about that day Rogan pleaded with me for his magic. I contemplate the finality I felt as I gave him what he was asking for, and I felt our souls say goodbye. This didn't happen that long ago, but in typical Osteomancer Osseous fashion, a shit ton has happened since then, and it's making me reexamine things. Maybe it's the impending death talking, but some of what happened doesn't feel as dire as it did before, it doesn't feel as finite as what's happened within the four walls of the church I'm trapped in.

Rogan was wrong.

Rogan was also very sorry.

And perhaps, contrary to my previous beliefs, some things are worth fighting for.

I've spent a long time looking at what my father did to me through a lens of abandonment and hurt. But as I sit here trapped in a cage that may be the last place I ever see, I realize that I haven't spent enough time looking at what he did through the eyes of someone who really understood love. He loved my mother. He wanted to be with her. Yes, I suffered because of that choice, but I know he suffered without her for a very long time too. It's just one of those things that sucks, but maybe it's not all so unforgivable as I've always thought.

When nothing happens, I start pulling and pushing with the tether again. I think of Tad and my Aunt Hillen as I go. I ruminate on how blessed I've been to have them, and realize I need to tell them more. The rest of my family pops into my mind, all my aunts and uncles spread across the country, and how amazing it is when we're all together sharing stories and laughing. If I get out of here, a family reunion is definitely in order, maybe I'll even invite Gwen and Magda.

Nah, they're still greedy bitches. I'm reminiscing, not losing my mind. No case of the Jamies here.

I feel a tug on my soul that makes me sit up and pay attention. I hold my breath, willing the feeling to come again.

One second.

Two.

Three.

It happens again, and tears prick my eyes as a warm burst of Rogan's magic fills me. I scramble to grasp the tether and shove an overload of magic his way to confirm that I feel him.

More magic is shoved at me, and I gasp with excitement, suddenly wishing I read a book about morse code or something, because I have no idea how to communicate with him other than to show him that I'm still here. I don't know if he can track me somehow. I thought he mentioned once that some tethered witches can, but I don't know how it all works.

I knew I should have slept with him before.

Maybe our connection would have been stronger then. Tad's going to love it if I ever get the chance to tell him he was right.

Lesson learned, always hop on that dick first, ask questions second.

I do the best I can wrapping my thoughts in magic. I focus on where I am and what it looks like. I think about Elon being here and show Rogan Jamie's face. I coat all of it with magic and then send that magic through the tether. I don't know if it will work, but it's worth a shot. I send him images of anything and everything that could help him find us. I even send him magic-laced visuals of what I will do for him if he gets us out of here.

You know, a little extra motivation.

I don't know how long I sit, trading power back and forth, but eventually it starts to taper and then stops completely. A strange emptiness swells inside of me at the loss of contact, and all I can do is hope with every fiber of my being that it's enough. That somehow I did something that will bring him and the Order here in time.

My stomach growls angrily, and I glare at it. "Fuck, I'd

kill for a Sloppy Joe right now," I grumble, my voice slicing through the baleful silence.

I look over to Elon. His legs are now stretched out in front of him, and his head is hanging as though he might be asleep. I'm sure sleep is hard to come by in this place, so I should leave him to it, but now that I've filled the grim quiet with noise, I find it oddly comforting, and I don't want to stop.

"You know that sandwich is named after a legit dude?" I ask no one, as though no one and I are having a legit conversation. "He was a cook or something, and he took the loose meat sandwich to the next level with some kickin' sauce, and boom, the Sloppy Joe was born."

I chuckle like I'm responding to something funny no one said.

"I know, ordering a *loose meat* anything does sound like some kinky back-alley innuendo. I'm totally going to call sex that now, just to freak people out. *Yeah, baby, give me that loose meat, please*," I declare—for some reason in a creepy South Boston accent.

I chuckle, thoroughly amused.

Okay, maybe I am losing it a little.

"Can you imagine if the Sloppy Joe was invented somewhere other than America though, like if it was created in some posh restaurant in the heart of London or something? There's no way it would have ended up with a backwoods name like Sloppy Joe. No, we'd be eating Untidy Josephs or something," I state in my best British accent. "I'll take an Untidy Joseph and a side of mushed peas," I mock and then stick out my tongue in distaste. "Who eats mushed peas past the age of two?" I ask, looking around as though someone is going to answer me.

"What is wrong with you?" Elon asks me, peeved, not

even bothering to lift his head up and look at me as he tosses the judgmental question my way.

I sigh. "So many things, how much time do you have?" I joke, picking at the cuticle of my nail, not bothered in the slightest by his annoyance.

"We just watched a witch get murdered and then burned to nothing, like the pile of ash that resulted was the whole sum of her existence..." Elon exclaims, pointing toward the altar and all the piles of ash on the dais, whose origins, appallingly, are no longer a mystery to me.

I wonder how many witches' bodies make up each gray pile, and then I shove that question away, because I'm not trying to fracture my mind beyond repair.

"I know," I tell him flatly, a hint of growl in my tone.

"If you know, then how the hell are you talking about Sloppy Joes like this is just any ol' day and people like Jamie aren't going to win."

"It's called compartmentalization, Elon. I'll have to work all this shit out in counseling later, but right now all I'm trying to do is not lose my mind before help gets here."

Elon barks out a humorless laugh and lifts his green eyes to mine. "Don't you get it? No. One. Is. Coming. We're in the middle of nowhere with a psychopath who's been planning all of this for most of her life. We're not making it out of here alive."

Not with that attitude, you're not, flashes through my mind, but I bite down on my tongue before I can say it and sound exactly like my Grammy Ruby.

"Maybe not," I agree solemnly, then after a beat add, "but I'm not going to spend the next day thinking about how I'm not going to make it. I'm going to talk about weird shit and hope somehow I can figure out a way to get out of this until that fucking knife is in my heart and it stops beating. And even then, I'm haunting the shit out of that bitch. If she thinks she's going to get away with this, she's got another thing coming," I tell him adamantly.

He shakes his head, although I don't miss the hint of a smile that tugs at one side of his lips.

"So, Elon Vesuvius Kendrick, tell me your deepest darkest secret," I challenge playfully.

He scoffs and rolls his eyes. "My middle name isn't Vesuvius..."

"Well, it should be, but that's neither here nor there. Stop stalling. Come on, spill it...and don't bore me with that *I came back from the dead* shit, I want seriously juicy gossip," I tease with the wag of an eyebrow.

The church falls silent for a moment, and Elon scoots closer to his barrier. "What did you just say?" he asks, his tone deadly calm but his eyes filled with warning.

I look around us and decide since Jamie didn't just come barging in and declare, *say whaaa,* that we're okay to talk about this.

"Did I not mention that Rogan told me about that? My bad. Yeah, I know about that. So I'm going to need you to dig a little deeper into your vault of secrets, mmmkay?"

Elon watches me like he doesn't know what to make of anything that's happening. "Why...why would he tell you that?" he presses, and I try not to take the question personally; it's clear this isn't something that gets shared at friendly gatherings no matter how much wine is involved.

I pull in a deep breath and study him. "Honestly, I don't know. I did technically ask him, and I did demand that he tell me the truth, but I'm not full enough of myself to think that's all it took to get this truth out of Rogan," I explain with a small shrug.

Elon takes me in as though this information changes everything. I can almost see a weight lift from his shoulders, and I can imagine he's been trapped in his head, worrying about what happens if he comes back from the dead again, or worse, what if he doesn't?

"Come on, let's hear it, what's something you've never told anyone?" I challenge again, inviting some levity to break up the heaviness of what just happened.

Elon gets lost in thought for a moment, and I hope he's thinking of an answer instead of getting lost in his own head again.

"Honestly, I don't know. Does it get deeper or darker than what it seems you already know? I feel like I've been set up for failure. Any stories of the candy bar I stole and never confessed to pale in comparison to *my brother and I survived death and we have no idea how it happened.*"

I bark out a laugh. "Yeah, I suppose that's true," I concede. "Okay fine, if you could eat anything right now, what would it be?"

Elon groans and rubs at his stomach. "At this point, I'd eat almost anything. But a massive garden burger and a baked sweet potato would start things off nicely," he declares, and it shows just how hungry I am, because I would normally side-eye those options, but right now my mouth is watering.

"What about you?" he counters wistfully, and I can tell his thoughts are stuck in yummy food-ville.

"Definitely an Untidy Joseph, oh...and a mountain of mashed potatoes with gravy," I admit, licking my lips.

"What adult eats Sloppy Joes?" Elon questions, and I scoff at his poor, deprived and ignorant ways.

I raise my hand and then point to myself for good measure. "Um, I do. They're like a weird comfort food in my family. If my Aunt Hillen is without a jar of her secret sauce, you know the world is about to end. I mean, *Manwich*, eat your heart out. Her sauce is so good, and she puts all these hidden veggies in it and serves it on a homemade roll... Ugh, it's pure chef's kiss," I tell him dreamily and then actually do a chef's kiss, because it's just wrong not to when you're talking about something so delectable.

"Damn, I must be starved, but that does sound good," he admits, and I smile, adding to the list of things that need to happen when we make it out of here: have Hillen make this boy her world famous Sloppy Joes. "But that's not what I was asking," Elon tells me, cutting into my list-making thoughts. "I want to know what the deepest, darkest secret you've never told anyone is," he asks, a snarky brow raised in interest.

"What? You get a pass, but I don't?" I counter.

"Pshh, no, you already knew mine, that's not the same as a pass. It's only fair that you dish too so we're back on an even playing field," he teases, and I huff, disgruntled because I can't find any fault in that logic.

So instead, I think about what the answer is. Typically, my go-to deep and dark is about my dad, but it doesn't feel right to still look at it that way, not with what I've been feeling lately. I study Elon's face and wonder if I should really tell him the thing I never thought I'd tell a soul. I mean, I've barely even admitted it to myself. I release a deep breath and straighten my shoulders as though it will give me the strength to admit the truth.

"The secret I've never told anyone, the one I've barely come to terms with is...I think I could fall in love with your brother," I admit, the words practically floating in front of me as though they're waiting for me to take them back, but I don't want to. "I say this after he's fucked me over twice and made it quite clear that he would save you over me time and time again, but even with all of that, I still care about him more than I should."

Elon is quiet, silently observing me and probably thinking I'm a mental case because I've only known his brother for a short while, and even then, it was because we were looking for him. "And why is that something you'd want to keep secret?" he asks me softly.

"Because I'm afraid that it makes me *that girl*," I explain with a generalized gesture to the side of me as though *that girl* sits to my right. "You know, the one who keeps tagging along after a man who doesn't treat her right and can't see her worth. The girl who makes excuses for the asshole and doesn't realize she loves the drama more than the man." I sigh. "I never thought I'd be that chick, but here I am caring about a witch who won't really ever choose me. And as much as it bothers me, the truth is, I could love him. Even though he may never love me back."

Heaviness settles in my chest as my confession swirls around me in the stale air. I always thought this shit was supposed to make you lighter, but really I feel even more weighted down by reality and what I'm probably never going to have. I was willing to settle for a physical connection, to read into his actions and tell myself there *could* be more, but then I'd be ignoring what Rogan told me himself, *I can't let myself get distracted, I can't put anything before Elon and his safety.*

"And no, you don't need to hide the rabbits, I'm not going to go all *Fatal Attraction* on anyone," I add when Elon is just a little too quiet for my insecure nerves to take. "Don't forget this was a secret, I never had any intention of telling anyone, so you just simmer down."

Elon chuckles, and half his mouth tilts up into a cheeky grin. "I see why he likes you," he tells me, and I shoot him a *get real* look while, inside, my heart is screaming, *do go on.*

"Don't look at me like that. Do you think he just laid all his shit bare for you because he doesn't care? You're a smart girl, Osteomancer, even you have to see that," he teases.

"I do not," I argue, really showcasing my maturity, and

have to stop myself from punctuating that declaration with a huff.

Elon chuckles and rolls his eyes. "Maybe he's not admitting it properly, but my brother doesn't trust anyone. If he trusts you with not just his secrets but *mine* too, it's huge. He's fiercely protective and loyal, and it may seem like it's just toward me, but I know him. If he's letting you in, you mean more to him than you know. I'm sorry he hurt you," he starts, and I wave him off like it's nothing.

"No, really," he continues, his eyes locked on mine intensely. "I am sorry. I know the only reason he would have done that is because he has a one-track mind when it comes to me and my safety. I wish I could explain what it did to Rogan when he found out I wasn't okay, that I hadn't been for a long time. You'd think he was the tougher older sibling with the way he is, but it rocked Rogan's world, tainted what he thought he knew about our family and our place in it. And since then, we've only really had each other.

"When my uncle attacked me, and then Rogan and I woke up after we shouldn't have, everything that came after just reinforced that it was the two of us against the world. He needs time to adjust to more. He needs patience. But, Lennox, he's worth it, I want you to know *that* above all else. He's the most decent witch and incredible friend and brother anyone could ever ask for," he tells me, a hitch of emotion catching in his throat. "I don't deserve him. He always tells me that's our fucked up uncle talking and I shouldn't believe it, but I really don't deserve him. Either way though, I don't know what I'd do without him, and I hope I never have to find out."

Elon wipes at his eyes, his green gaze unwavering and filled with steely conviction. It makes my own eyes tear up in response.

"He's coming," I reassure him with every ounce of conviction in my tired body. "He's coming for you."

Elon shakes his head. "No, he's coming for *us*," he corrects, and I wipe at a tear that falls down my cheek.

We both grow quiet in companionable contemplation. I keep going over Elon's words in my head, looking for loopholes and wavering certainty. Part of me wants to find fault in his declaration, to protect myself against the hope Elon's words have sparked in me. But I can't dismiss the heartfelt points he just made. Rogan loves his brother more than anything; if there's one thing I know about that witch, it's that. And Elon's right, if Rogan is trusting me with not just his secret but the secrets of the person he loves most in this world...well, there's no ignoring the meaning of that.

I release a weary exhale and choose not to abandon hope just yet. I mean, what do I have to lose? I've survived heartbreak before, I can do it again. Rogan is worth it, and so am I. A small smile takes over my face, and I look over to see that Elon is watching me. He smiles back as though he can read the thoughts in my head like they're his new favorite book. I shake my head at him and move to lie on my back.

"Fancy a game of *I spy*?" I ask randomly, and Elon chuckles and lies down too.

"I spy a church that needs to be burned to the ground," he states drolly, and I laugh.

"Touché, Osteomancer Kendrick, touché."

From your lips to fate's ears.

16

I'm exhausted. Not exhausted enough to actually fall asleep, which would be a welcome blessing at this point, but definitely enough to generally feel miserable and cranky. I thought I felt drained the day before with all the trying to find a chink in the armor of this demon magicked cage and from all of my attempts to discover a way to use my magic despite the excruciating pain it causes, but no. Now I truly understand what it is to feel spent and depleted. One night on a dirty stone floor in nothing but sleep shorts and a thin tank top has me feeling beyond wrecked. My eyes burn with fatigue, but just when my mind and body give into it, my ominous surroundings and the cold step in and cackle a *not so fast*.

Wind sneaks in from the still open doors of the church to tease the piles of leaves and ash that cover the floor of the dais. I'm not sure where Jamie went after she killed Brianne —and then I did my best to kill her—but she never came back. At first, I was relieved by this, but as the early hours brought with them a cruel morning chill, my shivering body started to wish that she'd show up just to shut the damn doors.

I figured out an incantation that helps me warm my bones—a nifty little spell my ancestors recorded in the grimoire that I remembered earlier—but the problem is that I have to constantly feed magic into that spell, so things like sleep are impossible because I can't shut my brain off enough to allow it to happen while also staying warm. Any time I did manage to doze off, I'd wake up shivering in no time.

I huff out a frustrated breath and once again try to relax enough to get some semblance of rest. I know I'm going to need it with what's going down today under the light of the harvest moon. That is unless a rescue party shows up before then, although, unlike Bonnie Tyler, I'm *not* holding out for a hero. I do my best to get lost in my thoughts, to conjure a daydream where I'm in a hammock, bathing in the sun as ocean waves lap against a sandy shore. The water is clear, clean enough to drink...aaaaand now I'm reminded of how thirsty I am and have been all night.

I groan and throw an arm over my eyes in an effort to block out the sun and convince my brain it's suddenly nighttime and now the perfect time for us to get some sleep. Unfortunately, it's been light outside for a while, not in a blue sky and beautiful sort of way, it's just bright enough to be annoyingly gloomy outside. However, none of that light has really breached the dark shadow that is the inside of this church. Certainly not enough to warm anything up anyway. If I didn't know better, I'd think the sun's rays are afraid of crossing the threshold and pissing off Jamie. Or maybe it's fear of the demon that owns her that's chasing away the warm tendrils of light that I'm so desperate for.

Elon lets out his own huff of frustration, probably because he's tired of my constant grumbling and rolling around the stone floor as though one piece of rock will be more comfortable than another piece of rock.

“The stone floor not to your liking?” he observes cheekily, his voice gravelly and dry, the sound rubbing against me like sandpaper.

“Oh the floor’s just fine,” I counter wryly. “You don’t happen to have a sleeping bag over there or a change of warmer clothes that I don’t know about? Ooooh, how about one of those fancy Purple mattresses that I always see ads for? I mean, *sold* if it really does give you the best night of sleep in your life,” I ramble, moving to lie on my side, the crook of my arm pillowing my head.

“Nope,” Elon chuckles and wipes at his face with tired, dirty hands. I hear the hair of his somewhat scraggly beard scrape against his palms, and for some reason it makes me cringe. Who knew I hated that sound as much as nails on a chalkboard.

Oh the things you learn in forced captivity.

“I heard you snoring up a storm last night,” I accuse playfully, even though inside I’m jealous as fuck. “Thought a bear stumbled in here and decided to hibernate, but nope, just you,” I tease with just a splash of annoyance in my tone.

I really shouldn’t be annoyed, I know that Elon’s been through a lot, and that’s definitely taken its toll. Really, it’s no wonder his body shut down the way it did. I’m sure mine will do the same soon, you know, if I’m not dead after tonight.

Elon glares at me with feigned shock. “Please, I demand receipts,” he declares like he’s some overacting lawyer on a prime-time TV show.

“Oh right, let me just pop out my phone and press play on the recording I took of your nocturnal emissions,” I joke, and then we both cringe. “Wait, that’s not right,” I correct, racking my brain for the correct phrase. After a couple beats, it still doesn’t come to me. “Listen, I’m too tired to come up with an alternative phrase that doesn’t sound like I recorded you jacking off, so let's both just pretend we know what I'm talking about," I offer with a shrug, rubbing my tired eyes with the palms of my hands.

Elon laughs. "Fine, but it never happened if you don't have video...of the snoring, not the jacking off," he corrects, as though somehow I'd be confused as to exactly what he's referring to. We both cringe again and then crack up. He lifts his hands in surrender and shakes his head. "Let's just erase this whole conversation," he suggests sheepishly.

"Done," I agree all too quickly with a giggle, and then we both fall quiet for a beat. "So you snore a lot," I start again, diving right into our convo-redo.

He laughs and lets out a loud gasp, as though he's never heard a more atrocious accusation in his life. "Oh please, women are always blaming men for snoring. It was probably you, but you simply refuse to accept it, because culturally women are supposed to be all delicate and prissy," he taunts, a cheeky grin stretched wide across his face.

"Um...you must not be hanging out with the right women, because the ones I know are badass and wild. Besides, what century are you living in? Women own their shit these days, we're even allowed to admit we fart now," I tell him with exaggerated excitement, as though this news is the best thing to happen to women since we started wearing pants and demanding equal rights.

I do a quick shiver as a gust of wind moves through the church. I adjust the magic I'm feeding into my magical internal space heater as Elon surveys my clothes...or the lack thereof.

"I'd offer you my pants, but I don't think your shorts would fit me, and I, uh, I don't have any underwear on," he explains, as though he caught me eying his cargos and wondering how I could steal them from him.

Totally haven't been doing that. Nope. Definitely haven't been staring at Rogan's brother, debating how I could get him out of his pants.

"Ew, you're one of those creepy commando dudes?" I razz, my face scrunching up in distaste. "Real talk, I never got that whole thing. Like, I know it's supposed to be sexy or whatever, but I've been a victim of chafing one too many times, and that shit hurts. How are you going to have your twig and berries just rubbing up against your jeans like that? Ouch."

Elon shakes his head, and I swear his cheeks just turned four shades redder under his beard. "No, I wear underwear, but the first week here, I ripped them up and used pieces of them as toilet paper," he explains, and the confession steals the levity from our lighthearted conversation and drops us right back into the reality of where we are.

"Ah," I chirp in understanding, the heaviness of our atmosphere once again settling over me.

Giving up on the idea of rest, I sit up with a groan. I double-check that everything I'm working with is tucked away like it should be inside the now stretched out fabric of my shirt. The moon knows I've woken up far too many times at home with a boob poking out of an arm hole not to be cautious. Nothing worse than chatting away to a fellow captive and then realizing your nipple was mean mugging them the whole time.

There's just no coming back from that tier of awkward.

"Alright, Elon," I call out with a resigned sigh. "On a scale from one to ten, how bad is the bed head I'm working with?" I ask, fluffing my curls, as though the worst thing I have to worry about in this place is an unruly mane.

Really, I'm just trying to distract myself from the fact that my body has betrayed me by creating urine even though I haven't given it anything to drink in over a day. The betrayer also seems to have forgotten the miserable fact that we only have a bucket at our disposal, which will then require the drip dry method for sanitation purposes. Because peeing in a bucket isn't bad enough, but sitting there while your bits dry really just escalates things to another level of awesome. Maybe Elon was onto something with this whole underwear toilet paper thing.

Elon surveys my hair. "Well, you have this little..." He brings a hand up behind his head and splays his fingers. "Peacock situation happening in the back, but I think it's working for you," he teases, and I roll my eyes at him and then quickly start to finger comb said peacock situation into submission.

Elon stands up and nudges his bucket into the back corner of his cell. I look away just as soon as I hear the distinct sound of a zipper being unzipped. Liquid hits the bottom of the bucket, and it's louder than I thought it'd be. I look over at my own bucket and grumpily come to terms with reality. I get up, my muscles and bones objecting to the change of position. Everything groans and pops like I'm the deck of a worn old pirate ship that's seen far too many days riding the ocean waves.

I nudge my own bucket into the corner and debate if it's worse to pee facing him to hide my ass or away from him to hide my cooter. I snort out a laugh at the word *cooter* and decide sideways it is. I look over at Elon to make sure his back is still to me and, with a sigh, surrender to the call of nature.

So this is happening. Where's a SheWee when you need one?

I hold my breath and pretend my pee isn't just as loud as Elon's. All in all, it's not as mortifying as I thought it would be. I can kind of sit on the rim of the bucket so my quads aren't dying halfway through. Truth be told, I've had worse porta potty incidents than this, I tell myself as the drip drying commences. I'm not ready to lose my underwear just yet, in part because maybe I can turn it into some kind of a weapon, use the elastic as a garrote or something. I ponder the possibilities while studying the lines of mortar and stone that work together to create the wall in front of me. I finish up, pull up my undies and shorts and then speed walk away from the bucket as though I just lifted its wallet and need to get out of dodge.

Wind whips through the church just then, and I swear I expect to see Jamie pop up in the doorway from the ominous sensation that's riding the chilly breeze. I look over at the bright open entrance, but no one is there. Hope that somehow she's off leaning against a tree, succumbing to internal injuries, bubbles up inside of me, but I don't let reality run off with the fantasy, no matter how much I wish it were true.

I reach inside myself and observe the tether.

He's coming.

He'll find us.

"Any idea what time it is?" I ask, my stare fixed on the doors that represent freedom but also death, depending on who walks through them.

Elon shakes his head no and doesn't bother offering a guesstimation beyond that. He stares at the entryway too, grass and trees just visible beyond the open doors. It's easy to see we're both anxious and apprehensive about what we know is coming. I try not to think about it too hard, but I can't help but wonder which of us she'll come for first.

I'm pretty sure after what happened last night that it'll be me. She'll want to punish me for attacking her so she can reestablish dominance. I suspect she'll save Elon for last, sticking to the *torture plan* she's been working with since before I showed up. Or at least I'm hoping this is how it's going to go down. There's a tiny voice of panic in my head that's terrified it might be Elon first. The thought makes me sick. But I've been working out ways in my mind to keep that worst case scenario from happening.

I've been thinking through all the possibilities since Jamie left the last time. There's the *wild card* hope that somehow whatever brought Elon and Rogan back from the dead when their uncle killed them could happen again. But what if it doesn't? There's no guarantee, which means it's better to be safe and sort through all outcomes than be sorry.

Swatting away the worry that's trying to claim my mind, I feed magic into Rogan's and my tether. I pull the power back less than a minute later, and I wait for Rogan's silent reassurance. I clutch onto the relief that swells in my chest when I feel him reach back out to me by mimicking what I just did.

He's coming.

He'll make it here before the moon rises and seals our fate.

He'll do it. He has to.

I pull in a deep breath and slowly let it go. Time to get back to it, no point wasting any more of the day.

"Okay, Elon," I chirp, followed by a *let's do this* clap. "It's going to hurt like a bitch, but we need to see if we can weaken these markings or possibly overload them. Which means we both need to be using magic and trying to find a way past whatever it is they do to stop us," I announce, stepping up to the front line of symbols that have me trapped.

Elon studies the open church doors for a moment longer and then looks over at me. He appears to debate for a second, and then he offers me a quick nod before pulling his hands from his pockets and shaking out his arms in preparation. "Okay, tell me what you want me to do."

I pace the lines of symbols that I now want to rip from the ground with my bear hands. Technically, I did try that, but the fuckers aren't going anywhere, no matter how *Hulk Smash* I tried to get with them. I stalk up one line, past another, and down the third, until I meet the wall and turn to retrace my steps. Like a caged animal, I stride up and down, frustration filling each footfall as I study the marks and try to make sense of them.

Elon and I have been fighting them for hours, looking for weaknesses, trying to understand how they work so we can figure out how to counteract them. But for all our time and effort, they're still dropping us to our knees in pain over and over again, with nothing else gained. I growl, fed up with our lack of progress and pissed that I can't figure out how to best some bullshit demon stones.

Elon is lying on the floor, still recovering from our last go, and I know he's close to his limit of how much more he can take. As much as I judged his previous resignation, he hasn't complained once or asked me to stop. Every time I come up with a new option to try, he's there, on the floor, screaming right along with me. But it can't last forever. And now I'm worried if I push much harder, he won't have anything to fight with tonight when he'll really need to.

I rake my fingers through my hair, practically feeling the seconds tick away. Minutes slip through my hands until they become hours that leave rope burns in my palms from how quickly they're pulled from my grasp. The light around us is already changing, and I feel in my bones that time is almost out.

We've been working all day, and silently I've been hoping that any minute now, Rogan and the Order will come walking through the open doors, and all of this will be over. They'll set a trap for Jamie, let Elon and I finish her in the end, and we'll all go home safe and sound. But as the arc of the sun dips closer and closer toward the horizon, I'm accepting that none of this is going to happen. It's just Elon and me against the psycho and her demon.

I now fully comprehend how torturous it is to tip an hourglass on its end and force it to count down. Each attempt to break through these demon bonds, every scream rent from our lungs either from pain or frustration, is like a speck of sand falling away and inevitably sealing our doom. Every time Elon and I fail to make any progress is like a dagger to the gut, because I gave us hope, and then it all slipped away.

I was certain we could find something that would help us, but the moon is threatening to rise, and we're no better off than when we first started. Jamie is going to walk through that door any moment, she's going to call her demon, steal more powers, and then she'll be back to finish us off one by one.

Impatiently I check the tether again. I watch it as though it's a phone and I'm willing the important phone call I'm expecting to come through right now.

Nothing happens.

Temptation to check on Rogan again tickles the back of my mind, but all I can tell from our tethered exchanges is that he can feel me and I can feel him. Sadly, there's nothing more to glean from those moments other than we're there for each other in one way, but it's not the way Elon and I need right now. I try to convince myself that the connection is feeling stronger and that must be because he's getting closer, but it's just delusional hope giving me something to cling to so I don't have to stare at my empty hands and feel the weight of what all of it means.

I stretch my neck and try to shake off the direction of my

thoughts. Yes, it sucks that there's no sign of help. But I'm plucky, dammit, and nothing is impossible.

There's hope.

We're not going to die.

I repeat it over and over again in my head as I pace the edges of my cage. Maybe if I say it enough, it'll be true.

An owl hoots somewhere outside, and it feels like the gong of a grandfather clock announcing that time is up. As though that thought conjures her from the growing fog outside, Jamie is suddenly standing in the doorway. I blink in quick succession, focusing on her silhouette and praying that it's just my eyes playing tricks on me. She steps into the gloom of the church, her bag of damnation and death once again slung over her shoulder. My attempts at staying plucky are plucked away when I see her arm is healed and that there's a new demon mark burned into the flesh where her damaged eye used to be.

Score one for me, I suppose.

Her sudden and silent presence makes my skin crawl, and it's as though she's sucked all the air and sound from the world around us. Everything is eerily quiet, and I can feel the menace pulsing off of her in waves. My heart thumps in my chest like it's banging angrily on a door and demanding to be let out. A ringing starts in my ears, and a silent chant of *this is it* whispers through my mind.

Rogan has until she comes back from her demon orgy all pumped full of magic, before it's too late. But he doesn't know that. Our stupid tether doesn't let me explain anything to him, and I'm terrified to even entertain the thought of what happens to him if he doesn't find us in time. It's not even just Rogan I worry about, but what happens to all the witches if Jamie pulls this off? I mean, I seriously doubt she'll stop at just bone magic. She's too much of an all or nothing kind of psycho. I hate that I'm even questioning it, but am I staring at the person who could single-handedly be the end of the witch race? What's worse is that no one, outside of the dead, will even see it coming. Just look at what she's done to Osteomancers, there's only two of us left.

I swallow down my dread as Jamie stands there, surveying the inside of the church as though she's surveying her kingdom. She starts to walk, her footsteps practically thunderous against the apprehensive silence pressing in against me. I breathe through my alarm and activate the only line of defense I have left...piss the bitch off and try to save Elon for as long as I can.

Jamie doesn't look at me as she closes the distance from the doors to the back of the church and the lines of symbols trapping me here. Her teeth are clenched, her eyes fixed on the altar, like the silent treatment is what's going to send me over the edge. She's so busy trying to ignore me as she walks by that she doesn't see me reach for my bucket and heave the contents at her.

Please let this go through. Please don't splash back at me.

I silently chant my pee-prayer as I watch excitedly as the liquid passes the symbols and splashes all over Jamie. I'm about to raise my hands in celebration and let out a hoot of approval when her head snaps to me, and she growls.

"*Sepha.*"

Torment explodes all around me. One second I'm standing there watching piss drip down part of Jamie's face, hair, and clothes, and the next it feels like tiny needles are being shoved into every inch of me.

I bite back a scream. I knew this was coming. Pushing her buttons was always going to come with retaliation, but as hard as I'm trying to keep it in, a whimper escapes me as I crumple to the floor as the bucket goes bouncing away. Elon's yelling; at me or her, I'm not sure. I want to tell him to shut up, to keep her attention on me, but my mouth can't do anything other than grit through the pain. I push to raise my head through the agony attacking me and glare at him. He's too busy snarling at Jamie to notice. It seems Elon has a plan of his own, and it doesn't involve saving his own ass; he's trying to save mine.

Ugh. Doesn't he know Rogan needs him more than he does me?

I considered the selfish route. Thought about the fact that as the *source*, I have all the power, and it might be better if I last longer in this sacrifice scenario, but I've spent all night and day tossing it all back and forth, and I just can't. Saving myself at the cost of someone else will never sit right with me. So here we are.

"Shut the fuck up!" Jamie screams, bringing her hands up to her ears and covering them as though it will be enough to block out whatever Elon's growling at her.

Her voice rings with unhinged panic, like everything is becoming too much, and I get the impression that Jamie's teetering on the edge of control, like her breaking point is just on the other side of a narrow ledge.

Now if I can only push her over.

The pain stops as Jamie loses her focus and tromps up to the dais. She moves as though she can't escape fast enough, and I wonder what's happened since she was here last. She seems far angrier and more subjugated than she was before. The bag practically gets slammed down on top of the altar, and Jamie just stands there, her breathing quick and ragged. She looks up after a moment, her one teal eye settling on me as she wipes piss-soaked strands of hair from her face.

"I'm going to destroy you," she seethes at me. "You'll be screaming in the afterlife, that's how badly I'm going to fuck you up," she threatens vehemently.

I shoot her a cheeky grin and try to cover up my shaky

limbs as I push up from the ground. "Your mama," I snap back without hesitation.

Instantly I want to facepalm.

Really, Lennox, that's the best you've got?

In my defense though, I'm insanely thirsty, and I was just lightly tortured.

Elon snorts out a laugh that says even he's judging me. I dismiss his appraisal with a look that says, *I know, I know. Give me a minute to warm up.* I get to my feet and look back at Jamie. There's wild mania gleaming in her eye and insanity etched into her features.

"What are you waiting for then?" I challenge. "Let the screaming begin. Let's find out if all this is going to work the way you want it to. I mean, there's *no way* your dumbass has accounted for everything. You didn't even know the others' magic would trace back to the source instead of going to you," I ridicule. "You really thought you could throw a little bitch fit and the magic would just cooperate, but you forget, Jamie, you have to be worthy of it, and you and I both know that's never going to happen."

An angry twitch reveals itself in her top lip.

Looks like I just struck a chord.

"What are you going to do when the magic keeps eluding you? How much space is left on you for more ugly ass demon promises?"

"Guess we'll find out," she snaps at me, pulling new candles from her bag and angrily setting them all around. "You're so typical, *Osteomancer Osseous*," she mocks. "You think you're so much better than me because you have a little power running through your veins. You want to know who else thought that?" she taunts, a wicked smile on her face. "Every other dead Osteomancer that came before you, that's who. Go right ahead and talk all the shit you want, we'll see how brave you are when you're up here bleeding for me, begging me to stop, as you piss and shit yourself."

"Look forward to it, you rabid cunt. At least I won't be the only one up there covered in *my* piss," I provoke, flipping her a lovely set of twin birds.

Jamie lets loose an annoyed screech and starts rifling through her bag more aggressively.

Nerves flutter through me like frenzied insects, but I breathe through it and pat myself on the back. Definitely redeemed myself from the *your mama* catastrophe.

"What are you doing?" Elon whisper-growls, as though Jamie can't hear every word he's saying.

I give him a noncommittal shrug, and his green eyes start to study me, like my plan is suddenly tattooed all over my skin. I don't say anything else, and he shakes his head at me like some disapproving parent who didn't see this coming. *This* is why I didn't fill him in on what I was going to do in the first place. He would have argued with me about how, as *the source*, I shouldn't be handing my power over to Jamie, and technically he'd be right if it weren't for the whole *immortal* thing. That trumps what I could be handing over to Jamie completely.

Even though it's possible Elon might not come back this time, I can't risk what happens if he does. To me, that is a far worse power for Jamie and her demon to get their hands on. I know Rogan is coming. I hope he'll get here in time to save both of us, but if not, Elon's secret is far more important to protect than the power running through my veins. I know he wouldn't agree with me about that, which is why I said nothing. I didn't want to give him time to figure out a way to try and stop me.

Totally called that right.

I look away from him and, in my head, start saying my goodbyes. I don't want to wait until it's too late, and I might be in too much pain to do it right. I may not be able to look the people I love in the eye before I go, to tell them face-to-face what they mean to me. But I can put it out there into the universe, hoping my love, my gratitude, my words, find their way to the hearts of those they're meant for.

I picture Tad and Hillen, all the laughter and tears, hugs and special moments we've shared throughout my lifetime. I don't know where I'd be without them, and I know this will be the hardest for them to come to terms with. I hate thinking about what life will look like for them when I'm gone, but I know they'll have each other and the rest of the family and that they'll all help one another when things feel like they're too much. I think of Rogan and hope that I play this right so that when he finally comes, Elon is still here, and everything he went through to find him isn't for nothing.

I give myself a moment to lament what I'm losing, not just the time with the people I love, but *my* future. A future I hoped would someday be filled with love and babies, laughter and adventure. A future, it seems, that was never meant to be. Sorrow sticks in my throat as I look up and watch Jamie set up. She reaches down and seizes a handful of ash and spreads it around the base of the altar as she murmurs something.

Please don't let all their loss be for nothing, I plead with the universe.

Jamie works, focused on the task at hand, and I try to banish the fear settling in me like drying cement. I know it's going to hurt, that I'm going to wish I was dead long before I actually am. I'm trying to be ready for it, but I don't know if anyone can really be ready for something like this. Slow, measured, slightly shaky breaths move in and out of my lungs. I work to make them even, to come to terms with my life and the impending loss of it.

With a dirty-looking rag, Jamie wipes something on the altar, and I try to recall how long it took her to summon her demon the last time she did it. I do my best to guess how long she was gone before she walked back into the church ready to kill Brianne. I work out the time table, as though knowing I have exactly forty-three minutes will make all of this more bearable.

I look over at Elon, and his eyes are filled with fire and determination. The dude is definitely pissed.

"Are you giving up?" he accuses, a taunting sneer on his face and frustration filling his gaze. "What happened to your fight, Osteomancer? Where's that unwavering determination that's grated on my every nerve since you showed up inside those demon marks?" he demands, but I know what he's doing. It's written in the tears I see start to well in his eyes, in the anguish etched into his weary face. He knows what's coming as much as I do, and we're both fighting to keep the other alive.

"You're a good witch, Elon," I tell him, a hitch in my throat that I quickly clear.

"Stop it," he snarls, panic painting his words as he starts to pace restlessly at the inner edge of the demon symbols boxing him in. "You have to fight, Lennox. Rogan's going to need you," he pleads with me, but I shake my head and swallow past the tightness in my throat.

"Not me, you," I counter, shaking my head as he opens his mouth to argue. "He'll need you," I mouth to him, not trusting my voice to stay as strong as I need it to.

A bang pulls both of our attention back to the front of the church, and we see that the candles are already lit. My heart picks up, I'm not ready to see her rip apart another innocent animal. The first time was scarring enough.

I look back at Elon, his eyes jumping around the church like he's looking for help.

"Don't, Elon," I warn as I see him calculating what to do, what to say to tip the scales toward him. "I know you think you might have a get-out-of-jail-free card, but what if that only works once?" I tell him cryptically, and I can see how much he hates the truth of my words in his sorrow-filled eyes. "You can't take the risk. He needs *you*," I plead, my eyes begging him to think about Rogan, about what his loss would do to him.

The first time Rogan told me that I wasn't even a factor when it came to choosing Elon versus choosing anything else, it stung a little. I mean, I got it. It's his brother, and they'd been through more than I could really fathom at the time, but it didn't feel nice to hear nonetheless. But now, as I stare Elon in the eyes, plead with him to hold out for Rogan, to fight until he can get here to help him, it doesn't hurt like I thought it would. I don't feel second best or less than. There's no resentment or hard feelings. It feels right. I get it now. Elon was always someone worth fighting for, and I hope I honor him and Rogan by fighting for as long as I can against what Jamie is about to do to me.

Elon closes his eyes, as though it will block out the truth of what I'm saying, but we both know it won't.

"It's okay," I reassure him as a tear slips down his cheek. "I'm ready, and Rogan is right, you're worth it," I tell him as I look up and see Jamie tucking something in the back of her pants. She reaches back into the bag, and I know what's coming next, the bunny, the blood, the chanting...the wrongness of it all.

My hands start to shake as the specks of time that I still have left fall away one by one. I touch the tether with my magic, sending Rogan one last message. I beg the fates that he won't feel what I'm about to go through and that this tenuous little connection turns out to be the loophole that I hope it is. That all my magic and ability will transfer to him and not Jamie after I die.

I've given it so much thought since I realized that I was the source. I've gone over it and over it in my mind, working through every possible scenario I could think of for how to keep this magic away from such a heinous being. I can only hope that this connection between us really did happen for a reason, like Rogan's aunt said, and that somehow, even if Rogan can't save me, he can save the magic.

I let out a deep resigned sigh, ready as I'll ever be for when Jamie comes back and the second ritual begins. My gaze finds her still standing at the altar, but I don't see what I'm expecting to find there. There's no innocent animal clutched in Jamie's hands ready to be slaughtered and used to summon a demon. No, instead she's holding a savage looking silver dagger. My heart sinks and then starts to sprint when I spot the gold bowl on the altar. I look down to find a now empty bag on the floor that has the remnants of some poor Soul Witch's bloody heart.

My eyes snap up to Jamie's triumphant cruel glare.

Shit.

I thought she'd have to power up before we got to this part, but I was wrong. She's not setting up the ritual to call her demon, she just set up the one that kills me.

And just like that, I'm the top of the hourglass: empty, hollow, and completely out of time.

17

Elon rakes his fingers through his dirty hair as the realization that Jamie's jumped the gun, or rather the demon, hits him too. He starts to breathe harder, terror bleeding into his eyes. He paces inside his cage, looking like a savage lion ready to destroy anything that dares try to corner him.

If only it were that easy.

If only our will to stop this made it possible.

How many times has he had to stand there trapped and unable to stop the horrors taking place at the front of this cursed building? How many times has he been forced to endure the torture and live with the scars?

"Don't look, okay, Elon?" I warn, giving him permission to shut me and everything that's about to happen out. I don't want to add to his trauma. I don't want to be one more thing that chips away at his soul.

"You two are too cute, trying to save each other," Jamie coos venomously, her evil cackle echoing off the stone walls of the church. "As if anything you do would change what's already been decided," she jeers. And then, just like the first time I watched her murder another witch, she opens her mouth and snaps, “Delio!”

I do my best to quash the terror bubbling up in my stomach as I feel a pull in my gut. But then, I’m forced to watch in horror as the spell once again takes someone else.

No.

No, no, no!

I rush to the front of my cage and slam into it hard, as though the sheer impact will break the barrier separating me and Elon. I scream as he’s brutally yanked from his feet and dragged toward the altar. I ignore the pain that crashes through me as I bellow, “Nooooo!” my cry feral and filled with raw panic.

It’s supposed to be me!

He’s supposed to go last!

“Fight!” I order Elon, my enraged eyes moving to Jamie, who’s watching me like a vulture that’s just spotted its next meal.

“Take me first!” I scream at her, my words half warning, half plea. “I won’t fight, I’ll do whatever you want,” I promise her, but in a blink, I see that my declaration is a mistake.

Fuck! Stupid, Lennox! I berate, because that’s not a bargaining chip that will work for this nightmare of a soul. She wants us to fight, to suffer, to die anyway, despite all our efforts not to. She gets off on it. The disgusting truth of it gleams in her one eye, and I want to rip it from her face and crush her until she’s nothing.

“You fucking bitch, you stay the fuck away from him,” I snarl, slamming my hands against my magical barrier, breathing in the pain it causes me and using it as fuel for my fury.

Elon’s shouts ring all around me as he’s dragged up the few stairs that lead to the dais and lifted against his will onto the altar. I can see that every muscle in his body is tense;

he's fighting as hard as he can, but the demon magic is too much.

I scream and spit every possible curse and threat I can think of to try and stop what's happening, but it only seems to feed Jamie's cruelty. I screech in frustration, pulling at my hair and trying and failing to get past these evil markings. I watch Elon fight the magic that's pinning him down, but nothing is happening beyond the strain I see in his face, in his body. His eyes find mine, and the fear I see in them makes me shatter into a million pieces of rage.

I can't let this happen.

I have to stop this, but how?

Think, Lennox, think!

I shove my magic at the barrier again, but like all the other times, it ricochets back at me and punishes me for even bothering. I snarl through the pain as Jamie steps over to Elon and dips her hand in the gold bowl. Blood coats her skin as she fists the heart and lifts it out, moving to rub it all over Elon as she begins to chant.

I witness each crimson streak and scarlet splatter on his skin, when suddenly I no longer see the stain of someone else's life on Elon's skin, I see a way.

Elon's voice sounds off in my mind. *There's no way out of these unless Jamie wants you out. They're tailored to fuck with our magic...*

Our magic...

Bone magic...

I don't know how I haven't thought of it before, but the thing is, it's not just bone magic running through my veins anymore. Could that be it? Is that the key to break us out of this whole fucked up situation? It's possible that Elon meant witch magic in general versus demon magic, but for some reason, I don't think that's it. I think he specifically was pointing out that these cages are designed for Osteomancers.

I block out Jamie's chanting and the sounds of Elon struggling, and start searching my cage for a sharp piece of bone from the owl skull fragments I scattered all over. I shove a frantic, terrified message through the tether, hoping Rogan hurries the fuck up, and then I start pleading with my magic, with Rogan's magic, to show me what it can do.

I snag a thin but sharp bone fragment from the side of my cell and hurry over to the corner of my cage where two lines of demon symbols meet, the corner closest to the dais. Jamie's chanting changes slightly, and excitement enters her tone, and I look up to see her placing the blade of her knife against the skin of Elon's arm.

Shit, she's moving too fast. I need to slow her down. I rack my brain for what to do or say, and it hits me.

I start laughing loud and hard like I've completely lost it. My glee is beyond overexaggerated, but I need to get the nutcase's attention. I hold my side as though I have a stitch in it from whatever it is that I find so amusing. And when I look over, relief slams into me when I find Jamie's eye on me. I shutter my emotions, refusing to allow the relief to leak through and continue to cackle like a deranged hyena.

"You are so stupid," I announce loudly, pointing at Jamie and laughing. "I've been sitting here waiting for you to figure it out, but you just never did," I taunt, giggling so hard that the sound of it annoys even me.

"Do you really think the Order was just going to let me be taken?" I declare as I put my hands behind me and discreetly cut into my forearm with the piece of sharp bone. Heat pools along the cut, but I run the shard of bone over it again and again to ensure it's deep enough.

"What the fuck are you talking about?" she demands impatiently.

"You didn't think they'd have a backup, a way to find me just in case you had any more traps hidden around?" I ask her, with a raised eyebrow and a judgmental snicker. "Nice note by the way, the Order techs were very impressed with that piece of magic," I offer, hoping a little flattery will keep her listening and the blade of her knife away from Elon.

"They're coming, Jamie," I warn her, offering my own unhinged smile as I feel blood start to drip steadily from my fingers. I begin to pace the line of demon symbols that have me trapped, doing what I can to make it look like a slow contemplative prowl and hiding the fact that I'm spilling blood on the line as I go.

"You're only going to get time to take the magic from one of us," I tell her confidently. "And then the Order is going to be here to try and stop you. You really want to waste your time on Elon?"

She glares at me, clearly not buying it, so I tsk at her and shake my head.

"You're running out of time, Jamie, and you don't even know it. I'm offering you a trade. Put Elon back and take me. It's the only way you're going to stand a fighting chance against what's coming," I tell her, and I hope with everything I have left she believes me.

Her demon marks are lit up just like they always are when she uses their magic, but the rest of her looks ashen, like she could crumble to nothing if the wind pushed too hard.

"You're lying," she counters, and I laugh in response.

Of course I am, but as much as she wants to believe *that*, I see a speck of doubt in her eye. There's a *but what if* debate happening in her demented mind, and I hope against hope that she might actually listen to me.

Elon is panting on the altar, his eyes trained on the knife

in Jamie's hand. "Lennox, don't," he growls out, wincing as Jamie presses the knife into him harder.

"You don't care if I survive the Order," she snarls, the wheels in her head turning slowly and finally arriving at this conclusion as proof of my deception.

"No, I don't, I hope they find a way to flay your very soul and make you suffer for eternity," I admit, vitriol spilling out of every syllable. "But I do care about Elon. This is about helping him. I will sacrifice myself and give you my magic if you will let me trade places with him right now. But the Order *is* coming either way, so now you have to decide which is more important: the power you say you want or torturing an innocent witch because you don't like his mom."

Her demon marks flare with my words, and her grip tightens around the handle of the knife. She studies me for a second and then another, as though my words are sluggishly sinking into her and fucking with all of her plans.

"Tick tock," I mock as I make another pass with my bleeding arm inside the black demon marks etched all around me.

"You're just trying to save him," she accuses, her gaze suspicious but hesitant.

"Of course I am, you stupid bitch, that doesn't mean I'm not telling the truth though," I snap at her. "You want to risk it?" I challenge. "Are you going to miss your opportunity to kill the source?"

Her nostrils flare with anger, but thankfully the knife doesn't move any closer to Elon.

"If I'm lying, you kill me and then you kill him," I tell her with a casual shrug, "but if I'm not, they'll stop you, and I'll watch them gut you while the demons you owe rip your soul apart," I tell her, annoyed that she's still debating this. My logic is fucking sound, but *this* mental case isn't. I don't know if she's going to fall for it.

My foot catches on the edge of an uneven stone, and I stumble, my arms shooting out to catch me at the threat that I might fall down. I recover quickly, but Jamie's eye drops from my confident stare down to the blood spilling off my arm. She moves away from Elon, taking a step toward me, her features pinched with mistrust and anger.

"What are you doing?" she growls, her gaze shifting from my arm to the now bloody symbols on the ground.

"Coming for you," I growl right back, and I don't miss the fear that flashes across her face before fury takes over.

The doors to the church slam shut with a resounding boom as though she's magically barricading us in here. I know right away that I've lost her, and she shoots me a glare and then moves back toward the altar.

"I'm going to rip your soul out of you myself!" I bellow at her as she once again presses the knife against Elon's skin.

She starts to chant, and Elon screams in pain as she slashes the knife down his arm. I'm lost to the desperate fire growing in my body, Elon's cries spurring me on. I call on my magic, begging for answers. My blood decorates the inner line of demon symbols, seeping into the grooves and bends like my essence is reclaiming them in a way. I stare at the marks intensely like they're a puzzle I know I can solve if I just find the right angle, and that's when words pop into my mind unbidden. I start weaving them together, spelling and chanting, empowering the words with my magic and will and then feeding it into the blood. The marks respond to my use of magic, but it's not at the same level of pain as when I tap into my natural Osteomancer abilities. I pick up the pace, weaving and chanting even faster. I don't know exactly what I'm doing, but I put my faith in my magical instincts, trusting the blood magic just as I've always trusted the bone magic.

Elon screams and begs for Jamie to stop, just as the symbols all around me start to steam and hiss in reaction to what I'm doing as my blood works to take over. I shove more magic into everything, ignoring the pain as Elon's forlorn cries push me to press even harder and work faster. My words and spell weaving would give the best auctioneer a run for his money, and I feel a strange climax starting to build in the magic itself.

A loud crack rents the air, making everyone jump. Jamie stops her chanting and cutting, and looks to the door, the blood draining from her face. I, however, study the now bloody symbols at my feet and see that one of the stones is now cracked where once it was whole. I take it in and then test what I think just happened, by shoving a bleeding hand through the space above the symbol. I wait for the pain to slam into me when my hand starts to cross the barrier that was just there, but nothing happens.

Shock slams into me.

Holy shit, it worked.

I quickly move my hand over to the stone that still has an intact demon mark, and pain rushes through me like a tidal wave with the contact. I yank my hand back, but all I need is to crack a couple more stones, and I can get free. Elation hammers through me with the revelation, and I look up at Jamie, vengeance and triumph written all over my face.

Satisfaction blooms in my chest as I watch panic quake through Jamie, her stare grows worried, and she rushes to double down on what she's doing, chanting faster as she once again starts in on Elon. I focus back on the trail of my blood, chanting just as fast. The Mancer spills off my tongue like a vicious waterfall of magic, pouring my will into my blood as stone by stone, I fight to take back my freedom.

Another stone cracks, but I don't stop to celebrate as Jamie and I race against each other for Elon's life. Tension tightens every muscle in my body as I rush to get the fuck out of here and stop Jamie from finishing the ritual with Elon. Another stone cracks, and I know I only need one more, and then I'm going to annihilate her and the demon who made all of this fucked up shit possible.

"Stop," Jamie screams, and I look up to see she's holding the knife to Elon's throat with a shaky hand. "Don't you dare break one more symbol, or I'll kill him right now," she threatens, and I freeze. The manic gleam is back in her eye, and I know she means what she's saying.

I slip my arm out of the magicked cage, the threat clear. I may not be able to get out yet, but enough of me can to try and stop her if she tries anything.

"Don't move," she growls, pressing the knife into his throat harder as she glares at me.

I glare right back, but I stop, worried if I say anything or move anything, it'll make her too jumpy and Elon will pay the price.

"How the hell do you have blood magic?" she demands, her voice just shy of a shriek. "Your grandmother didn't have blood magic, and no one else in your family had any other branches," she declares, clearly knowing way too much about me and the people I love.

I recall her talking about doing research, and it makes me wonder just how deep she dug into everyone she's taken.

"No, she didn't have blood magic," I agree evenly and calmly as though I'm trying to calm a spooked horse. "Before *you* started taking Osteomancers, I didn't either," I tell her cryptically as I silently and cautiously push magic out into my freed hand and try to feel for her bones or for her blood.

"So how the fuck do you have it then?" she snarls impatiently.

Elon flinches against the blade being pressed into his neck as he looks at me with rage etched into the planes of his face and pleading eyes, silently begging me to stop her. I try to search for a way to magically do that, but even though I'm straining to get my hooks in her, I can't find a way. It's as though her essence, her physical body, isn't standing right in front of me. Maybe the demon magic has cloaked her somehow, and I try not to show the worry in my face that I feel over the fact that my magic still might not be enough to stop this.

"Because I'm tethered to a Blood Witch, how do you think the Order is tracking me?" I tell her, doubling down on the lie.

Jamie's face whitens before my eyes. I can physically see the horror that runs through her at my declaration. I had no idea what a tether was before Rogan, but it's clear that Jamie knows exactly what I'm talking about, and she's terrified.

I should feel some sort of gratification from her reaction, take delight in the raw fear I now see written all over her face, but she's still holding the knife to Elon's throat, and I'm afraid she's going to slip and hurt him. I tell myself that I'll use the blood magic to stop the bleeding if it comes to that, but if the wound's bad, I might not be able to do enough to save him. There's also still the issue of the magical dead zone that seems to be wrapped around Jamie and Elon.

"I'll still trade places with Elon," I offer calmly. "There's still time for both of us to get what we want from this," I remind her, my eyes dropping from her unhinged stare down to Elon.

I try to offer him what reassurance I can with a look, and

then I look around at the base of the altar and around the dais for anything that might still be blocking my magic.

A thunderous boom sounds off all around us. I have to fight to keep from jumping out of my skin, and my head snaps in the direction of the church entryway, because that sure as hell wasn't me. The large wooden doors bow like they're on the verge of admitting whoever is on the other side. I stare at it completely stupefied as astonishment slowly sinks in, and relief starts to bubble up inside of me.

He's here.

I don't know how I know, but I do. Rogan is fighting to get in. He's so close and yet so far away, but he's here. He's here and *we're* still alive. My eyes well with tears, and I turn back toward the dais, my eyes eagerly searching for Elon's. I go deadly still when I realize that Jamie's pointing a gun at me with one hand, and the other hand is still gripping the knife, only the blade is poised over Elon's heart instead of resting against his throat.

He looks over at me, his green eyes filled with tears, and terror and rage war inside of me.

Jamie laughs as another massive crack booms through the doors behind me, but I can tell they still haven't made it through.

So close!

"You thought you'd won, didn't you?" she asks jeeringly.

I hold my breath, screaming inside for them to break down the doors and stop this psycho.

Another thunderous crack pounds through the doors.

Hurry!

Jamie's smile turns sadistic, and she cants her head to the side. "Too bad you were wrong, Lennox."

No!

A soul-shattering scream tears out of my throat as Jamie's eye hardens and her finger squeezes the trigger. The sound of the gun discharging drowns out everything, and I shove a raging pulse of magic at Jamie, desperate to stop what she's trying to do, but my magic slams up against a barrier protecting the dais. This time, when the pain explodes in my body, it's not from the symbols carved into the stones at my feet, it's from the bullet that rips through my chest.

Agony tsunamis through me, but the bitch isn't done. She raises the sharp knife above Elon's chest and, with no mercy or hesitation, plunges it down through Elon's heart. He gasps as she buries the blade in his chest, and then I'm forced to witness his body as it relaxes in that horrible way that only death can cause.

I bellow a keening cry so visceral and broken that my magic responds. My heart cries out to Rogan as I pour the loss and need for retribution out of me so forcefully that with a flash and sonic crash, the stones at my feet explode.

My scream is cut off with a gurgle, and I suddenly taste blood in my mouth. I refuse to look down at the damage I know has torn through me, and another splintering crack from behind me spurs me on. I force my body to lumber closer to Jamie. She eyes me, her stare panicked as she starts to chant, shoving her hand in the blood pooling at Elon's chest and wiping it down her face.

I immediately recognize what she's doing, and wrath burns through my veins. She's calling her demon. She's using Elon as her sacrifice and calling him to take her away. I use everything I have inside of me and shove another pulse of magic at her on a choked scream. Just like with the symbols that comprised my cell, stones erupt in a line at the base of the stairs that lead up to the dais and the altar. I can suddenly feel Jamie and Elon with my magic, and satisfaction hammers through me now that the demon marks protecting her from me are destroyed.

The doors burst open behind me with such force that it throws me forward against the floor, fucking up my effort to try and get to Jamie. Noise and chaos erupt all around me, and I struggle to pull air into my lungs and to find the strength to push myself up off the ground. It was all I could do to stay on my feet after she shot me, and now I'm not sure if I can command the cooperation of my limbs.

Something slams into Jamie, and she's thrown away from Elon and the altar. I hear Rogan scream, and the sound rakes through my soul and calls to my sorrow.

Stone cuts into me as I drag myself closer to the altar. I need to get to Elon to keep her from using him to escape. I couldn't protect him when he was alive, but I will in his death. I refuse to let this demon-stained bitch use any more of him than she already has.

Each inch is a struggle, but I grunt and cough and force myself closer. There's some kind of fight happening behind me, and when I turn to see what's happening, I'm shocked by what I find. It's as though the shadows themselves have torn themselves away from the walls and corners of the church and are now fighting the team of Order members who are here to rescue us. Everything moves so fast, there's so many of them, and I can't make out faces or pick out Rogan amidst the mayhem.

Rage boils inside of me, and I push even harder to get to Elon.

Come on, body, it's just a flesh wound, we got this.

Movement catches my eyes, and I see Jamie struggling to get to her feet. I latch on to my magic, but something about the connection is wrong. It's like my magic is blinking in and out of service. I pull in a deep wet breath and focus on the power that's always been so steady and strong inside of me. The connection evens out, and I push magic through my body to stop the bleeding as much as possible. I try to repair what I can, and then I take some of what's left and reach out to Jamie. She's closing the distance between her and Elon, the demonic chant pouring from her chapped lips. I feel the bones in one of her legs, and with a thought, I crack them to stop her progress.

A pained scream rings through the church, but it quickly gets lost in all the commotion.

"Thought you had won, didn't you?" I growl out as she goes down, my voice lost in the noise echoing off the walls of the church.

I magically reach for Jamie again, but my access to my ability blinks out, and a fit of choking coughs demands my immediate attention. I hack up blood as I pull myself up to the altar. Magic flicks to life again inside of me, and I waste no time calling to the powdered bones in the piles of ash now all around me. One flick of my wrist has them morphing from piles on the ground to clouds in the air. I shove the remains of the people Jamie has killed at her as she struggles to get up. Ashy mist surrounds her, and I do my best to suffocate her with it while I command another cloud of ash to pull Elon's body down from the altar.

Jamie screams, and I shove ashes down her throat until all I hear are her coughs and the gagging as she fights a cloud of retribution. I want to do more, to make her suffer more, but I can already feel my access to my magic flickering out again, like my batteries are going out and need to be replaced. I refocus everything I have on getting Elon down to me, and then I ask the ashes to pull us away to the wall under the massive, dirty, stained glass window that marks the front of the church.

I hold onto Elon with every ounce of strength that I have, relieved that I have him now and Jamie can't get to him anymore. At the same time, I'm completely broken over the fact that she murdered him so senselessly when Rogan was just outside the doors. Power shuts off inside of me again, but we're almost to the wall and still partially hidden in a fog of ash. I drag us until the stone of the front of the church keeps me from going any further. I stop and check for a pulse. Finding nothing, I try to listen through my wheezing for any sign that Elon's breathing. His chest doesn't move, and it's clear that he's gone. There's nothing there.

Tears stream down my face as I try to pull the knife from his chest. It takes me three tries and a serious effort to fight the agony that courses through me from the gunshot wound, but I finally get it out, setting it down beside me in case I need it. I feel my strength wane, and I pull Elon to me and crouch over him protectively, and then every ounce of ability drains out of me like I'm a sieve. It's as though I bargained with my body to give me everything so I could get to Elon, and now that I have him, there's nothing left in the tank for me.

In.

Out.

I practically force my lungs to inflate and then deflate, but it's getting harder. Sounds of the Order winning the fight should spark hope in my bones, but instead, they're drowned out by my grief and sorrow. I can't even think about what Rogan will do when he finally finds us, just to discover that he was seconds too late. I block out everything as I hold Elon's body, my tears dripping down my face and mixing with the blood that's still pouring out of my chest.

I should feel alarmed, but I find I can't feel much of anything, and even though I'm trying to tap into my magic, I can't find any to try and make the blood stop. I'm no Soul Witch, and as much as I wish I could, I can't repair all the damage or hide all the evidence of the horror that both Elon and I endured in this place at the hands of a power hungry psycho.

I push a lock of dirty hair out of Elon's face and reach up to close his eyelids. I can't even look up to see who from the Order has come to the rescue. I feel too ashamed and devastated that I'm the only one left here to find.

"Lennox! Elon!" Rogan bellows out, his powerful voice searching, the hope in it breaking my heart. But like the moth I've always been to his flame, I look up, drawn to him even against my will.

He's going to hate me. Hate that I'm here instead of Elon. And I feel as though I'm being crushed under the weight of that knowledge as my wrecked gaze searches through the fighting and finally lands on a pair of moss-green eyes.

Useless hope surges through me as I take in his face. He's still searching the church for us, and I wish I could call out that I'm here, but I don't have it in me. I watch the perfect planes of his face frantically looking as he fights away shadows that dare to get too close to him and the others around him.

I'm here, I whisper in my head, and as though I just screamed it at the top of my lungs, Rogan's eyes immediately find mine. I see a flash of relief in his gaze before a trio of Order soldiers step in the way, fighting off a handful of shadow creatures who growl and snarl and move as fast as a flash, leaping from here to there in a blink. I know that when Rogan finally gets to me, the relief he's feeling will get ripped away, and it's my fault. If I'd only thought of the blood magic earlier...I could have stopped so much.

A demonic snarl tears through the church, and Jamie rises from the literal ashes, floating on the air like some harbinger of doom. Her marks are as bright as the sun itself and, from what I can see, just as hot too. The demon magic is burning through her, reminding me of the way Eleanor started to crumble from the demon curse she accidentally absorbed.

I wait for Jamie to turn and aim her demonic rage at me, but instead she focuses on the Order members now treading on her hellish sanctuary. I spot Prek and his team, along with several others including Marx and the Major as they dispatch shadow creature after shadow creature and move collectively closer.

Jamie screams, the sound something more akin to a Ring Wraith than a human. Her hair burns away as she floats in the air, a deep and steady chant falling from her melting lips. It feels like there's a collective intake of breath before all at once, her chanting grows louder and the church all around us starts to shake ominously. I cover Elon protectively with my body, palming the silver blade I set next to my thigh.

Pieces of Jamie start to fall to the ground with sickening splats as she focuses all her borrowed magic on whatever it is she's trying to do. I can't tell if she's trying to bring the church down on top of us or call something up from underneath it, but either way, I can see that the magic she's using is incinerating her inch by psychotic inch. I watch her, wishing I had enough power to end her once and for all, but from the looks of it, she's already doing that to herself.

All of a sudden, the shaking stops and Jamie goes crashing to the ground of the dais. She hits it so hard that the stone vibrates underneath me from the impact. At first, I think she's out cold from the hit, but then she rolls over, tilts her head in that creepy way she does, and turns to look at me. She takes me in, a sickening smile on her marred face, only it's not Jamie I see staring out of her gaze, it's something else entirely.

Her one teal eye is now bright orange, and the pupil is slit horizontally like a goat's. Every single one of the demon marks branded onto her body glows that same fiery orange as her one eye.

"Osssteomancerrrr," it practically hisses, using Jamie's melted lips to speak my title.

I reach for my magic instinctually and try not to panic when it doesn't come.

"Yoooou're minnnneee," it wheezes, and I stop myself from flipping it the bird.

Must not piss off demons you can't protect yourself from.

Instead, I shoot it a glare. "Run, asshole," I warn, calling on all the rage and need for vengeance I can. "We're going to take your little pet alive, and when I find out who you are, I won't stop hunting you until you and everyone who helped this happen is fucking dead," I snarl, gesturing to Elon and the church.

The demon studies me for a moment and then starts to laugh. "See you sssoon then, Lennniiii." And with that, Jamie blinks, and the demon disappears. I'm once again staring back into a gaze that's one half teal and the other half demon mark.

Jamie looks shocked and starts chanting, "No, no, no, no, no!" A blood-curdling scream fills the air, then another, and another, and then all at once, the shadows that are fighting the Order turn and run toward Jamie. My first instinct is that they're going to spirit her away, and I open my mouth to try and shout out a warning. But before I can, the shadows converge on her. She starts to fight them, begging and screaming, and it's obvious the demon is tying up loose ends. Good, but if he thinks that will save him, he doesn't know who the fuck I am. Like piranhas, the shadow creatures rip apart what's left of the woman who sold her soul, while her demon marks turn on her and burn the rest of her to cinders.

Rot in hell, bitch.

I watch her meticulously reduced to nothing, without an ounce of pity in my heart for what's happening to her. Far too many people laid on the altar she built, begging for the same mercy she just was, and did any of them find it at her hands? No. I hope she spends eternity paying for the magic she tried to steal and all the innocent lives lost because of her greed. Screams turn to gurgles, and then just like that, she's gone, and all the shadow beings are gone with her. All that's left is a bubbling puddle of rotten blood and black tar.

I fight to pull a relieved breath into my damaged lungs. I close my eyes and absorb the solace and finality that comes in knowing she's gone and she's not coming back.

Ding dong, the bitch is dead.

18

With serious effort, mostly because it feels like an elephant is parked on my chest and I'm pretty sure most of my blood is now on the floor all around me, I turn away from the puddle of sludge. I try to fight off the flash of images that play through my mind as I settle back against the front of the church, do my best to block out all the horrors I witnessed within the stone walls of this place, but I can't seem to turn them off no matter how hard I try.

I hope they let us burn this tainted place to the ground before we leave.

My hold on Elon slips a little, and I try to pull him tighter to me, but my hands don't seem to want to work. I try again when suddenly I feel Rogan nearby. I look up, terrified to see what's in his eyes as he takes me in, struggling to hold onto the body of the one person who meant more to him than anything.

A choked sob tears out of his throat as moss-green eyes study first Elon and then me. I clutch his brother to me, still trying to protect him and also shield me from the heartbreak I know Rogan is drowning in.

"I need help!" he bellows brokenly, and then he's on his knees in front of me, hands up as though he's not sure where it's safe to touch.

I look down and finally take in what's causing the horror to seep into his face. Both Elon and I are covered in blood and battered beyond repair.

"Oh god, what did she do to you?' he asks, grief choking his words as tears fill his beautiful green eyes and spill over onto his cheeks.

I want to reach up and wipe them off, but I don't want to let go of Elon. I know I failed Rogan, and there's nothing I can do to change that, but I won't let Elon go until I know he's once again in safe hands.

"I'm sorry," I whisper, a sob stealing away the conviction in my voice.

Rogan's horrified stare bounces up to mine, and all I see there is agony.

He was so close. So fucking close, and it all went to shit in less than a blink.

"Somebody help me!" Rogan screams again, and this time several Order members come running. They take one look at us and freeze for a moment as though shock has stolen their ability to move and speak.

"Help her!" Rogan snarls as tears drip down his face, and the command breaks the unfamiliar Order members from their stalled stupor.

An older blond man crouches down next to me and tries to lift Elon from my arms. I tighten my hold on him and choke out a pitiful growl of objection. Rogan's face crumbles with grief, but I watch as he shoves it away and fixes his intense gaze back on mine.

"It's okay, you did so good, Lennox, let them take care of him now," he encourages, and the lie that slips right out of his mouth makes my heart ache.

I didn't do good. I failed him.

I shake my head, rejecting his praise, and try to breathe through the sorrow that slams into me. "I tried to make her take me first. I tried to stop her," I tell him so he'll know how sorry I am, how hard I tried to keep this from happening.

Heartbreak fills Rogan's eyes, but he doesn't look at Elon as the trio of Soul Witches reach for him again. His eyes stay steadily fixed on mine, despite the pain I know he's in from losing his brother.

"I know you did," he concedes, his eyes warm and understanding. "He's safe now, they're going to take him and take care of him, and we need to take care of you," he urges softly, as though I'm a wounded wild animal that needs to be soothed and coddled. I look down at my chest, at the damage ravaging my left side and the blood that's now slowly trickling out of me.

Dammit, I am *some wounded wild animal.*

I pull in a shuddering wet breath and, with a nod, release my hold on Elon. In a flash, he's pulled from my arms, and even though I said it was okay, a whimper of objection spills out of me as they pull him about ten feet away from me and lay him down and start checking him over.

My attention is pulled away from what they're doing when a pair of strong arms wrap around me and pull me protectively against a warm, hard chest.

A chest I'd know anywhere.

Rogan.

I wait for the pain of being jostled to hit me, but surprisingly, it doesn't, so I tilt my head back and look up into my favorite color of green eyes.

"I'm sorry," I tell him once again, but he shushes me and shakes his head like he doesn't want to hear it. I close my eyes and lean into him, finally safe from the horrors of this place.

"Open your eyes, Lennox, come on, stay with me, open your eyes!" he barks, and a small smile pulls at the corners of my lips.

"Bossy," I accuse playfully, and then a fit of bone-breaking coughs tear through me and try to drown me in my own blood.

Hands are suddenly on me, and I look at Rogan, scared that I'm being taken away. "I'm here. I have you," he reassures me, pressing his lips to my forehead as I feel the telltale rush of magic as it's shoved through me. I wait to feel the warmth that should accompany it, sense my broken parts as they knit together and heal, but none of that happens.

Panic fills Rogan's eyes as people bark orders all around me and more magic is shoved into my body, but I quickly realize it's not working. Someone shouts about a *spelled gun* and then orders a Contegomancer to come try and lift whatever shield is on me so that the Soul Witch's magic can work.

I close my eyes at their revelation. Of course the gun was spelled—it was Jamie's goal in life to fuck everything up beyond repair, why should I be any different?

"What are you saying? You can't help her? You're the fucking Order's Animamancers and you can't heal her?" Rogan snarls, and the fear in it makes my heart hurt. "Do something!" he cries out again, and then I feel him pull me closer as his deep, rich voice begs me to hold on.

"We have Contegomancers on their way, the two that were with us were both killed, Replacements are coming as fast as they can. With the nearby ley line, they'll be here in minutes," the Major assures Rogan, but we all know I probably don't have that long.

I force my lids to open, but it feels like it takes everything I have in me to make it happen. Devastated moss-green eyes stare into mine.

I try to talk, to tell him that it's okay, that I care about him and that I'm so incredibly sorry that all of this is happening, but there's too much blood in my throat and in my lungs, and I can't get the words out.

"Hold on, Lennox, they're bringing help. They'll figure out how to fix this," he reassures me, but it's not me who desperately wants to believe what he's saying. I knew the deal the moment my magic faltered. "Stay with me," he pleads.

I give him the most reassuring smile I can muster, nodding because this is exactly where I want to be. "You're going to be okay," he whispers confidently to me, his voice cracking with emotion. "I'm here, and you're going to be okay."

He scoops something from the ground and pushes it back inside of me while pressing his forehead against mine in that way that always made me feel all warm and gooey inside. I look down to see what he's doing and watch him cup blood from the ground and push it back into my chest, the desperate movement steady as he chants over and over again that I'm okay, that I'm going to be just fine.

I reach up and stop his hand, and our gazes meet, the undeniable truth spilling out of both of our eyes.

I'm dying.

Rogan shakes his head as though it will knock reality far from both of us, and I reach up and cup his cheek until he gives me his stunning green eyes again. A brokenhearted stare meets mine, tears spilling down his face as he takes me in. His lips gently press against mine, and I feel the love and the hope and the loss in his tender kiss.

I try to hold on to it, to use it to fuel the fight I know I have in me somewhere, but the cold is starting to seep into my bones, and it's getting harder and harder to breathe.

"Elon," Rogan pleads, and I ache for his loss I hear in his voice. "Elon, help me," he begs randomly, his strong chest shaking from the sobs spilling out of him.

My hand falls from his cheek, and when I try to lift it again, I can only manage to raise it a couple of inches before it flops back down to my blood-soaked abdomen.

"I've got you, Lennox," Rogan reassures me, holding me tighter to him as his tears spill down and warm my chilled skin. "I'm so sorry," he tells me on a shuddering sob as he pushes hair away from my face. "Please stay," he begs, and I feel my own tears slip from my eyes at the request.

"Elon, wake up and help me," Rogan growls brokenly, and I wish with everything inside of me it will happen.

Another presence appears at my side, but I can't make my head cooperate so I can look to see who. Short red hair dips into my line of sight, and I'm pretty sure whoever he is just put his hands on me, but alarmingly, I can't feel them. A second of silence passes, then another, and another. The witch looks up and shouts that he needs assistance. I focus on Rogan, on the tears and his beautiful face, on the hope and desperation I see in his eyes.

I lied to Elon. I didn't realize it until now, but I think the lie still counts. There's no *could* or *maybe* when it comes to loving Rogan, it's already a done deal.

"Please help her," he orders as more witches surround me, and Rogan's warm eyes once again settle on mine.

"Fight, Leni," he tells me, and then once again, it's quiet as it seems everyone around me holds their breath.

Rogan's eyes bounce back and forth between mine, and I try to tell him with just a look how much I care about him and how much I want to stay here in his arms.

"Shhhhh," he coos at me, stroking my hair and bringing

his lips softly to mine. "I know," he whispers against my lips, but when he pulls back, my blood has stamped his mouth, and fear starts to sink into the limbs that I can't feel anymore.

"There's too much damage. By the time we unweave the shield put on her, it'll be too late," a woman's solemn voice declares, and Rogan pulls me closer, his soft *no*s filling my ears as he fights the truth.

"I have a heartbeat," someone shouts in surprise, and the crowd gathered around me moves away to help whoever is still fighting for their life.

Rogan just stays and holds me as each breath gets harder and harder to take and the world around me starts to close in.

A small whimper escapes me, and Rogan kisses me softly again.

I mouth *I love you* against his lips, and when he pulls away, he nods as though he knows I'm trying to say something but he's not sure what.

"It's okay," he assures me, his tone gentle and kind as tears stream unchecked down his face. "I'll take care of Tad and Hillen. Hoot will stay with me, and I'll make sure everyone you love is okay. I promise, Lennox, I'll take care of them all. You can go if you need to...but I wish you would stay. I know it's selfish, but I have so much I need to fix, so much I still need to tell you. How can I let you go?" he asks on a sob, and all I can do is blink my own sorrow from my eyes.

There's a loud commotion somewhere close by, but I can't focus on what as someone steps into my line of sight, someone who shouldn't be here.

Grammy? I ask, mentally shocked to see her. She doesn't say anything, but she smiles warmly at me as though she can read the question in my mind. She gestures to the side of her, and I look over to see my mom and dad. I stare at them blankly for a moment as my emotions take time to catch up with how stunned I feel. My dad's warm smile has me crying like a baby. I've missed all of them so much, and now they're here. My mother opens her arms and holds them that way like she's waiting for me to step into her loving embrace, and as much as I want to go, I also want to stay.

Excitement and happiness explode inside of me, but I'm at war with the heart-wrenching loss I also feel. The possibility of so much more with this man sparks through me as I deteriorate in Rogan's arms, and I feel as though I'm being torn away from everything I've always wanted in life.

My Grammy offers me a knowing look and moves to stand with my parents. She's just like she was in life, giving me room and space to come to terms with things, never in a hurry to push me or force my hand.

I turn back to Rogan and try to whisper what I need him to hear before I go. I wish I could soothe his grief and chase away the distress he doesn't deserve. I'd love nothing more than to figure out a way to come back from this, but my body is broken beyond repair, and I can feel myself fading. Rogan leans down and presses his forehead to mine. I try to breathe him in just like I have so many times before, but my lungs no longer work the way they should.

I collect every ounce of strength I have left inside of me, and I whisper to him, "I love you," as I close my eyes, reveling in his touch and comfort.

"I love you," he reassures me, his tears sprinkling my face. "I love you so much, Lennox. I'm so sorry for everything," he laments, and I hear him plead over and over again...

"Come back to me."

His words sink into my soul, bringing with them weight

and warmth. I fight so hard, but try as I might, I can't make his words anchor me here.

I feel myself slipping.

Just as I try to tell him that I don't want to go, something severs inside of me. Everything around me disappears, and the last thing I hear is a mournful, "What have I done? Oh god, what have I done?"

EPILOGUE

I'm cold. Cold and uncomfortable, which is an odd combination to feel in heaven. Or maybe I'm not in heaven. I know I'm not in hell. I was a good person in life, but the fact of the matter is I'm cold and I feel like I'm lying on the world's most uncomfortable bed.

I try to open my eyes to take in my surroundings, but they don't feel ready yet. Which is another weird thing to think when you're supposed to be dead.

"Grammy?" I call out uncertainly.

I swear she was just here talking to me about something.

"Dad? Mom?"

My voice bounces around the walls of my enclosure, hammering me with the sound of my uncertainty. I know for sure I was just hugging my parents. I can still feel the tears on my cheeks as we embraced and I shed years of misunderstanding and resentment in a matter of minutes. It was beautiful and empowering, and yet here I am, now cold and uncomfortable, with no idea where they went.

I sigh and once again hear the sound of it echo all around me. My hand twitches, and my chest feels itchy and slightly uncomfortable. I pull in a deep breath, but I can't identify any particular smell that would clue me in to where I am. I squeeze my lids and then slowly try to coax them open. My first glimpse of my surroundings is dark. Very dark.

Shit.

Maybe there was a mix up and I accidentally got shoved down when I should have gone up. Or maybe this is some kind of weird ass initiation, like, *Surprise, you're in heaven! Aren't you extra grateful now that we scared the shit out of you?*

I look around me at the smooth walls of the small rectangular space that seems ideally sized to fit me. Maybe this is where we sleep in heaven? I guess that's assuming we do sleep. Although if we don't, how the hell did I just *wake up* in here?

I'm not sure what kind of establishment the gods or whatever are running here, but I gotta say I'm not super impressed right now.

I pause for a moment, worried someone or something might smite me for that thought, but when it doesn't happen, I relax. I start to press against the side and the bottom of this *thing* I'm in, looking for a way out or like a call button or something. I push hard against the wall above my head, and surprisingly, it pops open.

Bingo.

I look up through the now open door and see what I think is a strangely sterile and sparse looking space.

Fuck. Is heaven an alien spaceship? Wait. Do alien spaceships have linoleum?

It's a little disorienting trying to make sense of what I'm seeing upside down, so I roll over onto my stomach and attempt to make sense of it from this angle. The floor is gray linoleum, and the walls are a slightly lighter shade of *greige*—it's not quite gray, not quite beige.

Definitely not a spaceship.

I push out of the tiny space I'm in and see several other square stainless steel doors exactly like the one I just pushed open. There's several long fluorescent lights blinking down on me from the ceiling, and I'm completely thrown for a loop. I thought there'd be chandeliers or something a little more extravagant to greet new people with. My brow furrows with consternation, and I stare at the setup all around me, thoroughly confused.

And then it hits me like a runaway truck. I've never seen one before, but I'm suddenly certain I know exactly where I am.

Holy. Fucking. Moon shits, I'm in a morgue.

And the only thing that could mean is...I'm alive...again.

The End, for now...

ALSO BY IVY ASHER

Urban Fantasy Romance

The Osseous Chronicles

The Bone Witch

The Blood Witch

The Bound Witch

Dark Shifter Romance Standalone

The Savage Spirit of Seneca Rain

Rabid

Paranormal Romance RH

The Sentinel World

The Lost Sentinel Series

The Lost and the Chosen

Awakened and Betrayed

The Marked and the Broken

Found and Forged

Shadowed Wings Series

The Hidden

The Avowed

The Reclamation

More in the Sentinel World coming soon.

Hellgate Guardian Series

Grave Mistakes

Grave Consequences

Grave Decisions

Grave Signs

Shifter Romantic Comedy Standalone

Conveniently Convicted

Dystopian Romantic Comedy Standalone RH

April's Fools

ABOUT THE AUTHOR

Ivy Asher is addicted to chai, swearing, and laughing a lot—but not in a creepy, laughing alone kind of way. She loves the snow, books, and her family of two humans, and three fur-babies. She has worlds and characters just floating around in her head, and she's lucky enough to be surrounded by amazing people who support that kind of crazy.

Join Ivy Asher's Reader Group and follow her on Instagram and BookBub for updates on your favorite series and upcoming releases!!!

facebook.com/IvyAsherBooks
instagram.com/ivy.asher
amazon.com/author/ivyasher
bookbub.com/profile/ivy-asher

Printed in Great Britain
by Amazon

39061850R10157